"You're thinking you shouldn't be here with me."

His smile was s..le's
on a Friday r...
involved.... You want to leave, but you can't think of a
graceful way to do it."

"Believe me, Donovan, I don't need an excuse."

But Kira didn't want to leave. She wanted to stay here,
sitting across the table from Jake. Flirting with him.

The thought both frightened and thrilled her. She hadn't
been out with a man in months. Between her job and
her responsibilities at home with Lexie and Brian, she
didn't have time.

A wild, reckless mood swept over her. For one night she
wanted to be free. She didn't want to be the doctor or
the mother or the sister. She wanted to be Kira, a woman
who could enjoy a man's company for a few hours.

A man who was her client.

Dear Reader,

Every woman in today's world is an expert at multitasking. Whether you're a stay-at-home mom or the CEO of an international corporation, there never seems to be enough time for everything. But no matter what our responsibilities, our families always come first. Our husbands and wives, our children, our siblings and parents are the linchpin of our lives.

And not all families are linked by blood. Some of us have families we've made, forged together by shared pain and shared joy, by a love as deep as any bound in DNA.

But no matter how our families are created, we are willing to sacrifice anything, do anything, risk anything for them.

In *Family First*, Kira McGinnis's world revolves around the small family she's made for herself—her daughter, Lexie, and her stepbrother, Brian. Sexy, seductive Jake Donovan is an irresistible temptation, but how will he change the delicate balance Kira's created in her life?

Some of you may remember Jake from *In Her Defense*. I had too much fun with him in that book and I couldn't forget about him. So I gave him a story of his own. And as I got to know Jake better, I found a complicated, complex man hidden beneath his carefree exterior. A man who was perfect for intense, driven Kira McGinnis. I hope you enjoy their story.

I love to hear from my readers! You can e-mail me at mwatson1004@hotmail.com or visit my Web site at www.margaretwatson.com.

Margaret Watson

FAMILY FIRST
Margaret Watson

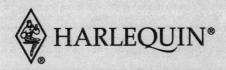

HARLEQUIN®

TORONTO • NEW YORK • LONDON
AMSTERDAM • PARIS • SYDNEY • HAMBURG
STOCKHOLM • ATHENS • TOKYO • MILAN • MADRID
PRAGUE • WARSAW • BUDAPEST • AUCKLAND

ISBN 0-373-71337-1

FAMILY FIRST

This edition published by arrangement with Harlequin Books S.A.

® and TM are trademarks of the publisher. Trademarks indicated with
® are registered in the United States Patent and Trademark Office, the
Canadian Trade Marks Office and in other countries.

www.eHarlequin.com

Printed in U.S.A.

Books by Margaret Watson

HARLEQUIN SUPERROMANCE

Don't miss any of our special offers. Write to us at the
following address for information on our newest releases.

Harlequin Reader Service
U.S.: 3010 Walden Ave., P.O. Box 1325, Buffalo, NY 14269
Canadian: P.O. Box 609, Fort Erie, Ont. L2A 5X3

For my family—Bill, Katy, Chelsea and Meg.
Now and always, first in my heart.

Thanks to my sister, Nancy Good, and Sheila Krippner
for so patiently answering my questions about therapists.

CHAPTER ONE

WHAT WAS he trying to hide?

Kira leaned back in her chair and watched Detective Donovan roam her office, his hands jammed in his pockets. Nervous energy poured off him as he studied the pictures on her wall, stared out the window, nudged a chair with the toe of his shoe. Finally he picked up the statue of the young girl fishing. He studied it for a moment, then set it back down on the table with too much force.

"This is all bogus, Doc." He slouched into a chair and focused on the wall behind her head.

"What's bogus?" she asked calmly.

"All of this." He waved his hand around the office. "Needing to talk to you. To make sure I'm *handling* the shooting. You've already talked to McDougal and A.J. You know Doak Talbott's was a righteous shooting."

"Yes, I've talked to Mac and A.J. But they didn't shoot Talbott, Detective. You did."

"I did what I was supposed to do."

Kira watched Jake jiggle his foot. "Shooting a civilian is something the department takes very seriously." She held up her hand as Donovan tried to interrupt her.

"Yes, I know the facts. I know what his alleged crimes were. But you still killed a man."

"Did they tell you about the 'alleged' bruises on his kid? And his wife?" Donovan met her gaze, his eyes blazing. "Did they tell you about the 'alleged' gun he was holding to a civilian's head?"

"I know all the *alleged* facts of the case, Detective. I need to know how you feel about what you had to do."

"I feel like I did my job. Period. End of story." His expression was defiant.

Kira threw her pen on her desk and leaned back. "You know how this works, Detective Donovan. I can't release you for active duty until I'm certain this shooting hasn't affected your ability to do your job. You can make it easy and cooperate with me, or you can do it the hard way. It's up to you."

Donovan studied her for a long moment. She could almost see the wheels turning in his head, as he relaxed in the chair and gave her his patented sweet-talk-the-pants-off-you smile.

"I choose easy, Doc."

"Good choice," Kira said. She nodded, encouraging him.

"Okay, so here's what happened. You know the story—Doak Talbott was wanted for domestic abuse and the murder of a waitress at the country club. He was afraid his son had seen him burying bloody clothes, so he had to get a hold of the kid. He found out where Jamie was staying…" Jake rubbed his side, the spot where his gun normally rested. "He tried to take Jamie's aunt hostage and was threatening everybody—his kid, the aunt and A.J. He wouldn't put down his gun. In my judgment, he was prepared to shoot all of us. I had to kill him."

"And how did you feel about that?" Kira asked again, patiently.

"It doesn't matter. I had no choice. If I hadn't killed him, he would have killed the kid. Or the kid's aunt. Or A.J. Or Mac. Or me." Donovan spread his hands and smiled, his sleepy eyes crinkling at the corners. "So you can sign off on me and take it easy for the rest of the hour."

"Nice try, Detective." Kira noted the tension behind his smile. "But I have to tell you, you're not being real original. At least half of the police officers who walk in here tell me the same thing." Her lips twitched. "The last time I was surrounded by so many selfless people, I was in grade school with the nuns."

"Very funny, Doc." Jake scowled. "You're a real comedian. What do you want me to say?" His gaze drifted to the picture of snow-capped mountains beneath a full moon. "I did my job."

"That's the point, Detective. In the course of doing your job, you killed a man."

He froze for a fraction of a second, then shrugged. "I feel good. The bastard didn't deserve to live."

Kira closed her eyes and wondered, again, why she'd taken this job. "Detective Donovan," she said, giving him a level look, "do you want to go back on active duty?"

"What do you think?"

"What do I think?" she repeated. "I think you'd

better get something straight. Unless you want to spend the rest of your career with the Riverton Police Department riding a desk, you'll respect both me and this process. So can we start over without the smart-ass answers?"

"You don't like smart-ass?" Instead of the defensiveness she expected, Donovan's mouth curled up in a wicked grin. "I'm thinking you're not a lot of fun, Doc."

"That would be correct, Detective. So why don't you knock off the lame attempts to make me forget why you're here? The quicker I can complete my report to the oversight board, the quicker you can get back to active duty. Unless you *want* to work a desk indefinitely." She cocked her head, waiting for his answer.

"That's very sexy, Doc. That no-nonsense, I-like-to-play-hardball attitude."

Despite the grin, she saw raw discomfort in his eyes. And something that might have been fear.

"Jake, nothing you say here goes beyond these doors," she said gently. "You know that, don't you?"

"Sure."

"Then what's the problem?"

"What do you want to hear? That I went home and puked my guts out after I shot Talbott? That I rode the porcelain bus all night?"

"Is that what happened?"

He grabbed a stapler from her desk, tossed it from hand to hand. "Of course not. Why would I get so upset about that loser?" He didn't meet her gaze.

"What *did* you do that night?"

"I watched the ball game, had a beer or two." His grin looked shaky. "That would be the White Sox. I'm not one of those yuppie, wine-drinking Cubs fans."

"Duly noted." She tilted her head, determined to keep him on track. "How did you sleep that night?"

He raised his eyebrows. "That's pretty personal, Doc. Are you looking for details of my...sleeping habits?"

"Oh, for heaven's sake, Donovan." She slapped the desk, her temper slipping.

Glancing at the clock, she said, "Your time is up. Would you like to make an appointment for our next session?"

Donovan frowned. "What do you mean, 'next' session?"

"Just what I said. We didn't make much progress so we'll try again. When would be convenient for you?"

She opened her appointment book, watching him fume.

"No time would be convenient," he finally said, scowling again. "Mac has been working overtime for the past week, doing both of our jobs. He needs a break. I need to be back on duty."

"Then maybe next time you'll be more cooperative."

Standing, he stared down at her, anger gathering in his face. Kira kept her gaze fixed on his simmering blue eyes. She watched as he struggled for control, watched as the heat faded.

"I'll have to check my schedule," he muttered.

"Fine. Get back to me when you can."

He slammed the door so hard her desk shook.

Kira pushed away from her desk and rubbed her eyes. Charming, sexy Jake Donovan—legendary in the Riverton Police Department for sweet-talking whatever he wanted from criminals and coworkers alike—was the last thing she needed right now.

Once again, the contract she'd signed with the police department to do psychological assessments came back to haunt her. She stuffed her folders into her briefcase as she glanced at the clock, hoping she wouldn't be late. Again. She'd do the job she was paid to do. Even if it involved spending several more hours with such a difficult man.

JAKE TURNED into the men's room and gave the water faucet a vicious twist, then splashed cold water on his face until his eyes stopped burning. He yanked paper towels out of the dispenser, pressed them to his forehead.

With a hissed oath, he shoved the wet wad into the trash can, scraping his knuckles on the edge as he drew back his hand.

The rage he'd tried so hard to control burst free in a blur of red and black. He kicked over the can and then ripped the dispenser off its bracket and heaved it at the wall. It bounced off the tile, hit the sink with a whine of metal, then crashed to the floor. Dented on one side, the handle broken off, it slid to a stop beneath the door of a stall.

When he stormed out of the washroom one of the patrol officers was at the door.

"You okay, Donovan?"

"Just peachy," Jake snarled.

The officer cleared his throat. "I…ah…heard something fall in there. You sure you're all right?"

"I'm fine." Jake pushed past him and threw himself into his desk chair.

"Hey, Jake," his partner Mac said, looking up from his work. "Doc McGinnis clear you for takeoff?"

"No." Jake cursed. "I have to go back."

Mac came over and propped himself on the edge of the desk. "What happened?" he asked in a low voice.

"Nothing." Jake grabbed a file and thumbed through it without seeing it. "She was pushing and pushing, trying to make me spill my damn guts to her."

Jake slammed the file onto his desk. "I don't do the gut-spilling thing. With anyone. Let alone a psychologist." He snorted. "She said I wasn't taking her seriously. How can anyone take that crap seriously?"

"Really? She thought Jake Donovan wasn't being serious?" Mac's lips twitched. "Obviously she's mistaken you for someone else."

A patrol officer led a man dressed in an expensive suit into the room. His hands were cuffed behind him, and Jake turned away to tune out the perp's loud protestations of innocence.

"Screw you, McDougal."

"Come on, Jake. She's not Barb."

Jake glared at his partner. "This doesn't have anything to do with Barb."

"No?"

"Why would it? Barb is ancient history."

"Jake. Your ex-wife, who just happens to be a psychologist, tap-danced on your head. And you're telling me you're not thinking about Barb when you're supposed to talk to another psychologist?"

"You're a shrink now?" Jake asked, his voice dripping with scorn. "You take a mail order course? Or is A.J. giving you lessons?" He picked up an empty paper coffee cup and slammed it into the wastebasket. "If I was engaged to a woman like A.J., I'd sure as hell have better things to do with her."

"You're a bright guy, Donovan," Mac said. "You know what the doc needs to hear. Fill in the blanks for her."

"I suppose *you* liked her poking around in your head?"

"Hell, no. But she made it as painless as possible." Mac returned to his chair. "Just get it over with. Maybe if you're straight with her next time, she'll cut you loose."

"Not likely," Jake muttered. "She's the type that won't let go. That woman has major control issues." His mouth twisted. "As she would say."

"Yeah, well, I'm going to have a control issue myself pretty soon if you don't get back to work. The cases are stacking up like flights into O'Hare. What have you been doing with your time, anyway?"

"I've met with my high-school group a few times."

"Troublemakers Anonymous?"

"Knock it off, Mac. They're just kids. Some of them don't have fathers around. They need guy time."

"You can give them all the guy time you want when you're off the clock. Between nine and five, you're supposed to be covering my rear end."

"I'm trying to make sure this group isn't the Future Criminals of America Club. Think of it as rear-end-covering in advance."

Mac raised his eyebrows. "You're not a babysitter, Jake. You're a police officer. A detective. Have you forgotten that?"

"Of course not." Jake frowned as Mac's words found a target, deep in his heart. "I'm just saying those kids are important. That's all."

"Yeah, they are. But *this* is your job." He gestured at the police officers milling around the room. "So stop screwing around and get yourself cleared. I need some help."

Jake swiveled and stared at the smear of dirty handprints on the wall. "What if she says I'm not 'psychologically fit' to be a cop? Or not 'temperamentally suited' to be a detective?"

"Is that what you're worried about?" Understanding lit Mac's eyes. "For God's sake, Donovan. You're one of the best detectives on the force. You've cleared more cases than just about anyone. You were born for this job."

Jake heard his father telling him the exact same thing and tried to ignore the memory. "McGinnis doesn't care about that."

"As I said, Kira McGinnis isn't Barb, Jake. She's not going to mess with you."

She already had. And if he gave her half a chance,

she'd force his doubts and fears to the surface, make him confront them.

No way would he allow that.

How could anyone who looked like Kira McGinnis be so dangerous? An image of the sexy doctor lingered in his head, her sable hair pulled back into a smooth coil, her whiskey-colored eyes darkening as she struggled with her temper.

He wondered what she'd look like when she wasn't sitting on the other side of a desk.

He didn't care, he told himself. He'd learned his lesson about psychologists and relationships. He didn't need a refresher course.

GOING MUCH too fast, Kira turned onto the quiet suburban street. She was late. Again.

She stepped on the brake, slowing her car to just above the speed limit. Houses crept past her window too slowly, and she drummed her fingers on the steering wheel. Finding a parking spot, she pulled in and dashed up the sidewalk to the bright-red front door and knocked.

"Hi, Kira," said Shelley. "Come on in."

Kira stepped into a child's paradise. The simple living-room furniture was all child-friendly. And the brightly colored bookshelves were stacked with books, toys, blocks and games.

"Mommy!"

Lexie threw herself into Kira's arms, and she hugged her daughter tightly as she pressed a kiss to her sweet-smelling, baby-fine hair. "Hi, sweetie. I missed you. How was your day?"

"I wrote my name!" The girl bounced out of Kira's arms. "Want to see?"

"Of course I do."

L-E-X-I-E. The letters were misshapen and took up the whole sheet of paper, but it was her daughter's name.

"Wow, honey," Kira said, pulling her daughter close as she studied the crooked letters, her throat swelling with emotion. "That's wonderful. I'm so proud of you." The realization that she'd missed another of her daughter's firsts pinched her heart.

"I did it all by myself," Lexie said proudly. "Shelley hardly helped me at all."

"We need to take this home and put it on the refrigerator," Kira said. "Why don't you get your bag and we'll go find a place for it?"

"Okay."

Lexie scampered off and Kira rose to her feet. "Thanks, Shelley," she said to her friend, shaking her head. "Another milestone. One step closer to kindergarten. I guess she's ready."

Shelley smiled. "She's growing up fast, isn't she?"

After they said goodbye, Lexie chattered all the way home. Kira gradually relaxed as she listened. For these few minutes, she could pretend she had nothing to worry about, nothing to do but listen to her daughter talk about the castle she'd built with blocks that day and the game she'd played with the other kids in Shelley's backyard. For these few minutes, nothing existed but Lexie.

As they turned onto a street lined with bungalows and tidy two-story houses, she scanned the cars parked at the curb, looking for Brian's old junker. Her heart sank when she realized it wasn't there.

But there was a basketball sitting in the middle of the driveway, and Kira's spirits lifted. If Brian was shooting baskets, maybe he was going to start working out with the team. She fervently hoped so. He needed physical activity and a focus for his restless energy.

She stopped and picked up the basketball, tossing it through the hoop with one hand, then carried it to the garage. As she opened the door to the house, the dogs barked wildly and launched themselves at her. Lexie dropped her bag and wrapped her arms around the larger dog's neck. "I missed you, Henry," she said, and Kira's heart pinched a little more.

"You, too, Scooter," Lexie added, giving the small dog a pat on the head. "I wrote my name today. Want to see?"

She pulled the paper out of her bag and held it in front of the smaller dog's nose.

"See, Henry?" she said, showing it to the other one. Henry sniffed at it, then tried to take a bite.

"All right, guys, into the yard," Kira said, opening the back door and shoving the dogs out.

"Uncle Brian!" Lexie called. "I wrote my name."

Kira knew Brian wouldn't answer. Where was he?

Suddenly, she smelled burning food and heard the hiss of water hitting a hot surface.

Kira ran to the kitchen, leaped for the stove and turned off the burners. Water boiled out of one pot and sizzled into steam as it hit the burner. Bottled spaghetti sauce simmered in the other, burned into a black mass on the bottom of the saucepan.

A white note had fluttered to the kitchen floor when she'd dropped her briefcase on the table. Picking it up, she read, Hey, Kira. I went to a friend's house. I started dinner.

She closed her eyes and tried to rein in her temper. Brian had thought he was doing her a favor. But she wanted to shake him. Didn't he know better than to leave the house with food cooking on the stove? What was he thinking?

He wasn't thinking at all. One of the results of his head injury was that her stepbrother didn't think before he acted. The trouble he'd gotten into recently was vivid proof of that.

For the hundredth time, she examined her actions over the past six years. Had she coddled him too much since the accident? Had she made too many excuses for him?

Had she kept him from growing up because she wanted to protect him from any more pain?

She sank into a chair and rubbed her temples. She needed to gear up for another battle with Brian about seeing a therapist.

It would be ironic if it wasn't so painful. She, a clinical psychologist, couldn't convince her own brother he needed help.

As Lexie pounded down the stairs, calling her name,

Kira forced a smile. She wouldn't let worry interfere with her time with her daughter.

She had far too little of it as it was.

CHAPTER TWO

THE SATISFYING impact of his fist on flesh shuddered through Brian's arm as he watched his opponent stagger backward and stumble to one knee. The sudden silence in the bar barely registered as he stood with fists clenched, waiting for the other man to stand.

Jenny grabbed his arm. "Stop it, Brian," she said. "It's not a big deal."

Rage blurred Brian's vision. "Stay out of this, Jen. Get out of my way."

"No!" She pulled at him, trying to drag him away. "You're scaring me, Bri."

Brian shook off her hand. His opponent scrambled to his feet and backed away, trying to staunch the flow of blood from his nose. "What's your problem?" the guy asked, his voice indistinct. "Are you friggin' crazy?"

"You think I'm crazy?" Brian clenched his fists tighter. "Touch her again and I'll show you crazy."

The bleeding man edged away, Brian following. He needed to hit him again, to wipe away the memory of the jerk mauling Jenny.

A heavy hand landed on his shoulder. "Hold it, kid."

Brian swung around, his fist ready, but a stocky police officer grabbed his wrist and slapped on a handcuff. In moments he'd fastened Brian's hands together.

"You going to settle down, kid?" the cop asked, his eyes hard. "Or do I have to put you on the floor?"

"No," Brian muttered. "I'm okay."

"Thank God you're here!" Blood streaming from his nose, the man he'd punched stepped forward. "This guy attacked me! Arrest him! I want to press charges."

Another, younger, police officer stepped between Brian and his opponent. "I'll call an ambulance," he said, his eyes cool and assessing.

"I don't need an ambulance." The guy wiped the blood from his face with the back of his hand.

"Are you sure?" the young cop asked.

"Yes! I just want you to arrest this lunatic."

The police officer holding Brian looked down at him. "Did you hit this guy, kid?"

"Yes," Brian answered, his voice defiant. "He…"

"Save it," the old cop answered. "What's your name? "Brian Johnson."

"Well, Brian Johnson, you're under arrest." He recited the Miranda warning in a monotone.

When the other cop cuffed the bleeding man's hands behind his back and Mirandized him, the man's voice rose. "What the hell are you doing?" he yelled. "*He* hit *me*."

"We're going to straighten this out down at the station," the older cop said. He glanced at Jenny. "Are you with one of these guys?"

She nodded. "Brian."

"We'll need a statement from you." He looked at the beer in Jenny's hand. "And I'll need to see your ID," he added. Taking Brian by the arm, he steered him through the staring crowd. "Let's go, tough guy."

The young cop followed, holding on to the guy with the bloody nose. The night air was still hot and humid, and the metallic smell of blood filled Brian's nose.

One squad car stood at the curb, its lights still flashing. More sirens approached, and Brian's stomach churned with fear. As another squad car swung around the corner, the cop tightened his grip on Brian's arm.

That squad car and two others rolled to a stop and more uniformed officers jumped out. "Load these guys and take them to the station," the cop holding Brian said. "We need to get statements from the witnesses."

Rough hands patted Brian down, removing his wallet and keys, then bundled him into the back of one of the squad cars. The hard plastic seats were unyielding and cold against his cuffed hands and the odor of urine and vomit hung in the air. The door slammed shut behind him and the car pulled away from the curb with a jerk. Brian toppled onto his side, smashing his cheek into the hard seat.

He had to swallow back the sour taste of that last beer he'd chugged. Lights from the street whirled sickeningly above him as he pushed himself upright. For the rest of the ride, he struggled to keep his balance and control his fear.

He'd *had* to hit that guy. He hadn't had a choice. The creep had grabbed Jenny. He'd brought her to the bar, and it was his responsibility to protect her.

But his fear swelled when they reached the police station. The handcuffs chafed his wrists. The bright lights hurt his eyes and made the dizziness worse. Without saying a word, the cop pulled him into a brightly lit room, removed the handcuffs, administered a Breathalyzer test and took Brian's fingerprints. Then the cop stood him in front of a camera and took a picture.

It was the kind of photo he'd seen in the newspaper plenty of times, with some poor sap staring straight ahead, a dazed and shocked look on his face.

Now *he* was the sap in the photo.

What if Jake saw the picture? Brian wanted to disappear through the floor.

The cop who'd arrested him stood in the doorway. "Let's go, kid," he said. He didn't sound mad. Mad would have been better than the contempt Brian heard.

Before he could say anything, the cop pushed him into a cell and closed the door. Brian rubbed at his wrists as the lock clicked into place with an ominous finality.

Instead of the bars he'd always imagined, the front of the cell was a solid wall with a small window in the door. The only sound he heard was the frantic pounding of his heart echoing through his head.

A quick scan of the cell revealed a bed fastened to the wall and a mattress with no sheets or blanket. A stainless-steel toilet was attached to the opposite wall. There was nothing else.

He could see a set of speakers mounted in the ceiling, along with what looked like a video camera.

"Hey," he shouted at the camera, panicking. "You can't just throw me in here and close the door."

The only answer was his own voice echoing off the walls. "What about my phone call?" he yelled.

Through the small window in the door he saw only another window in the door across the aisle. He banged his fist on the window and shouted again.

When no one appeared, he paced the cell, his panic building. He was in jail. He charged the door again, scrabbling for a fingerhold, frantic to pull it open. The door fit so tightly he couldn't even get his fingernails into the crack.

His bowels churning with fear, he finally retreated to the bed and sat down. He eyed the toilet, but the thought of using it with unseen eyes watching made him cringe.

The walls of the cell spun in front of him, reminding him of the beers he'd downed. Reminding him of all the things he shouldn't have done. He shouldn't have taken Jenny to the bar. He shouldn't have been drinking. And he shouldn't have lost his temper and hit the jerk in the bar. Even though he *had* grabbed Jenny's ass.

THE TELEPHONE rang just as Kira was finishing the last book from the stack Lexie had brought to bed. Her daughter's eyes were half-closed, and she drew her tattered teddy bear closer as Kira bent to kiss her.

"Sweet dreams, honey," she whispered.

"Is Uncle Brian going to kiss me goodnight?"

"Uncle Brian will come in and kiss you when he gets home," Kira promised.

"Okay." Lexie's eyes fluttered. "'Night, Mommy."

"Good night, sweetie."

Kira inhaled the scent of her daughter's freshly washed hair as she kissed her head, then she slipped out the door. The phone was still ringing when she reached it.

The phone number on the caller ID was from the police station. Was there an emergency? "Hello?" she asked.

"Is this Ms. Johnson?" an unfamiliar voice asked.

Her hand tightened on the phone. This was no call for her professional services. "This is Kira McGinnis," she said, her voice shaky. "What's wrong?"

"Are you related to Brian Johnson?"

"Is Brian all right?" she asked, dropping into a chair like a stone. "What happened?"

"How are you related to him?"

"He's my brother," she said, fear punching her in the gut. "What's wrong? Is he hurt?"

"He's not hurt, Ms. McGinnis. But he was arrested at Sweeney's. He was in a fight."

"What?" She sucked in a breath.

"Can you come down to the station?"

"I'll be there as quickly as I can," she said dropping the phone into its cradle.

Kira wrapped her arms around her waist. Another fight. *Oh, Brian. What did you do?*

He'd been in an alcohol-fueled fight at a party the previous spring. He'd apologized profusely, promised to stop drinking and swore it wouldn't happen again. He'd been devastated when he was suspended from the track team at his high school. She'd hoped it was a learning experience that would help Brian grow up.

And now the police had arrested him because of another fight. This time in a bar.

How could she go to the police station? Kira thought with a surge of panic. She couldn't leave Lexie. And the last thing she would do was bring her along. She didn't want her five-year-old daughter to see the uncle she adored when he was drunk and possibly bloody.

Kira took several deep breaths. She could call her neighbor's teenaged daughter. The girl could stay with Lexie.

Ten minutes later, Kira ran out to her car after giving the teen her cell phone number and promising she'd be back as soon as possible.

The police station felt very different at night. Not so businesslike. Voices filled with anger and fear drifted down the stairs, and desperation hung in the air. The police officers who walked past her were grim and un-smiling. She didn't recognize any of them.

Her anxiety ratcheted higher as she stopped in front of the desk sergeant, a man she'd never met. "I'm Kira McGinnis. Someone called about my brother, Brian Johnson."

The man looked up from his paperwork, assessing her with cynical detachment. "Have a seat."

He picked up the telephone and punched in a number. After a moment, he said, "Someone is here for Johnson."

A few minutes later, she heard footsteps coming down the stairs. She stood, nervously brushing at her worn T-shirt and faded jeans. She should have changed into something more professional. But she'd been so distraught she hadn't even thought to change her clothes.

A man's khaki-clad legs came into view first, followed by a light-blue polo shirt. She started to walk toward the stairs, plastering a professional, pleasant look on her face. She stopped in shock when she saw the man wearing the khaki pants and blue shirt.

"Detective Donovan," she faltered.

"Dr. McGinnis." Despite his obvious surprise, his voice was as cool as his eyes. "I wasn't expecting to see you down here."

"You arrested my brother, Brian," she said. She was amazed at how calm and controlled her voice sounded. She was no longer a member of the department family. Instead, she was one of *them*, the relative of an offender.

Donovan stopped a few feet away from her, his face guarded. "I didn't personally arrest him. I just happened to be here when they brought him in." He paused, studying her. "He was fighting in a bar. The other guy's nose is probably broken. Brian was using a fake ID to buy beer."

Oh, Brian. "Is he all right? Was he hurt?"

His eyes thawed a fraction. "He's fine. It doesn't look like the other guy touched him."

"What happened?" She shoved her hands into the pockets of her jeans to hide their shaking.

"I'm talking to the girl he was with, trying to figure that out."

"He was with a girl? Brian doesn't have a girlfriend."

Donovan shrugged. "They were together."

Brian had a girlfriend? A girlfriend he hadn't even told her about? The pain that revelation caused was sharp and swift. "Who is she?"

"Maybe you need to talk to Brian about that," he said.

"Can you at least tell me her name?"

"Can't do that, Doc. She's a minor."

At the pity she saw in Donovan's eyes, she straightened her spine. "What happens to Brian now?"

Donovan leaned back against the wall, studying her. His gaze made her twitch with embarrassment. Finally he said, "The arresting officer needs statements from Je…the young woman, your brother and the victim. The guy with the bloody nose was making a lot of noise about pressing charges and he has the right to do that."

"Then what?"

"Then you can pay your brother's bail and take him home." Donovan's face was expressionless. "He was picked up for underage drinking and fighting a few months ago, and he's had some problems at school. I'm guessing the judge will recommend anger-management therapy."

"How do you know about his problems at school?"

"You'll have to ask Brian about that, too." He paused. "But anger-management therapy would probably be a good idea."

Humiliation washed over her in a hot wave. "Go ahead and say it, Detective. I force other people to talk to me all day, but my brother needs help more than any of them."

His eyebrows rose. "I wasn't going to say any such thing. But if the shoe fits…" He shrugged.

"My brother…" She swallowed the hard lump that lodged in her throat. "Thank you for your advice," she said. "I'm sure you mean well."

Donovan's expression hardened. "Have you talked to your brother lately?"

"I talk to Brian all the time," she shot back. "You don't know anything about his problems. I don't…"

No. She was not going to make excuses for Brian to anyone, let alone Jake Donovan. "I'm not going to abandon Brian to work out his problems alone."

"I didn't say you would." Donovan pushed away from the wall and ended up too close to her. "Have a seat," he said. "Your brother will be here for a while."

Kira resisted the urge to back away. Standing this close to Donovan emphasized his height and her lack of it. "Do you have any idea how long? I have to get home."

Scornful, he stepped away from her. "So much for not abandoning your brother. Get out of here, Doctor. I'll bring him home when he's finished."

"Wait a minute," she said, but Donovan disappeared up the stairs.

Kira rubbed her face with both hands. One of the balls she was juggling had just crashed to the ground.

And the rest of them were looking pretty damn wobbly.

CHAPTER THREE

AN HOUR LATER, Kira paced her living room. The clock ticked away the minutes as she second-guessed herself. She should have waited for Brian. Was Donovan right? Would Brian think she'd left him to fend for himself?

No. Brian knew she had to stay with Lexie. Brian would understand.

Both dogs lay on the floor, watching her. "What else could I do, guys?" Scooter tilted his head. "Brian knows why I couldn't wait for him. Right?"

After countless more minutes dragged past, a pair of lights finally cut through the darkness and a pickup truck pulled to the curb. Kira hurried to the door and yanked it open.

Brian shouldered past her without saying a word. Donovan stood on the porch, his face unreadable.

"Detective Donovan." Her hand tightened on the doorknob. "Thank you for bringing Brian home."

She began to shut the door, but Henry stuck his nose into the opening and muscled his way out. Kira lunged for him. "Henry! Get back here!"

The dog ran to Jake, shoving his nose into the detective's crotch. He relaxed into a smile.

"Those aren't exactly party manners, big guy," he said, rubbing Henry's ears.

"Sorry," Kira said, reaching for Henry. "He's an idiot." She turned and called, "Brian! Come help me get Henry inside."

"I've got him, Doc." Jake brushed her hand away and grabbed the dog's collar. "Come on, boy."

Instead of locking his legs, as Henry usually did when she tried to drag him back into the house, the dog trotted obediently through the door alongside Donovan.

Donovan closed the door, then leaned against it, speaking to Brian over her shoulder. "Looks like you need to train this dog, Johnson."

"Yeah," Brian answered, avoiding her eyes, "he can be a real pain." Brian cleared his throat. "Thanks for bringing me home, Jake."

Jake? Brian had gotten awfully friendly with the detective on the ride home.

Her brother was about to head for the stairs when Donovan stopped him. "I'll see you on Thursday."

Brian shrugged. "Yeah, I'll be there."

He mounted the first step. Kira touched his arm. "Brian…" she began.

"Don't start, Kira," he interrupted, his gaze defiant. "Not tonight, okay?"

She had no intention of arguing in front of Donovan. "Lexie wants you to give her a kiss."

His shoulders relaxed. "I wouldn't forget that."

After Brian disappeared up the stairs, silence stretched out uncomfortably between her and Donovan.

Henry broke the tension by sticking his nose in Donovan's hand, looking for attention. "You're a friendly kind of guy, aren't you?" Donovan crooned, scratching the dog's ear. Henry whined in ecstasy.

"Well." Kira reached around Donovan to open the door. "Thank you, Detective, for bringing Brian home."

"My name is Jake, and you're welcome." Donovan glanced around the living room as he spoke, and she cringed as her eyes followed his to the jumble of books and toys on the floor. She hadn't had a chance to put Lexie's things away before she ran out of the house.

"I didn't realize you had a family." Donovan's inquiring gaze settled on her.

"I'm not married," she said without thinking.

He looked back over at the toys on the floor.

"I have a daughter. That's why I couldn't wait at the station. My babysitter had to get home."

Kira clamped her mouth shut. That was as much of an explanation as he'd get. Any more would blur the lines of their professional relationship, and she'd need that control the next time he came to her office.

Donovan nodded. "I figured that when I saw the toys."

"I won't keep you then, Detective."

"You're not keeping me," he said innocently. "I'm off duty."

"So am I," she said, opening the door. "You shouldn't be in my house."

"Why not?" He glanced at the toys again, then at the open door, and leaned against the wall. "I have to reveal all my deepest, darkest thoughts but I'm not supposed to know anything about you?"

"Precisely. You talk to me in my office. You don't come to my house."

"You're throwing me out? Without asking any questions about your brother?" He raised his eyebrows.

"What questions would I have? You weren't the arresting officer."

"No. But I'm the officer who brought him home."

Without waiting for an invitation, he strolled into the living room.

"What do you think you're doing?" she said, her hand still on the doorknob. "I asked you to leave."

"You did, didn't you?" He turned to face her. "You have to watch that temper of yours, Doc. It's going to get you in trouble one of these days."

"Out, Donovan."

"Are you sure? We need to talk."

Kira closed the door, took a step toward him and stumbled on something soft. She picked up one of Lexie's colored ponies. "Talk about what?"

Donovan held her gaze. "Your brother."

"Brian is not your concern."

"No?" He rocked back on his heels. "I'll tell him you said so on Thursday."

She remembered Donovan's previous remark about seeing Brian. "Does he need to be in court then? I'll have to rearrange my schedule."

"You really don't know about Thursdays, do you?"

The pity in his eyes had her pressing her fingers into the soft pink plastic of the pony. "No, I don't."

Now he didn't bother to hide the pity. "Brian hasn't told you about the group."

"What group is that?" There was apparently one more thing she didn't know about Brian.

"Your brother belongs to a group that meets once a week at Riverton High. They're all kids who have been in trouble with the law. I set it up and I'm the adult in charge." He bent and picked up another little pony and set it on the coffee table. "Brian's been coming since last spring, and we met during the summer at Starbucks. You're supposed to know about it."

"I don't." Kira dropped into her oversized armchair and gestured for Donovan to sit. "He hasn't said a thing."

"No?" He shoved aside a pile of children's books and settled on the couch. "The kids had to have their parent or guardian sign a permission slip before they could join."

"Then Brian must have forged my name, since I'm his legal guardian. He didn't give me a permission slip."

"I can see Brian has some explaining to do."

His words implied a closeness between Jake and Brian that tore a tiny rip in her heart. Why hadn't Brian told her about the group and given her the permission slip? What had happened to the boy who used to spend hours talking to her?

"What kinds of things do you do with the kids?" Anger at her brother replaced her pain. Brian didn't know Donovan was her patient, but he'd still put her into a very uncomfortable situation.

"We talk. Other than that, I can't tell you. Sorry, Doc. Professional confidentiality. As you would say." He gave her a slight smile. "The kids and I agreed that what we say in the group stays in the group."

She tossed the pony to the floor. "That was smooth, Donovan. Subtle, but with a nice sting to it." She struggled for control. How could one man make her lose her temper twice in one day?

"I try." He leaned forward. "Don't blame yourself, Doc. Teenagers are tough to handle.

"Don't patronize me, Donovan. I can 'handle' my brother."

"Yeah, you've been doing a great job. That's why he was arrested in a bar tonight."

"That's it. Get out." She jumped to her feet, walked to the door and pulled it open. "Right now."

Donovan didn't move. "Sorry," he said, rubbing his hands over his face. "That was uncalled-for. It's been a long day." He looked up at her, and the smart-aleck expression was gone. She saw only weariness in his eyes and the lines around his mouth.

"We need to talk about your brother. Will it be tonight or do you want to meet tomorrow in the station?"

"I don't *need* to talk to you. You didn't arrest Brian."

"No. But I had the patrol officer transfer his sheet to me, since I already know Brian and have been working with him." He leaned back against the red plaid couch. "Your choice. Tomorrow in public. Or in private tonight."

"That's remarkably petty, Donovan," she said. "Will you enjoy having me sit in your office?"

"I don't have an office. I have a desk in the bullpen. And no, I'd rather not discuss this in front of everyone. But if that's what you want…" He shrugged.

The doorknob was warm to her touch. She wanted fiercely to throw open the door, tell him to leave.

Instead she closed her eyes and fought to control her breathing. After a moment, she pushed away from the door. "All right. We'll talk now."

She sat rigid in the chair, waiting.

He sighed. "I'm not trying to yank your chain."

"No?" She raised her eyebrows.

A tiny smile played around his mouth. "All right. Maybe I *was*. Just a little."

His admission deflated her anger, and she sank back into the chair, suddenly bone-tired. "Now that we have the pleasantries out of the way, what did you want to say?"

"Do you have anything to drink? A beer, maybe?"

"Sorry. I can't keep alcohol in the house because of Brian." She eased to her feet. "How about a soda? Or some iced tea?"

"A cola would be great. Thanks."

When she returned a few minutes later with a can of cola for him and iced tea for herself, she saw that Henry had his head on Donovan's knee. The detective was scratching Henry's ear, and the dog's eyes were closed, an expression of bliss on his face.

"Just push him away or he'll be in your lap," she said as she sat back down. "He thinks he's Scooter's size."

"He's fine. I miss having a dog around."

Scooter, more suspicious, lay next to the door. His

head tucked between his paws, he kept his watchful gaze on the detective.

I'm with you, Scooter. Donovan looked way too comfortable, sitting in her cluttered living room with her dog drooling all over him.

It was an oddly intimate scene, and it made her feel uncomfortable. She wasn't used to having a man in her house late at night.

"Let's start over. Thank you again for bringing Brian home," she said.

"You're welcome." His gaze catalogued the room, lingered on the pictures on the bookshelf. "I didn't think I'd be seeing you again so soon, Kira."

"Neither did I, Detective."

"Call me Jake. When you call me Detective, it makes me feel like I'm sitting in your office."

"Believe me, Detective, I know you're not in my office." She shoved a strand of hair behind her ear, embarrassed that her hand trembled.

He watched her hand, then her face as he tipped the can of soda to his mouth.

"What's wrong, Kira?" His voice thrummed across her nerves in the heavy silence.

"You mean besides Brian being arrested tonight?" She gulped her iced tea. "Besides that it's past midnight and a police officer is sitting in my living room?"

"Don't beat yourself up so much. He's not the first kid who screwed up, and he won't be the last."

"This isn't the first time he's screwed up."

"You have your hands full, don't you?"

"I'm not looking for sympathy, Detective. Don't feel sorry for me."

Jake took a swallow of soda. "Feel sorry for you? No, that's not what I feel," he said softly.

"The relationship between a police officer and the family of a person who's been arrested is always complicated."

"There's that, too," he said, his voice deepening.

She rolled her eyes. "Knock it off, Donovan. Flirt all you want, but it doesn't change anything. You're still my patient and you're still coming in to see me again."

"Hey, it was worth a try."

She told herself she should be angry, but his amusement was contagious.

"All right, Donovan. I'll concede this round." She stopped trying to suppress her smile. "Just remember that the next round's in my office."

She saw genuine interest stir beneath the teasing mask he wore. "You're good, Doc," he murmured, his eyes suddenly hot with intensity.

The moment stretched uncomfortably long. Finally Kira cleared her throat. "All right. Tell me what's going to happen with Brian."

He took a last drink of soda and set the can down, his intensity replaced by cool professionalism. "He'll have a hearing in front of a judge in the next few days. I'm going to recommend probation, with this arrest expunged from his record if he behaves himself for the next year. Do you have a problem with that?"

"Of course not. That's very generous."

He shrugged. "It's not generous. It's fair. If he can keep his nose clean, he won't have a permanent record."

Kira studied him. "You care about Brian, don't you?"

"Why are you surprised? I know Brian. I've seen him once a week for the past several months."

"I'm glad there's another adult in his life," she said. "I love Brian very much, but I'm not sure which way to turn with him."

"May I ask you a question, Kira?"

It felt as though he'd touched her. She set her iced tea down on the table, too hard. "Of course."

"Why is Brian living with you? What's the deal with your parents?"

Kira's gaze strayed to the bookshelf, to a picture of four people. The man and woman had their arms around each other, and the love they shared was obvious. The boy and girl stood close, smiling into the camera, a parent's hand on each of their shoulders. "My father and his mother were killed in a car accident when he was twelve. Brian was injured in the crash—he had a head injury and was in the hospital and then rehab for three months."

Talking about it stirred painful memories for Kira. "Brian's personality changed after his injury. He became more irritable, his temper flared for no apparent reason and he has attention problems at school."

"That's tough," Donovan said softly.

"He was slowly improving and was still the same basically sweet kid until seven or eight months ago.

That party last spring, the one where he was arrested, was the first time I realized there was a problem. And it's just gotten worse."

"What does Brian say?"

"He says he's fine and to get off his back. He goes ballistic if I mention the word *therapy*."

"In other words, he's a typical eighteen-year-old." Donovan ambled over to the bookcase, picked up the picture and studied it. "Is he involved in any sports at school? Or any other activities?"

"He was on the track team last spring, but he was suspended for drinking. He's been on the basketball team the past three years, but he hasn't been working out with them or playing in the summer league games." She sighed. "Anything I suggest becomes a power struggle."

"You need to keep him busy." He set the picture back on the shelf. "He still has his job, doesn't he?"

"Yes, he works at Digital City Electronics."

"He's still coming to the group," he said. "And he participates—he doesn't just sit there like some of the kids. That's a positive."

"I guess it is," she said, her voice low.

"You know, there's another way to look at what happened tonight. Brian shouldn't have hit that guy, but the guy did grab the girl he was with. Not everyone would put himself on the line to protect a woman. Brian said he did what he needed to do and I respect that." He glanced up the stairs to where the teen had disappeared. "He had the right idea. He just picked the wrong method."

"Thank you for saying that, Detective."

"It's Jake."

"All right. Jake."

His eyes twinkled. "Was that so hard?"

He was too close to her. She stood and slipped around him. "I can't keep you any longer, Jake. I appreciate your help tonight."

"Anytime, Kira." His expression was unreadable. "You know where to find me if you need anything."

"I do." She opened the front door. "Thanks again."

A smile hovered on his lips. "If I didn't know better, I'd say I was getting the bum's rush."

"You'd be right. It's late, and we both have to work tomorrow."

"All I'm doing is riding my desk." He watched her steadily. "Remember?"

"How could I forget?" She stepped in front of the door, smiling. "Since you have so much free time tomorrow, I'll schedule you for another appointment."

He cocked his head to one side. "There's more to you than meets the eye, isn't there, Doc?"

"That's true for everyone, isn't it? Thank you again for bringing Brian home. I'll see you tomorrow."

"Maybe you will." He lifted his hands. "Maybe you won't."

She closed the door behind him and leaned against it, listening to his footsteps fade away. What was she going to do about Jake Donovan?

CHAPTER FOUR

THE NEXT MORNING, the ringing of the phone roused Kira from a deep sleep. She opened her eyes and glanced at the alarm clock, then shot straight up in bed. She'd overslept.

She fumbled the cordless phone as she picked it up and pushed the talk button. "Hello?" Somehow she managed to sound composed and professional.

"Dr. McGinnis? This is Captain Crowley."

"Hello, Captain." Crowley was in charge of the detectives. Kira swung her legs out of bed.

"What's going on with Donovan? I need him cleared."

"He was in yesterday." Kira got up and stuck her head out the bedroom door, listening for Lexie.

"Good. Then he's set to go back on active duty?"

"Not yet. We need to talk about a few more issues."

The silence on the other end of the phone was heavy with disapproval. "What kind of issues?" he finally asked.

"You know I can't discuss that with you, Captain," Kira said.

"Donovan is one of my best detectives. I need him back on the street," the captain bellowed. "Yesterday."

Kira held the phone away from her ear. Crowley's hair-trigger temper was legendary in the department.

"I'm trying to arrange for Detective Donovan to see me again today." A bead of sweat rolled down her neck.

"Don't give me any of that 'trying' crap. I want him in your office today. And back on the street tonight."

"I'll do my best, Captain."

"Damn right you will. If you can't get Donovan cleared, I'll get someone else who can."

Kira flinched as Crowley slammed the phone down. Then she carefully placed the handset.

She rubbed the back of her neck, where a vicious headache was starting. Then she hurried into her bathroom. If she was quick, they might be only a few minutes late.

"Is Uncle Brian awake yet?" Lexie asked as Kira helped her get dressed.

"No, he's not." Kira had tried to open his door before she woke Lexie up, but it had been locked.

"I want to talk to him before we go to Shelley's."

"Uncle Brian is still sleeping," Kira said as she wrestled a shoe onto Lexie's foot. "You can talk to him when we get home."

"I need to talk to him now. I need to make sure he gave me a kiss last night."

"He did." Lifted her daughter off the bed, Kira took her hand. "We're running late this morning, pumpkin. Let's go have a quick breakfast."

"I can't talk to Uncle Brian?" Lexie's lip trembled.

Patience. "Uncle Brian is cranky if he wakes up too early," she said, keeping her voice upbeat. "You don't want him to growl like a bear at us, do you?"

Lexie giggled, the impending tears gone. "I would growl back at him."

Kira led the way to the door, "We'll practice our growls while we eat breakfast, okay?"

"Okay." Lexie skipped down the hall, slowing only to touch Brian's door. It was her ritual every morning if Brian was still asleep.

"Will Uncle Brian be here when we get home tonight?" Lexie asked.

"I think so," Kira answered lightly. He'd better be. He wasn't working today, and she'd written him a note, telling him to be there when she got back from work.

Lexie took a bite of her toast, then asked her mother what the bite mark looked like. Refusing to rush her daughter's breakfast, Kira forced herself to play the game. But when Lexie finally finished, she helped her wash her hands, grabbed the child's backpack and rushed her out the door.

She dropped Lexie off at Shelley's, then continued on to work, already fifteen minutes late. Lexie had gone happily with Shelley, and Kira should be thrilled. But today she just wanted to hold her close. She wanted to give Lexie her undivided attention.

It felt as if her tiny family was splintering. Brian was pushing her away, and Lexie was becoming more independent every day. Babies grew up—that's how it was supposed to be. But she wasn't quite ready for her daughter to move into the next stage of her life. And Brian wasn't ready to move into the next stage of his.

Her frustration only increased when she reached her office. One of her appointments didn't show up, and another called to cancel. When she phoned Jake, she got nothing but a terse voice-mail message.

Rubbing her temples, trying to erase her headache, Kira walked down the stairs and into the bull pen, smiling at the cops she recognized. Was she imagining it, or were the greetings more subdued this morning? Had word already gotten out about her brother being arrested last night?

Of course it had. Cops were the worst gossips around.

Avoiding the furtive glances, she headed for Donovan's desk. He wasn't there.

"Good morning, Mac," she said.

He looked up from a file. "Hey, Kira. How are you?"

"I'm fine. I'd be better if your partner was around."

Mac looked over at Jake's desk. "Yeah, me, too."

"You don't know where he is?"

Mac tossed the file onto a stack of folders. "He called and left a message, said he was taking a personal day. He didn't tell me why."

"If you hear from him, tell him to give me a call."

"I'm sorry about your brother," he said.

"Thanks." She glanced around the room, at the other cops trying hard not to pay attention to her. "I guess I shouldn't be surprised that everyone already knows."

"You know cops," Mac said with an easy grin. "No secret is safe from us."

"Oh, yeah," she said. "I do know cops."

Frustrated with Jake's absence, annoyed with herself for letting Captain Crowley's threats bother her, she turned to go.

"He's not a bad guy, Kira."

"No, he's not," she said. "He's just a cop."

"Cut him some slack," Mac said, lowering his voice. "Jake doesn't take well to being backed into a corner."

"There's a news flash," she said, remembering her session with Jake the day before. "I'm not trying to back him into a corner. But you know I can't clear him until he talks to me."

"Yeah, I know."

"Does he want to return to active duty?"

"Of course he does."

She shrugged. "He isn't acting like a cop who's itching to get back on the street."

"Are you two spreading gossip about me again?"

Kira spun around to face Jake who stood next to a pretty blond woman with her arm twined around his. Kira bumped into desk behind her. Then she straightened.

"Absolutely," she said, crossing her arms. "We love talking about you behind your back. I was just telling Mac how much I needed to see you."

Donovan's eyes gleamed. "That's what all the women say. They can't get enough of me." He elbowed the woman next to him. "Right, Lissa?"

The blonde rolled her eyes. "Oh, yeah, J.J. You're a real catch."

J.J.? Kira looked from Mac to the woman.

"Mac, you remember Lissa, don't you? Kira, this is my sister."

"Hi, Lissa," Mac said, struggling to hide a smile.

His sister. "Very nice to meet you," Kira said, reaching out to shake hands.

Lissa gave her a quick, assessing look that was disconcertingly like her brother's. "Very nice to meet you, too, Kira," she said, then grinned slowly at her brother. "Now I know why you were so hot to stop by the station."

"I knew I should have made you wait in the car," Jake said, but he smiled as he ruffled his sister's hair. "Kira is the department psychologist. We're professional colleagues."

"Whatever you say, J.J." Lissa winked at him and Kira heard Mac trying to suppress a laugh.

"Knock it off, Liss. Or do I have to send you to your room?"

Lissa stuck her tongue out at him, then wandered off to talk to a young cop she apparently knew.

"Her car's broken and I'm dropping her off at work," Jake explained, watching his sister.

"That's very nice of you, J.J.," Kira answered.

Jake crossed his arms. "That's what she called me when she was a baby, and it stuck." He glanced from her to Mac. "And if anyone in this building calls me J.J. again, revenge will be swift and deadly."

"Your secret's safe with me," Mac said, clearing his throat. "J.J."

"You'll die a slow and painful death, McDougal," Jake warned. "I promise."

"I see now why you have all those women after you," Mac added. "Who can resist a man named J.J.?"

"Speaking of women being after you," Kira interrupted, "how about getting together with me this afternoon at one-thirty."

Jake turned away from her. "Sorry, Doc. I just came in to grab some files. It'll have to be another day." He pulled open a file cabinet.

"You're not afraid of me, are you Donovan?" Kira leaned against Mac's desk. Her smile held a challenge.

"Afraid of you?" His eyes slowly traveled down her body, then back up again. "No, I'm not afraid of you."

Kira held his gaze. "Sure seems that way."

"In your dreams, Doc." He made a production out of looking at his watch. "I'm a busy man. Places to be, people to see."

"That means he's getting together with his baby delinquents," Mac translated.

Kira swung around to face him. "One of those so-called delinquents is my brother."

"Jeez, Kira, I'm sorry, Mac said, clearly embarrassed. "I was just joking around. I didn't know your brother was in Jake's group."

Jake shot Mac a dirty look. "Nice going, Ace."

Jake gathered up a handful of files. "Well, kids, it's been fun talking to you, but I've got to run. Come on, Lissa," he called to his sister. "You're going to be late."

"Wait a minute," Kira said. "You told Brian last night the meeting was Thursday."

Jake shrugged. "I changed it." She saw pity in the

blue depths of his eyes. "One of the kids called me this morning and asked if we could move it up."

"Brian?"

"You know I can't tell you that," he answered. "You'll have to ask Brian about the group."

She stared after him as he and Lissa clattered down the stairs.

"I'm really sorry, Kira." Mac said from behind her. "I honestly didn't know about your brother. You want to slap me around a little? Be my guest."

"You're not the one I want to slap around."

Mac's lips twitched. "You want to knock my partner on his butt, get in line. I'm first, and Crowley is right behind me."

Kira smiled reluctantly. "I think Crowley has jumped to the head of the line. He called me at home this morning. He's not happy with Jake. Or me."

"Why did Crowley call you and not Jake?"

"Maybe he thinks he can intimidate me," she answered.

Mac laughed. "Shows you what he knows. I'll talk to Jake. I'll make sure he comes to see you tomorrow."

"Thanks, Mac, but don't worry about it. Jake's a big boy. And I can fight my own battles."

An idea percolating in her mind, Kira glanced at the stairs. "I'll talk to you later, Mac."

Without waiting for an answer, she ran to her office, checked her schedule to make sure she didn't have an appointment in the next hour, then grabbed her purse and hurried out of the building. Ten minutes later she pulled into a parking spot near the Starbucks closest to the high school.

JAKE STRETCHED his legs out and leaned against the back of the chair, enjoying the rich smell of coffee, the hiss of the espresso machine and the quiet clicking of computer keys. He studied the three kids huddled across the table from him. They were talking to each other in low voices while Brian stood at the counter, waiting for his order. He jiggled his foot and clenched and unclenched his hands in his pocket as he gazed at the group, then looked away.

Clearly, Brian was having second thoughts about asking to meet today. He'd blurted out the request in a late-night phone call, after having woken Jake from a restless, uneasy sleep. Brian had back-pedaled in another phone call this morning, which was why Jake had volunteered to pick the kid up. There was nothing like a captive audience.

Brian walked back to the table holding two cups of coffee. He handed one to Jenny, then sat beside her. Jenny smiled encouragingly and patted his arm.

"Okay, guys." Jake sat up in the velvet easy chair. "Brian asked us here, so he'll start us off."

Brian took a deep, shaky breath. "I was arrested last night."

Jenny reached for his hand and twined her fingers with his, and Brian flashed her a grateful look. The piercings in her eyebrows, nose and ears gleamed in the subdued lighting. She shook her dyed-black hair out of her face and crossed one thin leg over the other as she leaned toward him. "Tell them why, Bri."

"I was fighting in a bar."

Jake held Brian's gaze. The kid sighed. "And drinking. Jen and I were both drinking."

"What kind of stupid dork are you?" Alex scowled and slouched lower in his seat. His angry expression was partially hidden behind the popped collar of his polo shirt.

"The guy was grabbing Jen. All right? And he was hassling her about the way she looks. He was calling her a vampire and asking her if she'd suck his blood."

"You shouldn't have been there in the first place, man."

"You think I don't know that?" Brian glared at Alex. "I screwed up, okay? I made a mistake. But the guy wouldn't stop. He wouldn't leave Jen alone."

"He told the guy three times to stop," Jenny added, gripping Brian's hand.

"What the hell were you thinking, Jen?" Ronnie, one of the other boys, slapped the table. Both knees of his jeans were ripped out and his T-shirt had a hole beneath one arm. His hair looked as if it hadn't been combed in several days. "You guys were supposed to watch out for each other. You were supposed to keep each other out of bars."

"Not so loud," Jake said. "We're in a public place."

Brian turned to Alex. "So what do you do when you want a drink real bad?"

Alex grimaced. "I look at the yearbook."

"What for?"

"I look at the picture of the soccer team. And I don't see my picture there. The coach threw me off after I was arrested. If I want to play this year, I have to stay clean." He gave Brian a speculative look. "Don't you play basketball?"

"I did last year. But I probably won't make the team this year," Brian answered. "And I don't care."

Jake leaned forward. "You told me you were going to start working out with them, Brian."

Brian avoided Jake's eyes. "It doesn't matter now. After what I did last night, Coach Ryan won't let me be on the team even if I wanted to. Which I don't."

Jake made a mental note to talk to Brian's coach. Playing basketball would be good for Brian.

Ronnie jumped in with a suggestion, and Jake sat back, letting the kids talk. He wanted them to work out their problems together as much as possible. Suggestions had more power when they came from peers.

As he raised his cup to his mouth, he glanced out the front window and spotted a woman at one of the outside tables. She'd been looking into the shop, but when she caught his gaze, she jerked her head away.

Kira McGinnis.

He sat up too quickly, spilling hot coffee onto his hand. She'd followed him here. To spy on Brian? Or on him?

As he listened to the kids talk, he kept an eye on Kira. Thank God Brian was sitting with his back toward the front of the café. The kid was shaky right now. If he saw his sister watching him, he'd go ballistic. And Jake wouldn't blame him.

He'd been shocked that Brian's sister, the woman he'd described as an overbearing, interfering pain in the butt, had turned out to be Dr. McGinnis. He'd been equally surprised that she hadn't been the distant, professional woman he'd confronted in her office. She'd seemed human. Approachable. And far too attractive for his peace of mind.

Now, watching her outside the coffee shop, spying on them, he slid her into a less-threatening slot in his mind. Apparently she *was* interfering and overbearing.

Thank God.

He didn't need Kira McGinnis taking up residence in his head. He didn't want to think of her as anything other than the company shrink. After last night, the lines between professional and personal had blurred in his mind.

Those lines were once again sharply defined.

BATTLING HER FEELINGS of shame, knowing it was wrong, Kira watched, transfixed. Although she couldn't hear the words, the animation in Brian's gestures was unmistakable. It had been so long since he'd been enthused about anything. And she was amazed at how Jake held every kid's attention. When he spoke they hung on every word.

She stayed until Brian took the cup from the girl, stood and dropped it in the trash along with his own. When the rest of the group pushed away from the tables,

Kira stood, accidentally knocking her chair backward. She grabbed it and steadied it, then hurried away.

Sitting in her car, she took a deep breath and let it out slowly. "You are so out of line." Shame overwhelmed her as she watched the small group walk out of the coffee shop. She slid down in her seat, promising God she would never spy on Brian again. *Just please, please don't let him see me.*

After a few minutes, she saw Jake drive past in his truck, Brian and the girl seated next to him. Kira waited long enough for Jake to get well away from Starbucks, then she started her car and drove back to the station.

THAT EVENING, the front door opened while Kira was mixing together a batch of gazpacho. She heard Brian's steps heading up the stairs. "Uncle Brian," Lexie called, and she ran up the stairs after him.

"Hey, Lex," she heard Brian say. "What's up?" His voice was soft and gentle, full of love for his niece.

Kira walked into the living room and called, "Hi, Bri. I'll need you to set the table in a few minutes."

"All right." She heard his door slam.

She stood staring up the stairs, wondering where all his anger was coming from. Wondering why she couldn't connect with her brother.

As she headed back to the kitchen, she heard a knock on the front door. She was tempted to ignore it, not in the mood for solicitors, but at another knock, a little harder, she yanked open the door.

Jake stood on her porch, his eyes aloof.

"Detective Donovan. Jake. Come in."

She stepped aside as he brushed past her. "I need to talk to you, Kira. Can you walk around the block with me?"

"Um, I think so. Hold on."

She ran up the stairs and knocked on Brian's door. "Bri? Could you come downstairs and watch Lexie for a few minutes? I need to talk to Detective Donovan."

The teen threw his door open. "Why are you talking to Jake?"

"Because he said he needed to talk to me."

Brian pushed past her and ran down the stairs. "What are you doing here?" He stood too close to Jake, his fists clenched. "Why do you need to talk to Kira?"

"Because she's your guardian. There are things we have to discuss, and we're going outside to do it." Jake nodded at Lexie, who was playing with dolls on the floor. "Do you want the kid to hear what happened last night?"

Brian's face flushed. "No."

"Then cut the crap."

"You're not going to talk about today, are you?"

Jake laid his hand on Brian's shoulder. "What do we say every time the group meets?"

"Nothing leaves the group."

"Right. So, no, I'm not going to talk about today." He glanced over at Kira. "If you want your sister to know what you had to say, tell her yourself."

Kira was amazed by Brian's reaction. Instead of arguing with Jake, Brian nodded and moved away, dropping onto the floor next to Lexie.

She opened the front door and walked out, glancing back into the house before Jake pulled the door shut. Brian sat on the floor with Lexie, holding one of her dolls.

Her throat swelled with emotion. Brian was barely civil to her—she couldn't remember the last time they'd had a conversation. There were whole parts of his life he kept hidden. Jake knew more about her brother than she did.

"Don't look like that, Kira." Jake's voice interrupted her thoughts. "It's easier for kids to confide in someone who's not as close to them. It feels safer."

"I didn't even know he had a girlfriend."

"Maybe Brian needs some time to figure out the relationship before he tells you about it."

"Where did you learn so much about relating to kids?" she asked, running her hand along her neighbor's wood fence. "You don't even work the juvenile beat at the station."

"I'm the oldest of five kids," he said. "I helped raise my brothers and sister. And if it's any comfort, my siblings treated me worse than Brian is treating you."

"That's hard to believe," she said, trying to lighten her voice, blinking furiously to stop the tears. "Your sister seems very nice."

"Yeah, she is now." His voice was equally light. "It was a different story when she and my brothers were teens. I still have nightmares about some of the stunts they pulled."

By this time they'd reached the end of the block and

turned the corner. "You didn't want to talk to me about your siblings," she said, struggling to regain her professional distance. "What did you want?"

Jake shoved his hands into his pockets and looked down at her, his eyes cool. "I saw you at Starbucks today," he said. "What did you think you were doing?"

CHAPTER FIVE

"Starbucks?" she repeated, her voice faint.

"Yeah, the place with the coffee. Yuppie heaven. Where I was meeting with my group."

She could feel the heat of his accusation. "Yes, I was there." She stared at her shoes, her toes curling in mortification. "But I wasn't trying to intrude."

"No? You just wanted coffee and picked that particular Starbucks? Passing up two or three closer to the station?"

"No, I picked that one deliberately." She met his angry gaze. "I needed to talk to you."

"You could have talked to me at the station."

"Really? And when would that have been? When I found you at your desk this morning? When you called to return the messages I left you?"

"I knew what you wanted and I didn't have time for you this morning." He kicked a small stone on the sidewalk. "This isn't about me, Kira. It's about you. Do you think Brian is going to open up to you if you spy on him?"

She clenched her hands in her pockets. "I was wrong, Donovan. I admit it. I shouldn't have been there. But I'm worried about Brian. And I did need to see you."

"About what?"

"We need to schedule an appointment. Tomorrow."

"I'll do it when I get a chance."

"Fine. The next time Captain Crowley calls me, I'll explain to him about your busy schedule. I'm sure he'll be very understanding and supportive."

"Crowley called you?" He stopped and stared at her.

"This morning. He wants you back on the street."

"Damn it." He ran his hand through his hair. "He shouldn't have called you."

"I agree. He should have called you."

"I hope you told him to go to hell."

"Yeah, I chewed him out royally." She rolled her eyes. "Come on, Donovan. I need my job. I made polite noises and said, 'yes, Captain.'"

They passed the small park where she walked the dogs in the evenings. Finally Jake said, "I'm sorry, Kira. I had no idea he'd call you."

"He seems to want you out of my office pretty badly."

"Of course he does." Jake scowled. "He's a control freak. He can't stand someone else being in charge of me." A baseball from a game in the park rolled to the curb, and he picked it up and threw it back. It sailed over the kids' heads.

"I'm not in charge of you."

"Until I'm back on the street, you are."

"Then maybe I'll just order you back into my office, first thing tomorrow morning."

His lips twitched. "I won't pay any more attention to you than I do to Crowley."

"That puts me in my place." She suppressed a grin. "Maybe he needs you. He said you were one of his best detectives."

"He'd say anything to get me out of your office."

"You and Crowley have a lot in common, then."

"You're a real comedian, aren't you?" Jake shook his head.

"I try." She held his gaze. "So are you telling me you're not a good detective?"

"I'm a damn good detective," he growled. "Don't start with the therapist talk. I'm not on the couch in your office now, Doc. Stop poking around in my head."

"I don't have a couch in my office."

He raised an eyebrow. "You're a cool one, aren't you?"

"I have no idea what you mean, Detective."

He turned to face her. "All these sly questions about how I feel. I've seen that technique before."

"What technique would that be?"

"That technique of never letting up, of asking questions until I break. It's not going to work."

"I thought we were just having a conversation."

"We were," he said, dryly. "About you spying on your brother. How did we end up talking about my qualities as a detective?"

She shrugged. "I have no idea."

They turned the corner onto her block, and Jake slowed down. "Okay. Back to the important stuff. Brian."

"You think Brian is more important than your job?"

He sighed. "Nice try, Doc. You need to back off. You have to loosen the apron strings and give Brian more freedom. He's growing up."

"I'm not sure he's ready for more freedom," she said.

"He thinks he is."

"And you trust the judgment of an eighteen-year-old?"

He laughed. "Good point."

"I understand what you're saying. But I know Brian. I know what his problems are. And I don't think it's a good idea to turn him loose."

"I'm not suggesting you turn him loose." They were back in front of the house and he stopped to lean against the pole holding up her basketball hoop. "But ease up a little. Let him try and fail. It's not the worse thing in the world for a kid."

"How would you have reacted if someone told you to give your siblings more freedom?" she retorted. "Especially if they'd been getting into serious trouble?"

He grinned at her. "I would have told them they were out of their minds. I wouldn't have paid any attention."

"There you go."

His smile faded. "It's because of what happened with my siblings that I'm telling you to loosen up with Brian. Let him prove he's capable of making good decisions."

In her mind, Kira saw a younger Brian struggling with his rehab after the accident. She saw his frustration when he couldn't remember something, his temper when he failed. She saw his fear that he would always be a freak, different from everyone else. "You don't know how badly I want him to be a normal teenager, to have a normal teen's problems," she said in a low voice.

"Hey," Jake said, "these *are* a normal teen's problems. Probably three-quarters of the seniors in his high school have tried alcohol. A lot of kids get into fights. He's not reinventing the wheel here, Kira."

"I'd love to think he's just going through a normal teenage phase. But most of the other kids in his high school didn't have a serious head injury when they were younger," she explained. "Most of them don't have attention and concentration problems. The other kids will figure it out as they get older. I'm not sure Brian will."

"Brian is a bright kid. And he's basically a good kid. Don't give up on him."

"You're out of line, Detective. I haven't given up on Brian and I never will. I'm just being realistic."

"All kids should have such a passionate advocate in their corners." Jake leaned closer. "Brian doesn't know how lucky he is."

"I love Brian very much. And Lexie adores him. We're the lucky ones."

He stared down at her, the expression in his blue eyes warm. "Brian should thank God you're his sister."

The emotion she read in his face made her uncomfortable. "I think that might be asking for the impossible."

He put his hand against the pole and looked up at the

basketball hoop. "Brian was on the basketball team in school last year, wasn't he?"

"Yes, he was."

"It's nice that he has this hoop so he can practice."

"Who says this hoop is for Brian?"

"Who's it for? Your kid?"

"Why not?" she said, pretending to shoot a basket. "Lexie likes to play basketball."

"I played in high school. Maybe I'll challenge Brian to a game."

"I think he'd like that," she said.

As they walked to the house, Jake touched her arm. "Are you going to stop spying on Brian?"

"I wasn't spying!"

He just watched her, saying nothing.

"All right, maybe I was. Just a little." She gave in and let herself smile. "But getting caught has cured me."

"I hope so."

"Goodbye, Jake," she said.

"'Bye, Kira."

When she stepped into the house, Brian looked up from where he sat on the living room floor, playing with Lexie. "Where's Jake?"

"He left."

Brian ran to the door. "Hey, Jake." he yelled.

Kira could hear Jake coming back. "Yeah?"

Trying to give Brian some privacy, Kira knelt next to Lexie. She and Brian had taken the cushions off the chairs and the couch and arranged them on the floor.

"What are you playing?" Kira asked.

"Me and Uncle Brian are playing princess. I'm the dragon and I'm going to eat the princess." Lexie roared at Kira and waved her arms in the air.

"What's Uncle Brian?"

"He's the princess." Lexie pointed to a toy tiara lying on the floor. "This is his crown."

Kira stifled a laugh. "Is Uncle Brian a good princess?"

"Yes. The dragon thinks he will taste very good."

Kira picked up the tiara and ran her finger over the gold-painted plastic and the blue, red, green and yellow jewels. "You don't want the princess to step on her crown," she said, kissing Lexie. "You and Uncle Brian have fun. I need to finish making dinner."

Lexie roared as Kira retreated to the kitchen.

A few minutes later, as she made the garlic bread and added the finishing touches to the gazpacho, Brian came into the kitchen. "I asked Jake to stay for dinner," he said. "That's okay, isn't it?"

Jake appeared in the doorway behind Brian.

"Um, Brian, I'm not sure that's a good idea." She glanced at Jake, expecting him to chime in that he couldn't stay. Instead, he gave her an innocent look.

"Why not?" Brian demanded. "You always make extra."

It would be a breach of confidentiality to tell Brian that Jake was her patient. "Jake probably has plans."

"That's why I asked him to stay. There's something we have to do."

Flashing Jake an irritated look, she said to Brian,

"You're not running out of here with Jake after dinner. I told you I wanted to talk to you tonight."

Brian scowled. "We won't be long. I'll be back in plenty of time." He glanced toward the living room. "I figured you'd want to wait until Lex is in bed, anyway."

"What do you and Jake have to do that can't wait?"

"We have to get some flyers printed. To pass out at the high-school registration tomorrow."

Okay, this was what Jake was talking about. Ordinarily she'd question Brian about the flyers and ask for details. It's what she would have done yesterday.

"All right, you and Jake run your errand. But I'll expect you back early tonight."

His look of surprise made her feel a pang of remorse. Maybe Jake was right.

"I'll be back. So can Jake stay for dinner?" he wheedled. "That way we can get started earlier and I'll be back earlier."

Her lips twitched. "That was very smooth, Brian. All right, Jake can stay."

"Thanks, Kira."

Brian went back into the living room. She narrowed her eyes at Jake, who was leaning against the wall. "I couldn't tell him you were my patient. You should have said you couldn't stay."

He shrugged. "I'm not having dinner with the doctor. I'm having dinner with one of the kids in my group and his fascinating sister."

Fascinating? "What if I don't want to have dinner with you?"

He looked at his hands, then down at his clothes, and grinned. "I'm clean, I'm polite and I'm able to carry on a conversation. What about me will put you off your food?"

Her heart fluttered at his grin. Apparently she wasn't immune to the Donovan charm. "Don't flatter yourself, Donovan. I haven't met the man yet who can put me off my food."

"Is that a challenge?"

"Nope. Just a statement of fact. I'm only letting you stay because Brian wants you here."

"Hey, Jake," Brian called from the living room. "You want to play with Lexie and me? Or are you going to stay in the kitchen?"

"I'll play with you and Lexie," Jake said, glancing at Kira. "I think I'm bothering your sister."

"In your dreams," Kira muttered as she walked past him and dropped next to Lexie. "Lex, this is Mr. Donovan. Jake, this is my daughter, Lexie."

"Hi, Lexie," he said, folding himself onto the floor. "What are we playing here?"

"We're playing princess," Lexie answered.

"That's a good game. You look like a princess to me."

"I'm not the princess. I'm the dragon."

"Yeah?" Jake said. "Then who's the princess?"

"Brian's the princess," Lexie said happily. She picked up the tiara. "Put your crown on, Uncle Brian."

With a defiant look at Jake, Brian set the tiara on his head. It was too small for him and it slipped sideways. Kira's heart swelled as she watched him straighten it. Brian would do anything for Lexie.

"It's a good look for you," Jake said, grinning.

"Darn right it is." Brian pushed the tiara into place and turned to Lexie. "What can Jake be?"

Lexie studied Jake for a moment. "He can be the princess's horse," she said. "The princess can ride on the horse when she fights the dragon."

"Good choice, Lex." Brian grinned. "Jake will make a good horse for me to ride."

Kira retreated to the kitchen. As she tossed salad, she listened to the sounds of Lexie and Brian rolling around on the floor, fighting. Lexie shrieked with laughter as Brian begged for mercy in a falsetto voice, both dogs barking. And Jake neighed and snorted and pawed the ground.

By the time Kira went into the dining area to set the table, the battle was over. Lexie had her arms around Brian, her face buried in his T-shirt. When Brian saw Kira, he said, "The dragon is eating the princess."

Jake lay on the floor, arms and legs spread out. "The dragon already killed the horse," he said.

Laughing, Kira finished setting the table. "I hope the battle worked up an appetite, because dinner's ready."

The three immediately jumped off the floor and headed for the table. Jake reached for the chair next to hers, then hesitated, "Where do you want me?"

"How about beside Brian at the head of the table?" she said, giving him a gracious smile. That would put him as far away from her as possible.

Jake's eyes twinkled. "Can't take the heat?"

"I love the heat," she answered sweetly. "But you're Brian's guest. I assumed you'd want to talk to him."

Jake grinned as he bent his head for grace.

BRIAN OPENED the front door quietly later that evening, hoping Kira was reading Lexie her bedtime story. With any luck, she wouldn't hear him come in.

He was halfway up the stairs when Kira called from the kitchen, "Hello, Bri. You're not trying to hide in your room, are you?"

He sighed and reversed, coming down the stairs. "Hey, it was worth a try."

His sister was standing in the kitchen door, looking at him uncertainly. He stopped at the bottom of the stairs. "What's wrong?"

She shrugged as she sat in a chair. "Nothing's wrong. I appreciate you getting home early."

He shrugged. "I said I would."

"I know."

He looked away. She didn't have to tell him that he'd said he'd do a lot of things lately that he hadn't. He flopped onto the couch. "What did you want to talk about?"

"What do you think, Brian?"

She didn't sound mad. She sounded disappointed. Man, he hated when she got that sad look on her face. Like he'd let her down. He slouched lower on the couch. "Last night, I guess."

"What happened?"

"I heard Jake down here last night," he said. "I'm sure he told you all about it."

His sister studied him for a moment. "Jake didn't tell me very much. I want to hear your version."

Brian's knee began to jiggle and he looked away from Kira. "I was in a bar, all right? I know I shouldn't have been there, but I was." He'd wanted to show Jenny how cool he was. It had been stupid, and he'd known it as soon as they used their fake IDs to get a beer. But he couldn't back down. He didn't want Jenny to think he was a tool.

"Why did you start a fight?"

His face flushed. "Some guy was making fun of my friend." He cleared his throat. "The guy was calling Jenny a vampire and a freak. I told him to knock it off, but he didn't." And that was the worst part. Knowing that he'd been useless, knowing he hadn't been able to protect Jenny. "Then he grabbed her. So I hit him."

Kira didn't say anything for a long time, and he sneaked a glance at her. Her sad look made him want to disappear into the couch cushions.

"You said you know you were wrong to go to the bar…?"

He looked down at his hands, clamped around his thighs, and nodded.

"Then why did you, Brian?"

He shrugged. "I don't know."

"I thought…I thought you'd learned your lesson the last time were arrested."

Hearing a sob in her voice, he glanced up in horror. Why was she crying? Was she trying to make him feel worse than he already did? "I screwed up, all right?"

He heard the sullen tone of his voice, but was unable to change it. "Is that what you want to hear?"

"No, Brian. I want to hear why you did it."

"I don't know why," he said wildly. He would *not* tell her that he'd done it to impress Jenny. "I told you that."

"So this was just an impulsive decision. You went into the bar without a thought about the consequences."

"No, it wasn't impulsive. I thought…"

"You thought what, Bri?"

He *so* did not want to get another lecture about thinking before acting. "I thought it would impress Jenny. Okay? Are you happy?"

His sister sighed. "No, I'm not happy. But at least I understand."

Here come the questions about Jenny, he thought, wiping his sweating hands down his jean-clad thighs.

But Kira surprised him. "Why didn't you tell me about the group you're in with Jake?"

"Jake isn't supposed to tell anything about the group," he said, scrambling.

"He didn't tell me anything that happened in the group. He was very careful about that." She tried to hold his gaze but he looked away. "How come you never gave me your permission slip?"

He examined his sneakers, then looked over at the books Lexie had left on the floor. But when he looked at his sister, she was still watching him. Waiting.

"I was afraid you wouldn't let me join," he muttered.

"Why did you think I wouldn't let you join?"

He lifted one shoulder. "I figured you'd say I should come to you if I wanted to talk about shi…stuff."

"Oh, Brian. Of course I want you to feel like you can talk to me if you have a problem. But I wouldn't forbid you from talking to other people. I'm glad there's a group of kids you feel comfortable enough to talk to."

"Yeah?"

"Of course."

She smiled at him, but her eyes looked glittery. Like she was about to cry. He wanted to run upstairs so he wouldn't have to watch. He began to ease off the couch. "You're not pissed off?"

"No. I think Jake's group is a great idea."

"Uh, okay. Can I go?"

She blinked a bunch of times, then nodded. "When you feel like telling me about Jenny, I'm here."

"Jen's just a friend."

"Okay," she said. Her voice sounded shaky. "I'll see you tomorrow, Brian."

"Yeah," he said, fleeing up the stairs.

Safely in his room, he threw himself on his bed. Why did she have to cry? Why couldn't she have yelled at him? It was easy to tune her out when she yelled.

Man, he hated to see his sister cry. It reminded him of the time in the hospital, after the car accident. And that was a time he didn't want to think about, ever again.

The pain hadn't bothered him. He'd deserved the

pain. It kept the guilt away. But when Kira started crying, all that guilt came rolling back.

The guilt was why he couldn't talk to Kira. Because he hadn't just killed his mother. He'd killed her father, too.

CHAPTER SIX

HE KNEW she was in the office before he saw her.

Jake looked up and saw Kira walking over to one of the other cops sitting at a far desk. When she bent over to speak to Anderson, the short, dark blue skirt she wore tightened over her hips.

She said something and smiled, and the kid smiled back. Jake looked blindly down at the open folder holding Brian's arrest record.

"Hey, Jake."

A. J. Ferguson, the department victim's advocate and Mac's fiancée, eased herself into the chair next to his desk.

"Hey yourself, A.J." He forced himself to focus on her, closing the folder. "What's up?"

A.J. leaned forward. "Have you been to see Kira yet?"

Jake involuntarily glanced over at her. She was still talking to Anderson. "Did she tell you to bug me?"

A.J. followed his gaze. "Of course not. I was here early yesterday morning, and I overheard Crowley yelling at her."

"Yeah, she told me he called her. Crowley's just a jerk," he said, relaxing.

A.J. studied him for a moment, and the concerned look on her face made him squirm. "What?"

"Did Kira tell you what Crowley said?"

"He wants me back. That's not breaking news."

A.J. settled back in her chair. "I should have known she wouldn't tell you."

"Wouldn't tell me what? What did Crowley say?"

"He told her to make sure you were back on the street by last night. He threatened to fire her if you weren't."

"Fire her? Crowley said he'd fire Kira if I wasn't back on the street? That bastard." He jumped up from his desk and started toward the captain's office.

"Jake, stop it." A.J. grabbed of his shirt and yanked him back to his desk. "You don't need to get into a shouting match with Crowley. You need to go to Kira and get cleared."

"And this would be your professional opinion?" he said, tucking his shirt back in.

"No, you idiot. It's my opinion as your friend. Sit down and stop acting like you're five years old." She gave him a shove.

"I'd do it if I were you, buddy." Mac's amused voice came from behind A.J. "You don't want to mess with A.J. when she's got that look in her eye."

Jake threw himself into his chair. His pulse pounded behind his eyes as he pinned his partner with a look. "Why didn't you tell me this yesterday?"

"I didn't know yesterday. A.J. told me last night."

"Why didn't Kira tell me?"

"Figure it out for yourself." A.J. grinned as she watched Kira leave Anderson's desk and exit the bull pen. "Better yet, go ask Kira."

"Cute, A.J. Real cute. I hope you weren't trying for subtle there, because I have to tell you, it's not working." Jake slid lower in his seat.

A.J. touched his hand. "It'll be fine," she said quietly. "I know how hard this is for you, Jake. You want to get a beer when you're done?"

Jake forced himself to smile. "It's only three o'clock in the afternoon. Jeez, A.J. I figured living with Mac would be tough, but is it really so bad that you have to drink in the middle of the day?"

A.J. laughed as she stood up. "Don't make me hurt you, Jake. You're talking about the man I love."

Mac's gaze followed A.J. into her office. The adoration in his partner's eyes made Jake feel lonely.

"Don't you have something better to do than hang around my desk?" Jake snarled at Mac. "Are all the criminals in Riverton in jail already?"

"Nah, they're waiting for you to catch them," Mac answered. "So get up to Kira's office and make it happen."

It took a half hour to screw up his courage. The sign on her door said Come In. He shoved his hand through his hair and wiped a bead of sweat from the back of his neck. Then he knocked.

"Come on in," Kira called from behind the closed door.

Jake flipped the sign over so it read Not Available, then walked in. Kira pushed aside a pile of paperwork, smiling at him.

"Hi, Jake. I'm glad you came by. Have a seat."

"Why didn't you tell me what Crowley said to you?"

"I did tell you." She arranged a folder on her desk. "I told you yesterday that he'd called."

"You didn't tell me he threatened to fire you."

"Did Crowley tell you that?" she demanded.

"No. Someone overheard him."

"And you listened to gossip?" she asked, amused. "You *do* need to get back on the job, Jake. Clearly you have too much time on your hands."

"Are you denying he threatened you?"

"What Crowley said to me and what I said to him is my business. It has nothing to do with you."

"The hell it doesn't! If Crowley threatened to fire you because of me, that makes it my business."

Her knuckles turned white on her desk. "Thank you, Jake," she said after a moment. "I appreciate the thought. Really, I do. But I can handle Crowley."

He dropped into the chair, confused and intrigued. "I don't get it, Kira. If you had told me about Crowley, I'd have been in here yesterday."

"You think I should have guilted you into doing what I wanted?"

"Other people would have. It was my ex-wife's standard operating procedure."

She started to reach out to him, then drew her hand back. "I'm sorry, Jake. That's a rotten thing to do to anyone. And especially to a spouse."

"Yeah, well, it worked pretty well."

"That's not the way I work."

He almost believed her. And that was a scary thought. He hunkered down in the chair. "That officious little prick better not call you again."

"He won't have to," she said with a tiny smile. "Since you came to see me."

"Giving in to him never stopped Crowley from yelling at anyone." He looked outside the window. Clouds scudded across the summer sky, turning it a dark, bruised color.

"Do you want to talk about Talbott?" she asked.

"I'm here, aren't I?"

"All right. It's been over a week since the incident. Tell me what you've been doing since you shot him."

"Diddly-squat. And you know it."

"When you're not here. What do you do at home?"

He shifted in the chair, shrugged. "Same things as always. Eat and sleep."

"Are you sleeping well?"

He focused on the swirling clouds. "Some nights."

"And the other nights?"

Jake closed his eyes to block the memories of his violent nightmares. He'd woken last night, sure his sheets were covered with blood. He'd ripped them off before he'd realized it was a dream.

He didn't want to talk about that dream or any of the others. He didn't want to expose them to the light of day.

He didn't want to consider the possibility that his father might've been right. His father asking him why he wouldn't join the force. The unspoken suggestion that he was weak.

He turned back to Kira. "You sleep well every single night, Doc?"

"What's keeping you awake?" she asked.

He shrugged. Kira stood up and came around the desk. She sat on the edge, too close to him. "Are you having nightmares, Jake?"

His throat swelled and he stared without seeing at one of the pictures on the wall. "Yeah," he finally said.

"That's normal, you know," Kira answered in the same gentle voice. "I'd be concerned if you *weren't* having nightmares."

"Then I guess I'm really normal." He tried to sound as though he was joking, but was afraid he'd failed miserably.

"Do you want to tell me about them?"

He cleared his throat. "They're just your normal, run-of-the-mill nightmares. The usual blood and guts."

"It might help if you describe what happens. Talking about them takes away their power."

Talking about them was the last thing he wanted to do. It was bad enough to relive the scene in his mind. "Don't push it, Doc. They're nightmares. There's a lot of blood. Okay?"

"All right. We won't talk about them now. How's your appetite?"

He raised his eyebrows. "I ate two bowls of your soup last night."

He was impressed when she held his gaze and didn't so much as blink. "Do you eat when you're alone at home?"

He caught a whiff of her scent. It was mysterious, elusive and complicated. Just like Kira.

He shifted in the chair. "Doc, don't hover over me. I'm not going to run away."

"I didn't think you were," she replied. But she slid off the desk and walked around to her chair again. He couldn't stop himself from looking at her legs as she sat.

He took a deep breath. "Are we finished here?"

She shook her head. "No, we're not. About your appetite—"

"Yeah, I'm eating."

"What did you have for dinner two nights ago?"

"Hey, two nights ago the Cubs were on TV. I drank a couple of beers while I watched the game."

"That's it? You didn't eat anything?"

"Have you watched the Cubs lately, Doc? You need a couple of beers to get through the game."

She tried to hide a smile. "I thought you were a White Sox fan."

Impressed that she'd remembered, he forced a grin. "I lied. What can I tell you? In some circles, being a Cubs fan is an indication of mental-health issues. And you already had questions about mine."

"Very good, Jake. I like clever people who think on their feet. But I'm guessing you haven't been eating."

He drummed his fingers on the arm of his chair. "I need to lose a few pounds."

"Really?"

"I haven't been hungry, okay? Is that what you want me to say?"

"I know this is hard for you, and I appreciate the effort you're making." She tilted her head. "How has your relationship been with your significant other and your family?"

"My significant other? You want to know if I'm dating anyone, Doc, just ask."

The pen she'd been holding skittered off the desk and rolled onto the floor. It took her awhile to pick it up. "Let me rephrase the question. Who have you gone to for support?"

"I told you, I'm not big on gut-spilling."

"Talking about a problem can put it into perspective."

Right. As if it would help him get the image out of his head—Doak on the floor, blood staining the carpet, his life draining away from his body. "There is no perspective," he said. "I shot him and he's dead. That's not going to change."

"How do you feel about that?" Her voice was infinitely gentle.

He jumped to his feet, went to the window. The clouds had grown darker and the wind was rising. "The truth? I feel lousy," he said in a low voice. "It makes me sick. He was alive one moment and dead the next, and I did it."

He swung around to face her. "But it doesn't matter how I feel. It was my job to shoot him and I did it."

"It does matter, Jake. What's going to happen the next time you have to use your weapon?"

His gut heaved, but he only shrugged. "I'll do my job. Same as I did with Doak."

She studied him. "Are you going to be able to pull that trigger without hesitating? Your life or your partner's life could depend on it."

He paced the office, unwilling to sit in the chair, so close to her. "You think I haven't been asking myself that question ever since I shot Doak?" he muttered. "You think I haven't pictured myself in the same situation, tried to figure out if I could shoot again?"

"Have you got an answer?"

"Yes," he said, expelling a long breath. "Yes, I could pull the trigger again. If I hadn't killed Doak, someone I care about would be dead. That's the bottom line. If I have to use my gun on someone threatening a civilian or another officer, I will. I wouldn't hesitate."

"Thank you for being so honest, Jake." Kira stood. "I'll tell Captain Crowley you're making good progress and you should be ready to go by the beginning of next week."

"What the hell are you talking about?"

"I can't release you yet," she said. "Not while you're having nightmares and not eating and not talking to anyone about what happened. You're at risk for posttraumatic stress disorder and you can't go back on the street until we work through it. You're going to need to see me at least once more."

He felt an uncomfortable mixture of relief and anger. "That wasn't part of the deal. You said if I met with you, I'd get my badge back."

"I said you couldn't get your badge until you met

with me. You did, and I'll make sure Captain Crowley knows you're cooperating."

"I didn't sign up for this. How long is it going to go on?" He didn't want to let Kira see any further into his mind. She saw far too much already.

"I can't tell you that, because I don't know."

"I don't mind talking to you, Kira. Hell, I like talking to you. But it won't change anything."

"Then I can give you a referral to another psychologist."

"You want me to go to someone else? So I won't be your client anymore?" He held her gaze. "So we won't have a professional relationship?" Heat surged through him, and an answering spark lit her eyes before she turned away.

"That's up to you, Jake. If you're not comfortable with me, I'll give you a referral."

He prowled her office, wanting to touch her, knowing he couldn't. The walls pressed in on him and he scrabbled desperately for an out. "Crowley is going to be all over you."

"I'll worry about Crowley. You worry about yourself."

"Crowley doesn't believe in talking about your problems," he muttered. "He's not one of your new-age, touchy-feely kind of guys."

She laughed. "Of course he's not. He's a cop. But he doesn't intimidate me. And he can't fire me."

He shoved a hand through his hair. "Damn it, Kira, I don't want to come back. It took me all freaking day to come in here. And now you expect me to do it again?"

She reached out to touch him, then pulled her hand back. "I'm sorry, Jake," she said, compassion in her voice.

"Fine. I'll be back when I can."

He slammed out of her office, then leaned against the wall. He'd managed to skate through this time. But Kira was too damned perceptive. And he was weakening. He wanted to let all the ugly feelings spill out, the pain, the guilt, the anxiety. The fear. When she looked at him, he wanted to tell her things he'd never told anyone else.

He couldn't do that.

He'd sworn that no one would ever have that much power over him again. And Kira already occupied more than her fair share of his head.

BRIAN PUSHED a broom along the concrete floor. The stockroom shelves held boxes with televisions, VCRs, DVD players, computers, cameras and all the other electronic toys people craved. By now he was used to the sight, and it no longer inspired awe and amazement. Just irritation at the litter the sales clerks left behind.

Last night he and Jake had made the flyers for the high school. Man, he wished he were doing something cool like that tonight, instead of working this stupid job.

He turned a corner and brightened as he spotted Jenny. Her broom leaned against the shelf as she thumbed through a stack of DVDs. There *were* benefits to working at Digital City, and working with Jenny was the main one.

"Hey, Jen," he called, giving his broom a little push.

Jenny whipped around, jumping away from the shelf when she saw him. She touched the small of her back. "Hi, Bri." Her smile was too bright. "What's up?"

Brian frowned. "What are you doing?" he asked her when he reached her.

She picked up her broom. "Sweeping, same as you. Do you think we'll be out of here in the next half hour? I'm supposed to be home by ten o'clock."

Brian ignored her question and focused on the way she didn't meet his eyes. "What's going on, Jen?"

"My father yelled at me for staying out too late. He didn't care that I had to work."

She kept sweeping, but Brian grabbed onto her broom. "That's not what I meant. What do you have behind your back?"

Jenny paled. "Nothing."

"Don't give me that crap. What was it, Jen?"

Jenny pulled free. "What are you asking me, Bri?"

"Don't give me that righteous pose. Did you steal something?"

"Nice question, Johnson." She shoved him so hard he stumbled backward. "Way to have faith in me."

Brian steadied himself against the shelving. "Oh, man, Jen." He swallowed a sick feeling. "Okay, it's not too late. Just put it back."

"I didn't steal anything, Brian."

"It's okay, Jen. We all make mistakes. Jeez, you think I'm going to get on your case for shoplifting again? I was in jail the other night. Drinking and fighting, that's a whole lot worse."

"Don't be a jerk, Johnson." She spun around and pushed her broom down the aisle with short, choppy strokes.

He dropped his own and ran after her. "Man, you do *not* want Jake looking at you the way he looked at me that night. Like you'd just kicked his dog. Please, Jen. I don't want you to get caught."

"This job sucks," she shot back. "I hate it here." She choked back a sob. "I thought we were friends. I thought you trusted me."

"I am. I do." He reached for her arm, but she yanked it away from him. "That's why I want to help you."

Jen stuck her chin out. "Anyway, if I wanted to take something, I would. Redmond owes me."

Before he could answer, he heard footsteps behind him. "What are you two doing down there?".

It was James Redmond, the assistant manager on duty. Brian scowled. He didn't like the way Redmond treated Jenny. He watched her all the time with a funny look in his eyes. And he made fun of the way she looked.

"We're sweeping the floors, just like you told us," Brian said, picking his broom up off the floor.

"It doesn't look like a lot of sweeping is getting done back here." Redmond's gaze moved past Brian and landed on Jenny. "What are you up to, Noretta?"

"We're sweeping. Just like Brian said."

Jen's voice sounded defiant, and Brian tensed, waiting for Redmond to explode.

Instead, his expression turned sly and mean. "Is that

so? There's a lot of valuable merchandise in this store-room. Have you been slipping things into your pockets?"

"Of course not." Brian knew his voice was too loud, and he shoved his hands into his jeans. Realizing how it looked, he pulled them out quickly.

Redmond noticed. "What's in your pockets, Johnson?"

"My hands." He raised them, palms out. "Now they're not. See?" He eased over so that he hid Jenny from Redmond's view.

"You're a real comedian, aren't you?" Redmond said. "Come here."

"You can't search me."

Redmond's face got red. "No? I can fire you."

Brian straightened his shoulders. "There's a proce-dure you have to use to fire me. It's on the bulletin board in the break room."

"Is that right, smart-ass?" He jerked his head at Jenny. "What about Freak Girl behind you?"

Brian wiped his hands down the thighs of his jeans. "Don't call her that. Her name is Jenny." He swallowed. "There's a procedure for sexual harassment on the bulletin board, too."

Redmond's face went as red as the blood in Brian's favorite video game. He pointed a finger at Brian. "You're a troublemaker. I warned the manager not to hire you. Now I'm going to do something about it."

He turned and stalked away. Brian listened, waiting for him to come back. When he couldn't hear the footsteps anymore, he slumped against the shelf be-hind him.

"What's the matter with you?" Jen whispered. She hit the back of his head. "Are you a total moron? Why didn't you just let him search your pockets?"

"Because then he would have searched you, too. Okay? And I didn't want him to find whatever you're hiding."

Taking his broom, he pushed past Jenny, moving too fast down the row of shelves. He saw Jenny reach behind her back, but he didn't look. He moved down one aisle and up another until he'd finished sweeping. Then, his throat thick and his head spinning, he punched out and stormed out of the store.

CHAPTER SEVEN

JAKE SPRAWLED in the corner booth at McGonigle's, picking the label off a bottle of beer while the jukebox played a weepy song. He scowled. Playing sappy songs in a bar on a Friday night ought to be illegal.

Jumping up, he shoved a handful of quarters into the jukebox and punched the buttons, selecting songs by Tom Petty, John Mellencamp and Bruce Springsteen. Then he threw himself back into his seat.

He had the beer bottle halfway to his mouth when the door opened and Kira walked in. His pulse sped up and he lowered the beer to the table. She kept going to a booth on the opposite wall, giving the man waiting there a smile.

The guy was a cop. What the hell was Kira doing with Anderson? The kid was barely older than her brother.

Anderson went to the bar, returning a few minutes later with a glass of red wine. At least the kid hadn't embarrassed himself by ordering white.

"Hey, Donovan." Tricia, a fellow detective stood next to the booth, an open smile on her friendly face. "How's it going?"

"Hey, Tricia. I'm not too bad. How about you?"

She grimaced. "I got the Crowley tantrum today. He doesn't think my clear rate is high enough."

"Yeah, Mac and I are getting the same static."

"I'm blaming all that bad publicity about the leak in the Talbott case for the pressure. Did you ever figure out who it was"

"Nope. Never did find out."

She stepped a little closer, brushed a hand through short, wavy hair. "You here alone?"

Jake shifted in the booth. "No, I'm waiting for someone." He forced a smile. "You think I'm the kind of loser who drinks by himself in a bar?"

There was a flash of disappointment behind Tricia's easy smile. She slapped her forehead. "Donovan, by himself? What was I thinking? Catch you next time."

"Yeah."

Tricia slid into a booth with two other detectives and Jake turned his attention back to Kira. She was leaning toward Anderson, and the conversation looked serious. Her attention was focused on the kid like a laser beam.

Was she dating him? Coming to McGonigle's guaranteed the whole department would know about it.

The last Jake heard, Anderson had a girlfriend. Jake took a gulp of beer. Maybe Kira was the girlfriend he'd talked about.

His cell phone buzzed and Jake flipped it open. The caller ID indicated it was another cellular call. "Hello?"

"Jake? This is Brian."

"Hey, Brian. What's up?"

"I need to talk to you, man. About work."

"What's going on?"

"Redmond is hassling me again. And Jenny. I don't know what to do about it."

"You want to get together tonight?"

"I can't. I'm watching Lexie. She's asleep, but I don't know when my sister will be home."

Jake glanced over at Kira. She'd put her hand over Anderson's. It didn't look like she'd be home any time soon. "How about tomorrow?"

"I have to work. Maybe after?"

"Sure. Call me and we'll grab a cup of coffee."

"Okay." Brian hesitated. He blew out a breath. "I'll see you tomorrow."

Brian disconnected, and Jake slowly closed his phone. Brian had talked about Redmond hassling him before. Now he was hassling Jenny, too? Did this have something to do with the fact that Brian and Jenny were dating?

Whatever it was, he'd hear all about it tomorrow. The kids could talk for hours about their romantic problems.

And speaking of romantic problems, it didn't look like Anderson had any. He was smiling at Kira and she was smiling back.

What would it be like to have a woman like Kira in his life? To have all of that caring, that concern, that sharp intelligence focused on him?

A woman who knew how to read minds and hearts would be dangerous beyond belief.

Anderson slid out of the booth, leaned down and brushed his lips over Kira's cheek. Jake's spirits rose. If the kid thought that was a kiss, he had a lot to learn.

It was Friday night and Kira's date had just left. Maybe he could interest her in a game of pool.

A friendly game between coworkers.

Jake stood and walked over to the bar, ordering two more beers.

KIRA REACHED into her purse for her notebook. She'd just finished scribbling some notes when someone eased into the seat on the other side of her table.

She looked up to see Jake lounging against the vinyl cushion, his arm stretched out across the top of the seat, two bottles of beer in front of him.

"Hey, Doc. Who would have guessed I'd see you in a dive like McGonigle's?"

He slid one bottle over to her. "But since you've apparently gone over to the dark side, how about a beer?"

"Hi, Jake." She looked down at the beer, sweating in the heat, and then at Jake, his eyes crinkling at the corners and his dark blond hair shaggy and a little too long. Suddenly she felt too warm.

"So." His grin was wicked. "You come here often?"

She smiled back, determined to keep it light. "It's a cop hangout, isn't it? And I'm part of the department."

"Yeah, we're one big happy family." He pushed his bottle from side to side. "I've never seen you here."

"You must not have been looking, then." She raised the beer and took a sip of the cold, smooth beverage.

He smiled, pleased with himself. "I knew you had to be a beer drinker."

"You're learning all kinds of new things tonight."

"I am. I'm suddenly a big fan of education."

The blue of Jake's eyes deepened and he leaned closer. She set the beer down on the coaster. Was she actually *flirting* with Jake?

"I should probably get going." She fumbled for her purse. "I need to put Lexie to bed."

"She's already in bed and sound asleep."

She looked up at him. "How do you know that?"

"I talked to Brian a few minutes ago. He told me he was watching her and she was asleep."

"Why were you talking to Brian?"

"He had a question for me." He shrugged, as if it was no big deal. "The kids call me all the time."

"Oh." She bit her tongue to keep from asking what Brian had wanted. She knew Jake wouldn't tell her.

As she was searching for another reason to leave, Jake smiled, making her heart speed up and her palms damp. "Relax, Kira. Brian is watching a movie and your daughter is asleep. You don't have to hurry home." He cocked his head. "Unless you and Anderson have plans for later."

"Anderson?"

"I saw you with him earlier." He took another swallow of beer. "I didn't realize you dated cops. Like you said, I'm learning all kinds of interesting things tonight."

"I don't have a date with Scott! We were…" She clamped her mouth shut before she could say Scott was her client. "It's none of your business what I was doing with Scott."

He leaned back in the booth with a heavy-lidded look. "You were pretty cozy for two people who aren't dating. But I'm glad to hear it."

He looked as if he was waiting for her to ask why he was glad, but she kept her mouth closed. She'd never been good at these flirting games. And she shouldn't be flirting with Jake.

"Don't you want to know why I'm glad?"

"Not particularly." *Liar.*

"No?" His smile told her he knew she was lying. "Okay, I won't tell you."

"Fine." She took too large a gulp of beer, then struggled not to cough.

"I know what you're thinking," he said in a low voice.

She raised her eyebrows. "You're a mind reader?"

"I can see it in your face."

She raised the bottle again, as much to hide her expression as anything else. "Okay, I'll bite. What am I thinking?"

"You're thinking you shouldn't be here with me in McGonigle's on a Friday night. Someone might think we're involved." His smile was slow and intimate. "You want to leave, but you can't think of a graceful way to do it."

"Believe me, Donovan, I don't need an excuse." But she didn't want to leave. She wanted to stay here, sitting across the table from Jake. Flirting with him.

The thought both frightened and thrilled her. She

hadn't been out with a man in months. Between her job and her responsibilities at home with Lexie and Brian, she didn't have time.

A wild, reckless mood swept over her. For one night, she wanted to be free. She didn't want to be the doctor or the mother or the sister. She wanted to be Kira, a woman who could enjoy a man's company for a few hours.

A man who was her client.

She would think of this as one of their sessions, she told herself. Maybe if they spent a few hours together tonight, talking, she'd be better able to help him when he came in to see her next.

"I'm glad to see you're not running away," he said.

She held his gaze, took another drink and said, "Why would I run away?"

"I can't think of a reason why you should." He drained his beer. "How about a game of pool?"

"Sounds good." She took her beer and followed him through the crowd to a table.

A haze of blue cigarette smoke hovered above the light. The green felt had flecks of lint on it, and all of the balls had blue chalk marks. The wood of the table was scarred with nicks and cigarette burns.

"You want me to pick out a stick for you?" Jake asked. "You need one that fits you just right."

Kira was examining the cues in the rack on the wall. She looked over her shoulder at Jake. Was he assuming she didn't know anything about pool?

"Sure," she said. "You can fit me for a stick."

He handed her the same cue she would have selected. She hefted its weight in her hand. "Feels good."

"Let me show you how to hold it." Jake stood behind her and crowded her close to the table. Her face grew hot when he wrapped his arms around her and positioned her hands on the cue.

The guys at the next table hooted. One of them called, "Hey, lady, don't make any bets with that guy. He's a shark from way back."

She stepped away from Jake's embrace and flashed them a grin. "Thanks for the warning. I'll watch my back."

"You do that, honey," the other one said. "Because old Jake there looks like he's moving in for the kill."

Jake straightened and gave the two a lazy smile. "Hey, if you guys want to watch and learn something, I don't have a problem with that."

Kira laughed as she adjusted the cue in her hands. Then Jake was back, his body closer this time, cupping his hands over hers. The blond hairs on his forearms glowed in the light above the table, and his long fingers completely covered hers. When she shifted her feet, she bumped up against his hard body.

"Okay, Kira. You want to hit the ball close to the bottom, like this." He drew her arm back and struck the ball firmly. He left his arm curled around her a moment longer than necessary. "We'll play eight ball. Do you want the solid balls or the striped ones?"

"I'll take the striped ones. They're prettier."

She could tell he was grinning behind her. "I've got the solid balls covered. Do you want me to break?"

"No, I'll give it a try."

"Okay. You want to sink all the striped balls without knocking in any of the solids or the eight ball."

"That sounds easy enough."

"It's harder than it sounds." He reached for the cube of chalk and applied it to the end of her cue. "They're all yours, sweetheart. Wrap your hand around that stick and let those balls fly."

Kira looked over her shoulder at Jake, lounging against the wall at the side of the table. "You have quite a way with words, Jake. You'll tell me if I'm doing this wrong, won't you?"

"I suspect you'll do just fine."

"Glad you have faith in me." Kira lined up her shot. The cue ball hit the others with a solid crack and two of the striped balls went in the pockets.

Jake pushed away from the wall. She ignored him as she methodically worked the table, sinking the rest of her balls. When they were all gone, she knocked in the eight ball. The tiny crowd that had gathered around the table murmured its approval.

"That wasn't nearly as hard as you made it sound," she said to Jake.

He wore an appreciative grin. "You hustled me."

She set her cue down. "That wasn't a hustle, Donovan. I don't see any money on the table."

"I'll be damned." His grin got wider. "You're a bigger shark than I am."

"Hey, lady, nice work," the guy at the next table said.

The other man snickered. "We learned a lot, Donovan."

"Did you see her run the table?" Jake slung his arm over her shoulder. "I think I'm in love."

Kira shrugged him off. "Another game, Donovan?"

"Oh, yeah." His eyes gleamed. "Shall we put a little wager on this one?"

"What did you have in mind?"

"Another evening together."

"Those are high stakes," she said. "That would have to be two out of three."

"You're on." He picked up his cue and chalked the tip. "Winner breaks?"

"We can alternate. I don't want you to claim I had an unfair advantage."

"Pretty cocky, McGinnis." His slow smile made her heart flutter. "I like that in a woman."

She stepped back, putting a safe distance between them. "Your break, Donovan."

He racked the balls, then broke them with an efficient shot. He sank three and was lining up the fourth. He was good, almost as good as her. Kira stepped closer to the table, smiling demurely when he glanced over at her. She leaned forward just as he hit the cue ball, and it skittered off to the side harmlessly.

"Nice try, Jake." She chalked her cue and lined up her first shot. She'd put five in the pockets and was setting up her sixth when Jake moved in. He didn't say a word, but she could feel his gaze on her, smell his scent in the smoky air.

Her hand slipped as she struck, and the cue ball bounced off the bumper, inches from the pocket.

He leaned in and murmured into her ear, "You have to focus, Kira." He quickly finished the game. "Your break."

They were well-matched, but she won the second game. Jake broke for the third game, but he missed after sinking only one ball. She took his place at the table and planned her attack.

As she bent over the ball, he moved behind her. "Do you really want to win, Kira?" he whispered.

She straightened so fast he stumbled backward. "Of course I want to win."

She turned back, but he and put both hands on the table, trapping her between them. "Sometimes you win by losing."

Angling to look at him, she saw that his mouth was inches from hers. "I don't like to lose, Jake. At anything."

"I can see that." The left side of his mouth lifted. "I like that kind of passion."

A bead of sweat rolled down his temple. When she found herself leaning forward, as if to taste it, she jerked away from him.

"Back off, Jake. Go stand over there." She pointed to the wall.

When she missed the pocket by a fraction of an inch, she wanted to slam the cue to the floor. Instead she moved away without looking at him.

Jake sank all the solid balls, then turned to her before going after the eight ball. "You want to make it double or nothing?"

"And give you another chance to cheat? No, thanks."

He turned and sank the last ball, then set down his cue. "Cheat? I don't think so, Kira. What do you call cheating?"

"Bending over me? Whispering in my ear just before I was going to shoot? That's what I call cheating."

He grinned. "I'm glad to know I can distract you. But you did it first."

"I did not!"

"Oh yeah, you did. Trust me, Kira." He let his gaze drift over her, pausing at the V-neck of her blouse and the short hem of her skirt. "You deliberately bent over the table in the first game."

"I wasn't trying to distract you."

He took her cue away and hung it back on the rack, along with his own. "Kira, you distract me whether you want to or not." He put his hand on the small of her back. "Let's get out of here."

The bar was noisy, crowded and smoky. A slow, romantic song played on the jukebox, and Jake raised his eyebrows. "Unless you want to dance?"

The thought of stepping into Jake's arms to dance made her shiver. "No," she said hastily. "I'd better leave."

They stepped outside into a perfect summer night. A few stars twinkled in the dark blue sky and a soft breeze blew away the stale smell of cigarettes and beer. She turned into the parking lot, and Jake fell into step beside her.

"You want to get a coffee?"

"I should head home," she said with real regret.

"Okay. I'll follow you."

"That's not necessary. I'll be fine."

"Probably. But I'm still following you home."

She slid into her car and rolled down the window. "Good night, Jake."

Instead of answering, he waved at her and headed toward his truck. She pulled out of the parking lot quickly, but he was right behind her.

He stuck to her bumper all the way home and pulled into her driveway after her. By the time she got out, he was standing next to her car.

"Oh, for heaven's sake, Jake! My door is five feet away!"

"A lot of things can happen in five feet," he said. His hand resting on the small of her back, he escorted her to the door.

She turned to face him and found him much too close. He propped one arm against the wall and watched her for a moment.

"Where did you learn to play pool like that?" he asked.

"In college," she said. "There was a pool table in my dorm." She gave him an innocent look. "I played a lot."

"Next time we'll play basketball." He nodded toward the hoop next to the driveway. "But don't worry, since I'm so much taller than you, I'll give you a handicap."

She glanced at the hoop. "You're on."

"You're something else, you know that?" He smiled slowly. "I can't remember the last time someone out-hustled me like you did. You played me like a pro."

She couldn't help responding to his smile. "You made it easy by making assumptions."

"Believe me, Kira, I won't underestimate you again."

"Darn," she said. "There goes my advantage."

"Oh, I don't know about that." His voice dropped. "You still have a big advantage over me."

"I thought we were pretty evenly matched."

"Not even close." He leaned in, and for a moment she thought he was going to kiss her. Then he straightened. "I'll let you figure out why."

He brushed his finger over her lips and stepped away. "Good night, Kira."

"Good night." she answered. She stood at her door, clutching the doorknob, and watched him drive away.

"What have you done?" she whispered to herself.

CHAPTER EIGHT

KIRA LOWERED the basketball hoop to its shortest setting. "Okay, Lex. Go ahead and shoot."

Lexie tossed the ball underhanded toward the basket. It veered left, not even touching the backboard. When it hit the driveway, Lexie ran after it.

"Can I shoot again, Mommy?"

"You can shoot as many times as you like."

She watched as Lexie heaved the ball toward the basket twice more, both times missing entirely. "Do you want me to help you?" Kira asked.

"I want to do it myself. I want to play basketball," Lexie said, stamping her foot.

"You're going to be a great basketball player, baby."

"Just like you, Mommy. I want to be just like you."

"You're going to be better than me." Kira ruffled her daughter's hair and moved to stand behind her. "Hold the ball like this," she said, positioning Lexie's hands.

A half-hour later, Kira and Lexie walked into the backyard and dropped down on the fragrant grass. "How about a Popsicle, Lex?" Kira asked. "All basketball players have Popsicles after practice."

"I want a green one," Lexie answered.

Kira fetched two Popsicles from the house, and they slurped the frozen treats contentedly. The dogs watched, waiting for Lexie to drop the last piece. When she did, Henry grabbed it.

"Henry ate my Popsicle," Lexie cried.

"I guess he likes Popsicles, too. C'mon, Lex, let's get washed up and figure out what we're having for dinner."

The summer sunshine swept into the house with them as Kira opened the back door. Lexie hurried to the bathroom, while Kira checked out the blinking light on their answering machine.

Had Jake called?

She rushed over to the machine, then stopped in her tracks. Of course the phone call wasn't from Jake.

Friday night had been a mistake, and it was forgotten. She hadn't really bet another date with him.

She'd been telling herself that all weekend.

She pressed the Play button. "McGinnis, this is Captain Crowley. I told you I needed Donovan back on duty." Crowley's voice got louder. "Why is this taking so long? What's he saying to you, anyway?" Crowley was shouting now. "I'll fire his ass, and yours, too, if you don't get him out of your office."

The machine recorded the sound of the phone slamming, then the hum of the dial tone.

Kira took a deep breath and deleted the message. That was extreme, even for Crowley. Why was he so upset about this?

She grabbed the phone, then set it down again.

She wasn't going to call Crowley. The things she had to say were better said face-to-face.

"Can I have a Fruit Roll-Up, Mommy?" Lexie interrupted, dancing across the room.

Kira hesitated. After the Popsicle, she should give Lexie a healthier snack. "Sure," she said. "It's Sunday. We'll be a little wild and crazy." She grinned at her daughter. "What flavor?"

"Strawberry."

Kira reached into the cupboard and took a packet out of the box. As Lexie began to unwind it, the flat red ribbon dangled in the air. Henry turned from his water dish and snapped at it.

"Oh, for heaven's sake, Henry," Kira said. She grabbed him by the collar and dragged him toward the back door. "Out in the yard. You, too, Scooter." She slipped her hand under the smaller dog's collar as he tried to lick the Fruit Roll-Up.

Kira was at the refrigerator trying to figure out what to fix for dinner when she heard the front door open, then slam shut. Footsteps pounded up the stairs.

"Brian?" she called. Her only answer was the slamming of his bedroom door.

Her heart sank. Brian was supposed to be at work until much later.

"Lex, after you finish your snack, wash your hands and look at your books for a while. Okay?"

"Okay."

Kira headed up the stairs and knocked on Brian's

door. "Bri? What are you doing home? I thought you were supposed to be working."

"Leave me alone."

"What happened?"

He yanked the door open and stood blocking the way. "I got sent home."

His eyes were red. Had he been crying? "Bri? What's wrong?" she asked, reaching for him.

His mouth quivered as she wrapped her arms around him. "Redmond said some cameras and computer stuff were missing, and he said I stole them. So he sent me home."

"What?" Kira leaned back to look at him. "Why would Redmond accuse you?"

"Because he's a jerk."

Brian wrenched away from her and started to close the door, but she caught it. "Did he fire you?"

"He can't fire me unless he writes me up, and he can't prove I took the stuff. So he can't write me up." Brian dashed his hand against his eyes. "Redmond couldn't prove his butt was connected to his leg."

Her stomach knotted with foreboding. "Oh, Brian. That's awful. You must have been so upset." She reached for him again but he slid out from under her arm. "Why would he accuse you of stealing? What set him off?"

"I don't know. Or do you think I stole the stuff, too?" He glared at her, defiance radiating from him in waves.

"Of course not! I didn't say that."

"Why don't you just ask me? Or maybe you want to

search my room. See if I've got a bunch of cameras hidden under my bed."

"Stop it. I don't think you stole anything. I'm just trying to figure out how to fix this."

Brian looked slid away from her. "You can't fix it."

"What are you going to do?" she asked, trying to hold onto her patience.

He shrugged. "Maybe I should just quit."

"Why should you quit if you didn't do anything?"

"Because I'll have to eventually. He'll send me home every time I try to punch in." Brian hunched his shoulders. "It's his way of firing people without going through the procedure. He's done it before."

"You're not going to quit. Let's go back to the store right now. We'll ask Redmond why he thinks you're the one who stole the cameras. We'll fix this together."

"No! You can't do that. You can't talk to Redmond."

"Why not? He can't just accuse you of stealing for no reason."

"It's none of your business, Kira. Stay out of it. I'll take care of it."

He tried to shut the door again, but she wouldn't let him. "How are you going to take care of it? By being sent home from work every time you punch in?"

"Leave me alone!" he yelled. "I said I'd take care of it. You're always telling me what to do. God!"

He pushed past her, taking the stairs two at a time, and flew out of the house. The floor shook as he slammed the door behind him.

Kira ran down after him and pulled open the door.

Brian's car engine revved, then the car jerked and the tires squealed as he pulled away from the curb. Going too fast, he turned the corner and disappeared.

Lexie came over and reached for her mother's hand. "Is Uncle Brian mad?" she asked in a tiny voice.

"He just had a bad day at work today," Kira answered. She eased the door closed and knelt in front of Lexie. "Sometimes adults get upset by their work."

"You don't get upset by your work."

"I do sometimes," she said, thinking of her sessions with Jake and the telephone calls from Crowley.

"Is Uncle Brian coming back?"

Lexie's lip began to tremble, and Kira wrapped her in her arms. "Of course he is!" Kira hugged her daughter tightly. "He'll be back soon." *She hoped*.

Lexie looked toward the door and Kira could see the doubt on her face. She needed to distract her. "Do you want to watch a movie?"

"Yes!" Lexie ran to the DVDs. "I want *Nemo*." She pulled the well-worn case off the shelf. "Nemo's daddy searches the whole ocean to find him."

Kira turned her head so Lexie wouldn't see the tears welling in her eyes. No wonder Lexie had been upset by Brian storming out of the house. She was afraid he wasn't coming back. She'd been fixated on fathers lately, asking why she didn't have one. She wanted a father desperately.

That wasn't going to happen. Jason had taken off the day she told him she was pregnant and she hadn't seen him since. Kira swallowed. She didn't miss the spineless worm, but she hurt for Lexie.

Thank goodness Lexie had Brian in her life. There was at least one man who loved her unconditionally.

Except he'd just run out the door.

Kira slid the movie into the DVD player. She watched the first few minutes through blurry eyes, feeling more alone than she had in a long time. Then, as Lexie curled up on the couch, she retreated to the kitchen.

Kira chewed on a fingernail remembering the sound of Brian's screeching wheels. Because he'd been so volatile, so easily distracted, she'd hesitated to let him get his driver's license.

When he drove away from the house angry, as he was doing more and more recently, she couldn't help remembering what had happened to their parents, seeing the wreckage of the car they'd died in—remembering what it had done to Brian. The twisted mass of metal had barely resembled an automobile.

She walked to the front door and looked out the window again. Brian's car hadn't magically reappeared.

She leaned her head against the door. She and Brian and Lexie had managed pretty well on their own for the past six years. But she was tired. Navigating Brian's teenage years on her own, making decisions for Lexie...

She was tired of trying to keep all the balls in the air, all the time, all by herself.

Brian shouldn't be driving. He shouldn't be on the road when he was angry and upset. Her hand shaking, she tried calling his cell phone. He didn't answer.

Where would he go? Would he go to a friend's house? Would he go to Jen's?

Would he go to Jake?

Quickly, before she could lose her nerve, she found the piece of paper with Jake's cell phone number in the pocket of her purse. She stabbed the number into the keypad on her telephone.

"Donovan." His voice was brusque and businesslike.

"Hi, Jake. It's Kira McGinnis." She drew in a trembling breath. "Is this a bad time?"

"Kira." His voice softened. "How are you?"

"I'm calling about Brian," she blurted. "Did he call you? Is he on his way to see you?"

"No," he said sharply. "What happened?"

"He was sent home from work today. The assistant manager accused him of stealing. We had a fight." Her voice broke and she closed her eyes, mortified.

"Hey, sweetheart, take it easy," he said in a soothing voice. "We'll figure this out together. Are you at home?"

"Yes, but Brian isn't. He took off in his car."

"Stay there. I'll be right over."

She swallowed hard. "That's not necessary," she began, but the dial tone buzzed in her ear.

She'd made a mistake. Her hand trembled as she replaced the phone. Brian hadn't called Jake. Now Jake was on his way over here.

She shouldn't have called him. It had felt so good, for a moment, to lean on him. But she couldn't afford to lean on Jake. On Friday night, he'd made it clear he was interested in her, and God help her, she'd responded. But they were looking for different things.

She had a young daughter and an impressionable, difficult brother.

And Jake wasn't looking for strings.

Besides, until his situation at work was resolved, she needed to keep the boundaries between them distinct. Instead, she'd blurred them. Again.

She picked up the paper with Jake's phone number and called again, but got his voice mail. Her hand was still shaking as she set the phone down.

When the doorbell rang fifteen minutes later, she took a deep breath to steady her nerves. If she were smart, she'd stay in the kitchen and ignore it. But that was the coward's way out. And she wasn't a coward.

"Hello, Jake," she said as she opened the door. "You didn't have to come over here."

Jake stared at her for a long moment. "Are you going to let me in?" he finally asked. "Or do you want to discuss Brian out here?"

"I shouldn't have called you."

He waited another beat. "Let me in, Kira."

He was asking for more than he knew.

It was a mistake, but she stepped aside and watched him walk into her house. His presence steadied her, calmed her. Henry trotted up and shoved his head against Jake's palm. Jake absently stroked the dog's head, waiting for Kira to shut the door.

She struggled against the temptation he represented. "Jake," she said, twining her hands behind her back to keep from chewing on her nails, "I'm sorry I interrupted your Sunday. This isn't fair to you. Thank you for coming over here, but we're fine."

He raised his eyebrows. "You're fine? Really?" He took her hand and ran a thumb over her fingers. "Is that why you have no fingernails left?"

She drew her hand away. "Go home. Enjoy you day off."

He leaned against the wall. "Maybe I *am* enjoying my day off."

"Right." She rolled her eyes.

"I tell all my kids and their families to call me if they need me. It sounded like you needed help. So it was good that you called, and I'm not going to leave. Now, tell me what happened."

The relief she felt was staggering. And frightening. Trying to regain her balance, she turned and said, "Come into the kitchen."

They walked past Lexie, sound asleep on the couch. "Rough day?" Jake asked.

"Too much fun."

"I'm glad someone had fun. It doesn't sound like you did."

"It was fine until a half hour ago. Then Brian came home, and…"

Unsure of where to begin, she picked up the glass of water she'd poured when they got home from the park, took a drink and set it down. She picked up the wrapper from Lexie's Fruit Roll-Up and threw it in the trash. She was searching for something else to do when Jake took her elbow and steered her to the table.

"Sit down, Kira. Tell me what happened."

She stared at her hands, remembering Brian's pain and anger. When she looked up, Jake was watching her, nothing but understanding in his eyes.

She summed up what had happened with her brother, then said, "He peeled out of here, tires squealing, and I haven't been able to reach him."

"Do you think he did it? Stole from the store?"

"I don't know what to think." She looked up at him, her throat swollen with emotion. "Brian's not a thief. He's never stolen anything. But he got so angry with me. So defensive. Like he was hiding something." She rubbed at her eyes impatiently. "He's done so many things recently that I didn't think he would do," she whispered.

Jake took her hand, wrapped it in both of his. His callused fingers brushed against hers in a slow, hypnotic rhythm. "For what it's worth, I don't think Brian is a thief. I'd be really surprised if he stole anything from the store." He hesitated. "He called me on Friday and said he needed to talk about something that happened at work. He was supposed to call me the next day, but when I didn't hear from him again, I assumed he'd gotten it all straightened out."

He ran his thumb over her palm. "I guess he didn't. But you're assuming the worst, Kira."

All her attention was focused on her hand in his, the sensations he was evoking. "He acted guilty, Jake."

"You said he was trying to hide something. That's not the same as guilt."

"What could he be trying to hide? Either he stole the stuff, or he didn't."

"Maybe he's trying to protect someone else."

"Why would he do that? Why would he take the blame for someone else's crime?"

"He's eighteen years old, Kira. There's no rhyme or reason to what an eighteen year old will do."

"He drove away like a bat out of hell. I'm so afraid he'll get into an accident." Her voice broke.

He held her hand firmly. "You both need to cool down. It's probably a good thing he's out of the house."

"But I'm worried about him."

"Welcome to life with a teenager." He eased away from her and pulled out his cell phone, punching in a number. After a moment, he said, "This is Donovan. Any auto accidents in the past forty-five minutes?" He waited. "How about in surrounding suburbs and the north side of Chicago."

There was a pause, then Jake said, "Thanks," and snapped the phone shut.

"No accidents. Okay?"

She took a deep, breath as he relieved her greatest fear. "Thank you."

"No problem."

Just then, Lexie walked into the kitchen, rubbing her eyes. "What's for dinner, Mommy?"

"I'm not sure, honey." Kira dredged up a smile.

"We'll figure out something later. I need to talk to Jake right now."

Lexie's lower lip trembled and Kira knew tears were on the way. "I'm hungry."

"How about a PBJ to tide you over?"

"I don't want that."

"You don't want peanut butter and jelly?" Jake asked, feigning horror. "That's my favorite."

"Peanut butter and jelly is stupid."

"It's not stupid," Jake protested. "It's ambrosia."

Lexie looked at him suspiciously. "What's a bro-sha?"

"It means how delicious it is."

"It's not," Lexie said, but the threatened tantrum never materialized. It hurt Kira to watch Lexie respond to Jake. Her child's hunger for male attention was painful to see.

"Then what do you like?" Jake asked.

"Pizza."

"Pizza is my other favorite." He looked at Kira. "Why don't you and your mom and I go have some pizza?"

Lexie brightened. "Okay."

"We can't do that, honey," Kira said. "We're eating dinner here and Jake has to eat dinner at his own house."

"No, I don't," he said, his voice cheerful. He didn't look at Kira. "I think pizza sounds pretty good."

"Jake, stop," Kira warned under her breath.

He glanced at the stove. "I don't see you fixing anything for dinner. So what's the problem?"

"You know what the problem is," she muttered.

"What?" He gave her an innocent look. "You're allergic to pizza? It makes you break out in hives? You swell up like a balloon?"

Lexie giggled and Kira turned to her. "Lex, why don't you go turn off *Nemo* and put the DVD back in the case?"

As soon as her daughter was out of the room, she turned on Jake. "Don't get her hopes up like that. We can't go out with you."

"Why not? Lexie is hungry, I'm hungry and you must be, too. Seems to me it solves a lot of problems."

"What if Brian comes home and we're not here?"

He lifted his shoulders. "Brian's never been alone in the house before?"

"You know what I mean."

"Brian needs to be on his own for a while, to calm down.

"Jake, Friday night was a mistake," she said in a low voice. "A mistake I can't repeat."

"Okay, I promise we won't go to a restaurant that has a pool table."

Surprised that he could lighten her mood so easily, Kira's mouth twitched. "Are you always this irritating?"

"Usually I'm a lot worse. Just ask Mac." His teasing grin disappeared. "If it makes you happy, think of this as a parent-teacher conference with pizza included."

"Parent-teacher conference? Now you're really reaching," she said, trying to hide a smile.

"Hey, I could be a teacher," he said, his voice light. But something flickered in the depths of his eyes.

"I'm ready to go, Mommy," Lexie announced. She'd put her shoes on the wrong feet.

Kira knew she was trapped. "All right. But this is strictly business."

"Yes, ma'am. No laughing or horsing around allowed." He winked at Lexie. "Right, Lexie?"

Lexie giggled. "Right, Mr. Jake."

Kira gathered her purse and locked the front door behind them. This was about Brian. It had nothing to do with the dangerous attraction she felt for Jake. She was a professional and she could ignore her personal feelings.

Let him in.

She was afraid she already had.

CHAPTER NINE

KIRA TOOK a last drink of her soda and set it on the table in Cheesy Pete's play area. At the top of the multi-colored maze of tubes, ladders and slides, Lexie waved and grinned. They'd had fun. And, despite her concern for Brian, she'd been able to relax.

Jake stretched his long legs out under the table, brushing against Kira's bare ones, sending a flare of heat through her. Jake stilled and she hastily tucked her feet beneath her chair.

"It's kind of crowded in here. We'd have more space in the other room," Kira said, edging her chair away from Jake's. "We could still see Lexie through the glass."

"Nah, I like it in here," Jake said. His knee hit hers. "Close to the action."

"You're a man of hidden depths, Jake. I had no idea you liked this kind of action. Kids screaming. Ripe gym socks flying through the air." She sniffed. "The subtle scent of a full diaper."

"Is it noisy in here?" he asked, his voice low. "Does someone's diaper need changing? I hadn't noticed."

She sucked in a quick breath but turned it into a throaty laugh. "Stop, Jake. You're embarrassing yourself. And I have to say, I'm disappointed. I thought you were Mr. Smooth. I expected a better effort than that."

She didn't see him move, but suddenly he was a lot closer. Close enough for her to see flecks of green in his blue eyes. "Believe me, Kira, you'll always get my best effort." He leaned in. "I guarantee you'll be completely satisfied."

"Really? You think you can turn Brian into a model citizen?" Her hands shook, but she managed to give him a quizzical look. "Because we *are* talking about Brian, aren't we?"

His mouth was inches away from hers. "Sweetheart, we moved past Brian a long time ago."

"I have no idea what you're talking about, Detective," she said, her voice prim. Part of her was enthralled. The rest of her was alarmed.

But it was hard to resist. Jake made her feel alive. He made her feel like there was more to her life than being a mother and a sister.

And what trouble could she get into here, in the play area of a pizza place?

Lexie came flying back to the table, breaking the tension and grabbed the cup of apple juice she'd left there. When she tried to dart away, Kira snagged her around the waist.

"Not so fast, cutie pie. Where are you going?"

"To play!" Lexie squirmed in her arms, and Kira set her down. "I need to go down the slide head-first."

"Whoa! What are you talking about?"

"Everyone's going down the slide head-first," she

explained, pointing to an enclosed slide that wound around a pole from the top of the play structure to the floor.

Kira held onto Lexie and watched as a child came shooting out of the slide, upside down. His face hit the floor and the boy began crying.

"I don't think you need to do that, Lex. It's time to go home, anyway."

"Your mom's right, kiddo," Jake said, standing up. "I know you like pizza, but you don't want to turn into a pizza face, do you?"

Kira wrinkled her nose. "Nice image, Donovan."

But Lexie thought it was hilarious. While she and Jake whooped it up, Kira slipped Lexie's shoes on the girl's feet. And when Kira took Lexie's hand and led her toward the exit, Lexie slipped her other hand into Jake's.

Jake shot Kira a questioning look. Kira tightened her grip on Lexie's hand and shrugged. She had to resist the urge to tug her daughter away from Jake. Lexie was clearly enjoying his company.

But she didn't want her child to become too comfortable with him. To assume he'd be around. Lexie barely knew Jake.

And neither do I.

By the time they got back home, Lexie was slumped in her car seat, fast asleep. Jake got out of the passenger seat. "Do you want me to carry her into the house?"

"I'll get her," she said. She hesitated, then handed Jake her keys. "Could you open the door?"

"Sure."

A few moments later Kira stepped past Jake sideways through the door, Lexie in her arms.

"Have a seat," she said. "I'll be down in a minute."

"No hurry," Jake answered. He picked up the remote control and turned on the television.

Kira paused on the stairs. The scene in her living room looked so ordinary and domestic—Jake sprawled on her couch, flipping through the channels, Henry lying close to him. Even Scooter, who'd barked at Jake earlier, was now resting on the floor.

The tableau was too tempting. Appealing. And that set off alarm bells.

She couldn't get used to Jake's presence. If she did, she would only set herself up for disappointment. And set her daughter and her brother up for a crushing blow. Everyone in the department knew Jake wasn't interested in long-term.

On top of that, he was her patient. At least until she cleared him. It was time she remembered that.

Turning away from the scene in her living room, she concentrated on her daughter. It took only a few minutes to undress her sleeping child, put on her nightgown and tuck her into bed. Lexie never stirred.

"Sleep tight, baby," Kira whispered, kissing Lexie's fine hair. Then she smoothed the bedspread over her and tiptoed out of the room.

In the second-floor hallway, Kira took a deep breath and tugged on the hem of her shorts. She could do this. She could ignore the pheromones in the air and have a rational, adult conversation with Jake about Brian.

When she reached the bottom of the stairs, Jake stood up. "Is Lexie asleep?"

Kira smiled. "Out like a light. She had way too much fun today. Thanks for taking us to Cheesy Pete's. That's her favorite place."

"It was my pleasure."

Kira chose a chair far from the couch and sat down. "I didn't mean to take up this much of your Sunday."

"It's okay," he said easily. "I didn't have any plans." He leaned toward her. "I'm glad you called. I enjoyed myself. Lexie's a great kid."

"Thank you." She hesitated. "Lexie doesn't spend a lot of time around men, other than Brian. She seemed to enjoy you, too. But she's very vulnerable."

"I wouldn't do anything to hurt her, Kira."

"I know you wouldn't hurt her. Not on purpose."

"But I might hurt her accidentally?".

"Of course you could. She'll start building fantasies about having you in her life. And when you're not in her life anymore, she'll be crushed."

"Are we talking about you or Lexie?" Jake asked.

"Lexie, of course." Heat flooded Kira's face.

Jake watched her for a long moment. "You're assuming that if I get involved with…Lexie, I'll eventually leave."

That's what men do. "Come on, Jake. Everyone knows you're not serious. I've heard the guys talking about Donovan's bimbo of the week."

"You listen to gossip? I'm shocked, Kira. Shocked."

"I was, too, when I heard the stories."

"So you're afraid that Love-'em-and-Leave-'em Donovan would hurt your daughter?"

"Exactly," she said quietly. "I can't afford to take that chance."

"Maybe I'm getting tired of the bimbo of the week."

She held his gaze steadily. "Are you telling me you're looking for a ready-made family?" When he looked away, she said, "I didn't think so. There's nothing wrong with a good time." She swallowed. "I'd love to have a good time. But I have two other people to think about."

"Why does it have to be all or nothing?" He moved closer. "You and I could have a lot of fun without raising Lexie's expectations. Have a good time with me, Kira."

"Sorry, Jake, I don't want to be your bimbo of the week." *Yes, I do.* She wanted to lose herself in his easy physicality, coax more of those sexy smiles from him, hear him laugh.

She wanted to be impulsive, wild, free.

She glanced up the stairs to where Lexie slept, reminding herself why that was impossible.

"Okay, bimbo is out. But I'm open to negotiations." His smile was devastating. "How about being my hot mama of the month?"

She struggled to suppress a grin. "It's a very tempting offer, Jake. Really. But I'm afraid I'll have to take a pass."

"Maybe next month," he said, his eyes twinkling. "The offer isn't going to expire."

"I'll keep that in mind."

"You do that."

A car sped by on the street outside and the hum of the refrigerator sounded extraordinarily loud as they stared at each other. Kira looked away first. "I thought we were going to talk about Brian."

"Before we do, as long as we're getting personal, you said Lexie doesn't spent a lot of time around men besides Brian. Doesn't she see her father?"

"Her father isn't part of her life," Kira replied.

"That's too bad. Does he live out of town?"

"No. He lives in Chicago."

Jake frowned. "Then why doesn't Lexie see him?"

"He didn't have time to be a father," Kira explained.

Jake's eyes darkened. "Bastard."

She shrugged. "Better no father at all than a reluctant, resentful one. And she has Brian. They adore each other."

"Yeah, I could see that the other night." Jake grinned. "I told Brian he was hot in that tiara."

"What did he say?" she asked, curious about Brian's reaction.

"He laughed."

Kira sighed. "If I had said something teasing like that, he'd have exploded."

"That's because you're the parental figure, and therefore a constant embarrassment and irritation. He is a teenager, after all."

"I don't remember being so touchy as a teen."

"Based on what you told me about his accident, Brian has had a rough adolescence all around."

There was a lot more to Jake than the easygoing guy he showed the world. "How do you know so much about teenagers?"

For a moment, she didn't think he was going to answer. Then he looked toward the pictures of her and Brian and their parents on her shelf. "My dad died when I was twenty-one. A junior in college. My mother was devastated by my father's death, and I have four younger siblings. She couldn't cope with them, so I dropped out of school to help raise my brothers and sister."

"Is that when you became a cop?"

"Yeah." Henry dropped his head on Jake's lap and Jake stroked him. "My dad was a cop. He'd told everyone since the day I was born that I was going to be a cop, too." He tried to smile. "So it was easy to get into the academy. Joe Donovan died in the line of duty and his oldest son wanted to be a cop. They fell all over themselves to get me in."

"What were you studying in school?" Kira asked.

"Does it matter? I'm a cop now." He shrugged, but he couldn't quite hide his sadness.

"I think it does matter," she said.

"It's part of the past. I can't go back and start over just because my life took a different turn than I'd planned." His gaze rested on her. "It sounds like your life did, too."

"Yes." She thought about Jason, about the life she'd had until the day she'd found out she was pregnant. She glanced up the stairs. "I certainly didn't plan on being a single mother, but now I can't imagine life without Lexie."

"I like Lexie a lot. Brian, too." He grinned. "Even though he'd be mortified to hear me say it, you've done a good job raising him. I know exactly how hard it is to jump in and take over as a parent, especially to a teen."

"They sure don't come with owner's manuals. And I think you're flattering me, Jake. If I were doing such a great job raising him, we wouldn't have all these fights. And he wouldn't be getting into so much trouble."

"There's where you're wrong," he said. "Every teen pushes the boundaries. It's part of the job description. And Brian has a lot more to deal with than most."

"I'm not sure I can make it through the next few years." She sighed. "I'm afraid there might be bloodshed."

"You think this is tough? You haven't had the real test yet."

"What's that?"

"When Lexie is a teen," he said. "Teenage girls are hell on wheels."

"Thank you for that cheerful thought." She liked being with Jake. His teasing, laid-back attitude made her relax.

He made her laugh. That was a precious gift.

Before she could weaken and take his no-expiration offer, she stood up. "I've used up enough of your Sunday. You should go while there's still some of it left."

"You mean I should go so you can sit and brood about what to do when Brian comes home?"

"Don't knock brooding unless you've tried it."

"Trust me, Kira. I have tried it. It doesn't do much good. But here are a few tips I learned the hard way. Limits are important. Make sure he has clear boundaries. Make him take responsibility for what he does and suffer consequences."

"Are you saying I should have left him in jail last week? Not bailed him out?"

"He was shocked sober by his few hours in a cell. And scared to death. Maybe you should have."

"Here's the bottom line." He unfolded himself from the couch. "It's really pretty simple. You love him. He loves you. Remember that and you'll be fine."

"Yeah, yeah, yeah. I've heard that before."

He reached out and took her hand, pulling her closer. "It *is* that easy," he murmured. He brought her hand to his mouth and pressed his lips against her open palm. "Forget about the ugly stuff that's happened and remember the good stuff," he murmured against her skin. "Brian is crazy about you. How could he not be?"

Pleased, she still tugged her hand away from him. "I'm not sure if that's enough anymore."

"It's enough," he said.

She brushed past him to the door, when Scooter sat down in front of her. "Thank you, Jake," she said, her voice low. "For taking my mind off Brian. For making sure he hadn't been in an accident. For cheering up both me and Lexie."

"It's all part of the service." He moved closer, and Scooter stood, the hair on his back raised. He glanced down at the dog. "I don't think Scooter likes me very much."

"Scooter isn't an attention sponge like Henry," she said, moving the dog aside with her foot. "He's more suspicious."

"I like a dog who watches out for his people." He bent down to pet Scooter, but the dog growled at him.

"I guess he's reserving judgment," Kira said.

"How about you?" Jake replied. "Are you sure you don't want to reconsider my hot-Mama offer? I'm holding the position open for you."

"I'm sure," she said, but she couldn't quite keep the regret out of her voice.

"You don't sound sure." He backed her up until she was against the wall. "Maybe you need a little persuading. What do you think, Kira?"

She couldn't think with Jake so close. She could only feel and need and want.

He braced his arms on the wall on either side of her head and leaned into her. No part of their bodies touched, but every inch of her burned for him. He smelled like passion and sex, and his scent wrapped around her chest, squeezing until she could barely breathe.

She ached to touch him. She wanted to lean into him, to feel his strength. She wanted to touch his chest, to explore the hard planes of his muscles.

She wanted to taste him.

Slowly she lifted her head and met his gaze. A fire burned deep in Jake's eyes.

He leaned forward and touched her mouth with his, sliding his lips along hers as if memorizing her. Yearning stirred deep inside her, a longing for the connection his kiss offered, the pleasure it promised.

She opened her mouth to him, wanting more. Needing more. "Kira," he murmured against her lips.

He wrapped his arms around her and pulled her close. She pressed against him, welcoming the feel of his hard muscles against her, the weight of her breasts pressed into his chest, the heat from his body.

His kiss deepened as his hands roamed her back, gliding over each bump of her spine and her hips. She moved restlessly against him. When he cupped her hips and fitted her more tightly to his erection, she moaned into his mouth.

His lips trailed over her cheek, and he paused to nibble at her ear before continuing down her neck. When he reached the neck of her T-shirt, he buried his face in her shoulder while he tugged the hem of her shirt out of her shorts.

Then his lips were on hers again, his tongue in her mouth, tasting her. As his tongue tangled with hers, he slid his hands beneath her T-shirt.

His hands on her bare skin were like matches to dry wood. Her world contracted to Jake's mouth, his hands, his body. A far-off part of her brain reminded her to think of Lexie, to remember what was at stake. But it was too late. It had been too late the moment he touched her.

He cupped her breasts through her bra and she

strained into his touch. And when he unhooked her bra and pushed it out of the way, taking her breasts in his hands, her cry was swallowed by his mouth.

He lifted her shirt and stared down at her bare breasts. When he reached out and touched one swollen nipple, it contracted into a tight, hard nub. He slowly swirled his thumb around it, and she thought her legs would buckle beneath her.

"You have no idea how many nights I've lain awake, thinking about this," Jake said, bending to take it into his mouth. She arched into him as he rolled his tongue around her nipple.

He swept her up into his arms. She wanted to beg him not to stop, but her tongue tangled in her mouth.

He lay her on the couch, then stretched out beside her. He pulled her T-shirt over her head and when she raised her arms to help him, her hand brushed against something hard and angular. One of Lexie's dolls.

Her hand stilled. Slowly she broke Jake's kiss and struggled to sit up. He slid his hands down her arms, then cupped her face.

"What's wrong?"

"I can't do this. I'm sorry," she said, forcing herself to meet his eyes.

He brushed a kiss over her mouth, lingered. "I'm sorry, too. I shouldn't have touched you."

He would have moved away, but she grabbed his hand. "You don't understand. I'm not sorry you kissed me. I'm sorry I stopped you. But Lexie could wake up. She could come downstairs and find us. And there's no way I'd hear her. Or Brian could walk in the door."

His hand tightened on hers for a moment, and he pulled her close for a deep kiss. Then he eased away and stood. Picking her T-shirt up from the floor, he handed it to her. Then he leaned around her and fastened her bra.

He kissed the nape of her neck as he fumbled with the clasp. "I had a lot more fun opening this than I am closing it," he murmured against her skin.

She turned to kiss him. "Me, too."

He rocked back on his heels while she pulled the shirt over her head. Then he touched her face. "You surprise me, Kira. Every time I'm with you, you surprise me." He smiled, studying her through heavy-lidded eyes. "I like surprises."

"I guarantee you wouldn't have liked the surprise of Brian or Lexie walking in on us."

He pulled her to her feet, then into his arms. "I think we'll stick with fun surprises," he said into her neck. He leaned back, pressed another kiss to her lips. "I'll see you tomorrow at work," he said. He kissed her once more, lingering before he pulled away. "Sleep well," he said with a grin as she closed the door.

What was she going to do? Jake had become one of those complications she didn't need in her life.

But she wanted him anyway.

CHAPTER TEN

IT WOULD END today.

Jake barreled through the door to the station and ran up the stairs. The dance he'd been doing with Kira had lost its appeal. The therapy needed to be over. He'd talk to Kira this morning and get cleared.

She wouldn't be able to use her job as an excuse.

They had enough other barriers to overcome. And he *would* overcome them. He'd been intrigued by her the first time he'd met her. After last night, it was impossible to keep his distance.

As he walked into the nearly empty early-morning bull pen, the towering stack of case folders on Mac's desk prodded his conscience. His partner had been carrying a heavy load, and it wasn't right. He'd get up to speed on the cases while he waited for Kira to get in.

When he heard Crowley shouting, he glanced toward the captain's office but he couldn't see the poor slob on the receiving end.

The low voice that answered Crowley made him clench his hands on the folder. Even muffled, he knew it was Kira.

They were probably arguing over him.

He jumped up from his desk. As he got closer to the office, he could hear Crowley more distinctly.

"I've had enough of your excuses, McGinnis. If Detective Donovan has too many 'issues' to be back on the street, maybe he doesn't belong on the police force."

"Sit down and stop shouting at me, Captain." Kira's voice snapped like a whip, and Jake stumbled to a stop.

"Thank you," she said in an even voice. "Now let me explain something. I'm the therapist. You're the police officer. That means I don't tell you how to catch criminals, and you don't tell me how to treat clients."

"I'm his boss," Crowley said, his voice rising again. "I need to know what's going on."

"And I've told you. Detective Donovan is progressing well with his therapy."

Jake watched Crowley's face turn an interesting shade of purple. "Don't you take that tone with me, Miss McGinnis. I want details."

"What we want and what we get are two different things."

"Is that right?" Crowley cleared his throat. "If you want me to buy this therapy crap, tell me what Donovan's been telling you." Crowley's had switched from belligerence to wheedling.

"I can't believe you're asking me that." Kira's voice was steel-hard. "That's privileged information."

"I'd be more understanding if I knew what he was saying."

Why the hell did the old windbag want to know

that? Jake stared through the window, trying to see Crowley's face.

"I'll do you a favor, Captain, and pretend I didn't hear that." Kira's slapped her hands on Crowley's desk as she leaned toward him. Crowley took a step back. "I wasn't hired to spy on your police officers."

Jake grinned. He'd never seen Kira in a temper before.

"What's going on?" One of the patrol cops nodded toward Crowley's office. "Who's he chewing out this time?"

"Dr. McGinnis. It looks like it's going to be fun."

The cop peered into Crowley's office. "Yeah?"

"We believe in teamwork in this department, Doctor," Crowley said. His voice hardened. "You're not much of a team player, are you? Maybe we need to look for a therapist with a different attitude."

"You want a different attitude? How's this?" Kira moved around the desk toward the captain, who took a step backward. She shoved his chair out of her way. "Any information I give you is a favor. As of today, you're not getting any favors from me. You can yell all you want. I'm done with you."

She'd backed Crowley into a corner, and now she poked him in the chest. "Unless there is a genuine emergency, don't call me at home ever again. Do you understand?"

Crowley pushed past her. His face was beet-red, and he yanked at the collar of his shirt, loosening his tie. "This *is* an emergency. I need Donovan on the street."

"No, it's not an emergency. This is a hotheaded, controlling bastard losing his temper and sticking his nose where it doesn't belong. Your detectives might let you get away with that, Captain, but it doesn't work with me."

"You're calling me a hothead?" Crowley blustered. "I'm not the one yelling and screaming in here."

"You think this is yelling?" Kira stuck her face inches from Crowley's. "This is a calm discussion, Captain. I'm not going to lose my temper over someone like you."

Several other patrol officers had joined the group outside the office, and two of them exchanged high fives. Someone elbowed Jake. He turned to find Mac behind him. "What set her off?" Mac asked in a low voice.

"Crowley's been calling her at home, yelling at her to get me cleared."

Mac gave him a disgusted look. "Then why aren't you in there? Why is Kira taking the heat for you?"

"Doesn't look like she's taking much heat, pal. Looks like she's the one dishing it out."

"Yeah, we're all getting a kick out of the show. But it wouldn't be happening if you'd just—"

Abruptly, Mac walked back to his desk leaving Jake to stand frowning after him until Crowley's voice reclaimed his attention.

"All right, Doc. Maybe I was out of line. I shouldn't have called you at home." Crowley tugged on his tie again. "If you can't clear Donovan maybe he needs to go on long-term disability."

"Where did you get a stupid idea like that?" Kira

pointed her finger at Crowley again. "Let me explain this one more time. I'll try to use simple words that you'll understand. I am the therapist. You are not. Detective Donovan does not need to go on long-term disability. I will decide when he goes back on active duty. You have nothing to say about it. Is that clear?"

"Perfectly." He stared down at Kira, and even through the half-closed blinds, Jake could see the spite in his eyes. "I heard about you and Donovan at McGonigle's. Word is, the two of you looked pretty damn cozy. Maybe you like getting together in your office. Maybe you're doing more than talking behind that locked door."

Jake lunged toward Crowley's door, but one of the patrol officers grabbed his arm. "Don't spoil it, Donovan," he whispered.

"All right, Crowley, that's it." Kira's voice was soft, but the anger in it made Jake stop struggling. "I tried to be reasonable. I tried to talk to you, to keep this between us. You just stepped over the line."

She clenched her fists. "If you continue to harass me about Detective Donovan—" she bared her teeth "—trust me, Captain. I will make your life a living hell."

She stalked out the door, slamming it behind her. The patrol officers scattered as she glared at them.

"Enjoy the show, Donovan?"

"Oh, yeah. You were hot in there."

"Get out of my way." She pushed past him and headed for the stairs.

She took them two at a time. Jake watched until she

disappeared. When he heard a door slam in the distance, he started after her.

"Don't go up there, Donovan. You'll be next in line," one guy called.

He nodded over his shoulder. "I'll try to hold up my end better than Crowley did."

He heard a series of dull thumps as he hurried down the hall. When he opened the door, he saw Kira send a metal wastebasket flying into the wall. It bounced off and she kicked it again.

"Stop, sweetheart." He reached for her. "I could hear that thing begging for mercy from down the hall."

Kira twisted away from him. "He made me lose my temper. I hate losing my temper." She glared at him. "Did you boys have fun watching?"

"We had a great time seeing someone bust Crowley's chops for a change." He grinned. "I think 'hotheaded, controlling bastard' was my favorite part. Although 'make your life a living hell' was right up there, too."

"You think it was funny, Jake?" She took a deep, shuddering breath. "That was about as unprofessional as it gets." She stalked to the window. "It seems to be my week for unprofessional behavior. Only this time it was in front of the whole department."

"And the whole department appreciated it."

"What's going to happen the next time those guys have to talk to me? They won't take me seriously."

"Oh, they will. Everyone's going to remember this and they'll haul butt to get in here." He stepped closer. "It got me in to see you. You're hot when you're angry, Doc."

He pulled her against him, but she pushed him away.

"Knock it off, Jake. I'm serious."

He grasped her upper arms and pulled her close again. "So am I." He bent and brushed his mouth against hers. "I didn't have a restful night, Kira."

For a moment she softened and leaned into him. Her breasts flattened against his chest and her mouth trembled beneath his. Then she jerked away.

"We need to talk about last night, too."

"Talking is overrated." He watched her pace the room. "What we *need* to do is pick up where we left off."

"For God's sake, Jake! We're at work. Focus, would you?"

"Trust me, Kira. I'm focused." He'd tasted her all night in his dreams, woken up aching for her. He'd never been more focused.

"Good." She sat down, rearranged a stack of folders. "Can we forget what happened with Crowley and talk about you and me?"

"Anytime," he said with a slow smile. "Seeing you with Crowley got me thinking about you and me."

"I shouldn't have gone in to see him this morning," she said. She grabbed a note from her desk, wadded it and threw it into the wastebasket across the room. "I should have calmed down first."

"Crowley doesn't respond to calm." He glanced at the wastebasket. "Nice shot."

"I trained for years to stay calm when I'm at work. To be cool and collected."

He watched her for a long moment, intrigued by the fact that she wouldn't meet his gaze. "You were trying to protect me, weren't you?" he asked slowly.

"You don't need to be protected. You can take care of yourself."

"You could have told him I refused to come in to see you. Then he would have hounded me instead of you."

"Did you expect me to throw you to Crowley to save myself? What kind of person do you think I am?"

"I'm beginning to see who you are," he said. "I like what I see."

"Thank you," she said, her voice softening. Her mouth turned up in a tiny smile. "I'm glad I'm changing your opinion of psychologists."

"I'm making an exception for you."

"I'm honored," she said, her voice light. "Is that why you're here? To tell me I'd surpassed your expectation of psychologists?"

"I came in here to get Crowley off your back." He settled into the chair. "Ask me anything you want. I'll do whatever it takes to be released today."

"Really? That doesn't sound like you. Why the hurry, all of a sudden?"

He didn't look away. "Why do you think?"

"Don't go there, Jake," she said. "Not here, and not now. Please."

"All right. How about this? I need to get back to work. Mac has too much to do. And I'm getting bored."

"That works." She studied him for a moment, then

stood up and walked around to the window. Staring out, she said, "You know I have to send you to someone else."

"The hell you do! I'm not going to another shrink." He leaped out of his chair and grabbed her. "I told you, I'll be straight with you."

She moved away from him. "I know, Jake. But I can't be your therapist."

"Why the hell not?"

She spun around to face him. "Come on, Jake! Because of what happened last night. There are rules about sleeping with a patient."

"We didn't sleep together. Believe me, I would have remembered if we did."

"It doesn't matter. As far as the ethics committee is concerned, there's not a lot of difference between almost making love and actually doing it."

"Oh, there's a difference," he said. "A big difference. And I'd be happy to demonstrate it to you."

"You know what I'm talking about. We have a personal relationship, and I can't continue as your therapist." She shoved her hands in her pockets and retreated behind her desk. "I should have terminated our professional relationship before I touched you."

"At least you're admitting we have something between us. I was afraid you were going to pretend nothing happened."

"I'm not a hypocrite, Jake. The word no never came out of my mouth last night. I wanted to kiss you. I wanted to touch you, and I wanted you to touch me."

"I can't believe you just said that."

"Why not?"

"You're supposed to be coy and play hard to get. That's one of the rules of being a woman."

"Not all women play games." She gave him a tiny smile. "At least not those kind of games."

"You feel guilty about what happened last night." He was incredulous. "Don't you?"

"Yes, I do. Last time you were in here, you really told me how you felt. And I betrayed your trust when I kissed you. When I touched you." Her voice dropped to a whisper. "When I let you touch me."

"You didn't betray anything," he said roughly. "What happened last night has nothing to do with this."

She set the trash can in its usual place. "A therapist has to be objective. She can't be involved with her patient. And a patient has to know that his therapist won't use what he says against him, won't throw it back in his face when they're having a fight."

"Damn it! Are you telling me I have to start over with this therapy crap?"

"Now it's crap? A few minutes ago, you were willing to do whatever needed to be done."

"Because I wanted this behind us. I wanted to get Crowley off your back. I wanted to knock down one of your reasons for keeping me at a distance."

She rubbed the bridge of her nose. "I told myself no one would ever know what happened last night."

"Crowley doesn't know what we were doing last night."

"It doesn't matter if Crowley knows or not. I know. You heard his crack about what we're doing when we're alone in here."

"That was Crowley being crude." Jake's laugh was forced. "You know how cops think."

"Yes, I do. And I don't want anyone snickering behind your back. I don't want anyone to say I released you because you got me naked."

"That would not technically be true, Doc. So if you're going to use that excuse, I think I need to get you completely naked."

She finally smiled back at him. "That's very smooth, Detective. And so romantic. If you keep up that kind of talk, I'll be swooning at your feet."

"Promises, promises."

She turned back to her desk and sat down. "Would you prefer to see a man or a woman, Jake?"

"I don't want to see anyone."

"I know that," she said, her voice surprisingly patient. "But given that you need to see someone else, would you prefer a man or a woman?"

"A woman, I guess. I'd feel like a complete idiot, saying this stuff to a guy."

"All right. I have someone in mind. I'll give her a call. I'll send over all the paperwork, and if she thinks you're ready to be released, she'll sign off on you today."

"You have this all thought out."

"I have to fix this. Don't you understand?" She flattened her palms on her desk. "I've made mistakes in my professional life before. But I've never gotten involved with a patient. That's about as bad as it gets."

"It's not the end of the world, Kira."

"Close enough." She opened the folder on her desk and pulled out a sealed envelope. "Take this with you when you see Sherry. It's a copy of my records and the papers she'll need to sign to get you back on active duty."

She pushed the envelope toward him, but he didn't pick it up. "What happens after that?" he asked.

"You're back on the street. Crowley is happy. Mac is happy. You're happy. Everyone lives happily ever after."

"What about you? Are you happy?"

"Of course. Another patient success," she said, her voice light.

"Happy enough to have dinner with me tonight? To celebrate this success?"

"I'm not sure that's a good idea," she said. "How is Brian going to feel if we're dating?"

He shrugged. "I have no idea. And it's none of his business."

"That's not true, Jake. He feels like you're *his* friend, not mine. You're an adult he trusts, an adult he confides in. The two of you have a special relationship. He'll feel betrayed and jealous if we get involved."

"You're not giving Brian much credit. He might surprise you."

"I would love it if he surprised me."

"Then give him a chance." Jake stood up and reached for the envelope on Kira's desk. "And give us a chance, too. Don't keep throwing up roadblocks and making excuses." She looked away.

"I'll see you later," she said in a low voice.

"Count on it."

CHAPTER ELEVEN

WHEN BRIAN pulled up to the curb on Monday evening, Kira and Lexie were on the driveway, playing basketball. Lexie flung the ball underhanded toward the basket, which Kira had lowered as far as possible.

He'd been barely older than Lexie when Kira had taught him to play. He smiled reluctantly. She'd lowered the basket once. After he'd objected loudly, they'd played with the basket at regulation height.

He got out of his car and strolled over to the driveway. "Hey, Lex, great outfit." She was wearing a pink ballet tutu thing with an orange sash for a belt and wildly clashing multicolored striped socks.

Lexie let the ball drop and ran to him. "Uncle Brian!" She leaped into his arms, and his throat swelled as he hugged her tight.

Swallowing hard, he set her down and straightened her sash. "Is your mom teaching you all the hoop moves, Lex?"

"I'm going to be just like you, Uncle Bri."

"Yeah? Are you going to be as good as your mom?"

"She's going to be better," Kira said as she walked over. "Hey, Bri. How's it going?"

Brian expected her to grill him about the way he'd run out of the house yesterday after he'd been sent home from the store. Instead, she smiled at him. "You want to play some ball with us?"

"Uh, maybe I should change my clothes first."

Kira glanced at his khakis, dress shirt and tie. "Yeah, maybe." She punched him lightly in the shoulder. "Unless you want to look like a total dork out here."

She handed Lexie the ball.

"Uh, Kira?"

She turned to him again. "Yes?"

"Aren't you going to ask me why I'm dressed up?"

"Do you want me to?"

"You usually do," he muttered.

She studied him for a moment. "Okay, Bri. Why are you so dressed up? I know you didn't have to work today."

"I was looking for another job." He shoved his hands in his pockets.

"Really?" Kira turned around. "Hey, Lex, why don't you go in the backyard and play with Henry and Scooter until Brian is ready to play ball with us."

"Okay." Lexie dropped the ball again and ran to the gate, where Henry and Scooter had been watching them.

The ball started rolling down the driveway, and Kira stuck out her foot, letting the ball roll off it and bounce. Then she grabbed it from the air.

"You want to sit on the porch?" she asked him.

"I guess."

Kira shifted on the cement step and he wanted to squirm. But all she said was, "Where did you apply?"

"At two of the grocery stores in town. And at the hamburger joint. A lot of kids get jobs there."

"Any luck?"

"I have two interviews scheduled."

"Good for you." She hesitated. "I thought you liked your job at Digital City."

"I liked the discount there," he said.

"Is this because Redmond is hassling you?"

He kicked a small pebble on the stair. "I guess."

"Have you talked to him? Asked him why he thinks you're stealing?"

"I know why," he muttered.

He expected Kira to question him, but she didn't say a thing. He saw nothing but sympathy in her eyes. "Don't you want to know why?"

"Only if you want to tell me."

"I mouthed off at him the other night," Brian said, staring at the scuffed toe of his shoe. "He was being his usual jerk self and wanted to search me. I blew him off."

"He doesn't have the right to search you," she said.

"That's what I told him." His sister looked mad, but not at him. She was angry at what Redmond had done to him. His throat started to swell again, and he rolled his shoulders.

"I don't think you should quit. Don't let him win."

He wasn't telling her all of it. He wasn't telling her about Jenny, and how she'd acted so guilty. Part of him wanted to confide in his sister. But he also wanted to protect Jenny.

He stood abruptly. "I'm going to change my clothes. Then let's play some ball."

"I'll be waiting."

He was back outside five minutes later. He could hear Lexie in the backyard, squealing as she played with the dogs. Kira was dribbling, cutting and shooting baskets. She didn't even realize he was back.

Kira was in her own world when she played basketball.

"Hey, pass that ball over here," he called.

She turned and grinned. "You ready for a good butt-kicking, Johnson? 'Cause I'm going to take you to school."

"Big talk, McGinnis. Let's go."

JAKE BRAKED his truck to a stop in front of the house next to Kira's. Two people were playing basketball on Kira's driveway. Brian and Kira. At least he was pretty sure the one with the dark ponytail was Kira. She was moving so fast, dribbling around Brian and cutting to the basket, he wasn't sure.

As he got out of the truck, he saw Brian step up and block her. She slipped around him and dropped a reverse layup into the basket, as smooth as silk. Then she tossed the ball to Brian.

"Your turn."

Brian started to dribble, and Kira began defending him. Suddenly Brian stopped and slammed the ball into the driveway. "Damn it, Kira! Stop it!"

She raised her hands. "What?"

"Stop backing off." He stuck his face into hers. "I'm not a baby. I'm not Lexie. You don't have to take it easy on me. I'm not some stupid kid who doesn't know anything about basketball."

Kira shoved a strand of hair behind her ear and wiped at the sweat pouring down her face. "I'm trying to give you a chance to get your feet under you."

"I don't want to get my feet under me. I want to play. Straight up. No gifts." Brian shoved the ball at Kira's chest, and Jake started forward. But he stopped when Kira shoved Brian right back.

"Fine. We'll play." She leveled a look at Brian. "I'm going to wipe the floor with you."

"You're going to try," Brian sneered.

"Let's go," Kira said. "Jump ball."

She tossed the ball into the air. Even though Brian was a good six inches taller than his sister, Kira snatched the ball before he could get it.

Brian got into her face, but it didn't matter. She danced around him, dribbling so fast the ball was a blur. When Brian lunged at her, she took a fade-away jump shot that fell through the net cleanly.

Then Brian got the ball. Kira anticipated his every move. He'd go in one direction, she'd be there before him. He'd back away and she was still plastered against him. When he finally threw up a shot in desperation, she swatted it away.

"One—zip," she said as she started dribbling again. "You are *so* going down."

Jake sank onto the grass to watch. Then he saw Lexie

scampering across the driveway. She saw him and changed directions.

"Hi, Mr. Jake," she said. "Did you come to watch Mommy and Uncle Brian play basketball?"

"I guess I did."

"I like to watch them, too," she confided. "Uncle Brian says bad words and Mommy doesn't yell at him."

"Yeah?" Jake looked at Brian and Kira again. Kira dribbled backward, away from Brian, and took a long-distance shot. It sank through the net with barely a ripple. "I think I'd say bad words, too, if I was playing against your mom."

"I was playing basketball with her before."

"I can tell. That looks like your basketball outfit."

"This isn't my basketball outfit," she said, giggling. "This is my elgant outfit. Mommy says we're having a week of elgance."

"Your mom doesn't look real elegant," he answered. The words on the back of Kira's sleeveless T-shirt were barely legible and her baggy shorts were faded. Her shirt was dark with sweat, and through the armholes he could see her bright red sports bra. "She looks good," he assured Lexie. "Just not elegant."

"She'll be elgant later."

Lexie clapped any time either her mother or her uncle made a basket. Brian made very few of them. Kira sank almost all she tried. And Jake heard Brian mutter more than a few of those "bad" words.

Finally, when Kira reached twenty-one points, she tossed the ball onto the grass. Then she and Brian slapped hands and bumped knuckles. "Not bad, punk. Especially for someone who hasn't played in a while."

After the whipping he'd taken, Jake expected to see Brian sulking. Most teenage boys wouldn't accept losing to their sister with any grace at all. But not Brian. "Yeah? It felt pretty good."

It felt good to lose to his sister by more than ten points?

Kira used her T-shirt to wipe the sweat off her face, and Jake got a tantalizing glimpse of creamy skin. Then she sauntered over, dropping into the grass next to Lexie.

"I thought you were going to play ball with the dogs," she said to her daughter.

"I wanted to watch you and Brian," Lexie answered. "Brian said six bad words."

"That's why you're supposed to play with Henry and Scooter," she said. She ruffled Lexie's hair and fell backward to lie in the grass.

She folded her arms behind her head and looked over at him. "Hi, Jake. What are you doing here?"

"Counting bad words with Lexie," he said.

Kira laughed. "It's the big attraction of basketball right now," she said.

Jake stared at Kira, her face flushed and damp with sweat, her eyes glowing. "You're amazing."

She shrugged. "I love basketball."

"You're pretty good at that, too."

"She's more than pretty good," Brian said, hooking an arm across his sister's neck. "She's the best."

"I used to be the best," Kira said. "Now I'm just pretty good."

"Kira taught me how to play," Brian said to Jake. "When I was eight."

"You looked okay, kid. But you're not in the same class as your sister."

Instead of the prickliness he expected, Brian only grinned. "Not even close. She played for St. Paul's in Chicago, you know," he said. "Full-ride scholarship. She was the star of the team."

Jake looked at Kira again. "Point guard, I'll bet."

"Yeah," Brian said. "She was amazing to watch. We went to all the home games…" His voice trailed off.

Kira reached for Brian's hand. "Brian was with our parents in the stands for every game until the car accident." She smiled at her brother. "Bri used to hold up a sign with my name and number at the game. It said, My Sister Is Awesome. I looked in the stands for that sign every game."

Brian clung to her hand for a moment, then he let go and stood up. "I'm going to take a shower."

Kira watched him disappear into the house, her expression soft. Then she looked at Lexie. "You want to shoot a few more baskets, Lex?"

"Can I say bad words when I miss, like Uncle Brian?"

"No, you can't say bad words when you miss." Kira laughed and stood up, lowered the basket and fetched the ball from the grass. As soon as she had it in her hand, she bounced it against the asphalt, as if it was second nature. Jake stretched out on the lawn to watch.

Ten minutes later Lexie dropped the ball and ran to

the backyard. "Henry needs me to throw sticks some more," she said.

Kira tucked the ball under her arm and watched her daughter scamper through the gate. Then she turned to Jake. "Dogs trump hoops again. I'm going to get a complex if no one wants to play with me."

"I'll play with you," Jake said. "Anytime."

"In those clothes?" Kira asked, indicating his work khakis and dress shirt. "I'm not that desperate."

"Some other time, then," he said, staring at her sleek legs. "I'd love to take you on."

She glanced back at him as she headed for the garage with the ball. "Do you play ball?"

"Not a lot since high school."

She grinned. "I'll take it easy on you, then."

"Believe me, Kira. The last thing I want you to do is take it easy on me."

She put the ball on a shelf in the garage. "Fine. Then I'll kick your butt."

"Probably. But the fouls would be a lot of fun."

"Fouls as fun. That's a new concept." She leaned against the shelf. "What are you doing here, Jake?"

"Trying to change your mind about having dinner with me. Your friend Sherry cleared me to go back on active duty. So the whole conflict-of-interest thing is history." After watching her play basketball, he wanted desperately to get her alone. Her body was amazing, all firm muscles and curved lines. Female. Delicious.

She pushed away from the shelving. "I already told you why I can't have dinner with you tonight."

"Did you think I meant just you and me?" He shut down the mental picture of the two of them alone. "I meant all of us—you, me, Brian and Lexie. Lexie seemed to like Cheesy Pete's."

"And I'm sure Brian would be thrilled to go to the place he describes as a hellhole filled with rug rats."

"Okay, maybe not Cheesy Pete's. There are a million other restaurants in Riverton."

"Why don't we compromise? Stay here and eat with us."

"Really? You want me in your house after all you said about protecting Lexie and Brian from me?"

"That's not what I'm doing and you know it. I'm protecting them from building false expectations."

"And if we stay here, you can pretend that I came to see Brian," he said shrewdly.

She nodded. "That's what he'll assume."

"All right, Kira. You've got a deal. I'll make nice with Brian while I pretend I'm not lusting after you."

"Fine. Come on in. Brian should be finished with his shower soon."

As she headed for the door, Jake noticed the faded letters on the back of her shirt again. "Hold on," he said. "What's on the back of your shirt?"

She spun around too fast. "That's nothing. Just an old nickname."

He turned her around, feeling the tension in her shoulders. "Wild Thing? That's your nickname?"

"It's a silly college joke."

"Wild Thing?"

She shrugged. "You know how goofy college kids are."

"I like the sound of it," he said, his voice dropping. "It brings to mind all kinds of possibilities."

"That was a long time ago, Jake."

"You were pretty wild last night," he said quietly.

"Don't say that!" She glanced toward the house. "Brian and Lexie might hear you."

"God forbid one of them might think I like you."

Brian was standing in the kitchen when they walked in. "Hey, Jake. You still here?"

"We were discussing your sister's nickname."

"Nickname?" He stared at Jake, puzzled.

"Wild Thing."

"Oh, that." Brian laughed. "It's from the basketball team. The announcer always used to play the song when Kira went into a game. The whole place would go nuts."

"Yeah? Why that song?"

"Because that was how she played. She dove for every loose ball, she made steals, she never let up."

"I wish I could have seen her play."

"You can—"

"Bri, will you keep an eye on Lexie while I take a quick shower?" Kira interrupted.

"Sure."

She disappeared up the stairs and Brian looked at Jake with a questioning expression. "Your sister asked me to stay for dinner," Jake said. "Of course, I had to throw out some pretty big hints."

"Yeah?" He glanced up the stairs to where Kira had disappeared, then gave Jake a speculative look. "Why did you come over in the first place? I didn't miss a meeting or something, did I?"

"Nope. I had some business with your sister. From work," he added. "And I wanted to see how you were doing."

"Cool. You want a soda?"

Fifteen minutes later, Kira came downstairs in a pair of shorts and a T-shirt. Her feet were bare and her hair was still wet. She flashed an impartial smile as she headed out the door. "I'll start the grill."

"Isn't that your job, Brian?" Jake asked.

"Nah. Kira does the cooking."

"Barbecuing is a man's job," Jake said. "Come on, kid. I'll initiate you into the brotherhood."

Kira's yard was a secluded oasis in the middle of the city. Shrubs and two large trees shielded the yard from the neighbor's view. There were flowers planted along the fence and a hammock strung between the trees. Lexie was throwing a bright-green tennis ball to Scooter. Henry was lying in the grass, panting.

Kira stood in front of a gas grill. "Hey, Kira," Brian called. "Jake says we'll do the barbecuing." He leaned close as he turned on the gas and it ignited with a whoosh, making him jump backward.

"Whoa," Jake said. "Wait for me, Bri." He nudged the teen aside and adjusted the burners. "Okay, kid, prepare to do manly-man work."

"Oh, yeah," Kira said with a grin. "And when you're finished with dinner, Bri, I have a lot of other jobs for manly men."

As she turned away, Lexie came running over. "Mommy, you're not elegant."

"No, I'm not elegant tonight. But we have company, Lex."

"But this is the week of elgance. You said so. You said we had to dress up every night."

"You're right. We did say that." Kira glanced at Jake. "Okay. I'll go get elegant."

"You have to wear the dress I picked out for tonight," Lexie said.

"Maybe I should wear that one tomorrow, honey."

"No. That's tonight's dress," Lexie insisted.

"Okay." As she walked away, she muttered to Jake, "Don't you dare laugh."

Five minutes later she was back. Jake didn't have to suppress a laugh. But he did have to fold his tongue back into his mouth.

Kira wore a long gown made of some clingy material with diagonal pink, white and black stripes. Held up by skinny straps, the dress was bunched below her breasts, molding them so that it was clear she wasn't wearing a bra. It left most of her back bare.

"Not a word," she warned him beneath her breath, glancing at Lexie, who was running around the yard chasing the dogs. Brian stood at the grill, his back to them. "I bought it secondhand when I was in college. Lexie is totally in love with it."

"I don't blame her. I can feel heart palpitations coming on."

"Knock it off, Jake."

He leaned closer, slid his finger over her shoulder and tugged at the skinny strap. "I'd rather *take* it off."

She stilled for a moment and sucked in a breath. "Don't make me hurt you, Donovan."

"Promises, promises," he said.

Just then Lexie ran up and threw her arms around Kira's legs. "You wore it!"

"I promised you I would," Kira answered. The look she gave Jake was equal parts regret and warning.

"Uncle Brian is making hamburgers," Lexie said.

"So I hear. I guess he's a manly man now."

"HEY, JAKE, come see the digital camera I want to get," Brian suggested after dinner. "I'll show it to you online."

"No, no! I want Jake to read my bedtime story," Lexie protested.

"Hey, guys, leave Jake alone," Kira said, pushing away from the table. She gave him a pointed look. "He probably has to leave soon anyway."

He could take a hint as well as the next guy. "Yeah, it's getting late," he said as he stood up. "I'd better get out of here before Kira throws me out."

For a few hours tonight, he'd felt like part of a family again. With everyone but his sister out of college, working and starting families of their own, his own family didn't get together as often as he'd like. He didn't realize how much he'd missed them. He'd teased Brian, joked with Lexie and flirted with Kira—outrageously enough that Brian and Lexie thought he was kidding. They laughed and teased him right back.

He'd enjoyed himself. Maybe it was time to rethink his rule against dating women with children.

Or maybe it was Kira's family he enjoyed.

"Hey, Kira, walk me out to my car. I never did ask you that question about work."

Kira turned to Brian. "Will you read Lex her bedtime story?"

"Sure." He grinned at Jake. "But you're up next time, Jake."

"Count on it," he answered.

They walked out through the garage into the dusk. The scent of nicotiana was heavy in the air, and the moon was a slender crescent against a navy-blue sky. "What did you want to ask me?" Kira said.

He drew her into the shadow of the bushes behind the basketball hoop. "Will you wear this dress again?" he whispered. He ran his hands over her shoulders, lingered on her bare back. "Sometime when I can peel it off you very, very slowly?"

"That doesn't sound like a work question to me." Her voice was a breathy whisper in the semi-darkness.

He pressed his hands against the curve of her hips and pulled her closer. "Should I have told them the truth? That I wanted to get my hands on you?"

Her mouth parted seductively. "Probably not."

He bent his head and nipped at her collarbone, nudged the skinny strap of the dress off her shoulder. The scent of her skin filled his senses. He ran his tongue along the top of her breasts, barely covered by the dress. She shuddered and her hands tightened on his shoulders.

He bent to kiss her and covered her breast with his hand. Her nipple hardened against his palm, and she whimpered into his mouth.

He pulled the bodice down and tore his mouth away from hers. Bending, he took her nipple into his mouth. She arched against him, her fingers digging into his shoulders.

"Ask Brian to stay with Lexie," he said, his voice hoarse. "Come home with me."

Before she could answer, his pager buzzed against his hip.

CHAPTER TWELVE

As KIRA WALKED into the bull pen, her eyes zeroed in on Jake's desk. He wasn't there. Again.

He hadn't been there for the past three days.

She'd seen him exactly once since that night—the night they'd stood in the shadows near the basketball hoop, making out like a couple of teenagers.

When his pager went off that night he'd snatched his hands away from her as if he'd been burned. With a muttered "gotta go," he'd run to his car. Almost before the door closed he was driving away, tires squealing, siren wailing and lights flashing. In seconds he was around the corner and out of sight.

She'd found out the next day that Jim Lewis, a patrol officer, had been shot during a domestic call.

The officer would recover. Whatever had been going on between her and Jake was apparently dead and buried.

Yesterday, he'd given her a brief wave when he'd walked out of the building as she'd walked in. Either he and Mac were really busy or he was avoiding her.

Her money was on avoiding her.

Maybe he'd decided that her baggage was more than

he wanted to deal with after all. Brian and Lexie had been hanging all over him at dinner, vying for his attention all night. For a man used to having his fun and walking away, it would have been an eye-opener.

It was good that he'd run now, she told herself. They weren't really involved. There had been some flirting. Some teasing. And those kisses on Sunday night, the steamy episode the next night. It hadn't gone any further.

But, damn it, she'd wanted it to.

She'd begun to think that Jake could be part of her life.

That's what she got for letting down her guard.

She gave Jake's desk a vicious kick as she passed it.

"Hey, Kira."

She glanced over her shoulder. "Hi, Mac," she said, and kept on going.

He hurried over to block the entrance to the stairs. "What's wrong?"

"Nothing's wrong," she said. "Get out of my way."

"Uh-oh. I smell trouble in paradise."

"Don't start with me," she warned. "Move."

"Does my partner have anything to do with your foul mood?" he asked with a grin. "Has love's young dream turned into a nightmare?"

Had Jake talked about her? Had she been so wrong to think he was an honorable man? "What has he said to you?" she demanded, her stomach churning with humiliation and anger.

Mac's smile disappeared. "Whoa," he said. "He hasn't said a thing. He didn't need to. I saw him looking at you." He put a tentative hand on her shoulder. "He's my partner, Kira. I know him as well as I know anyone."

"That's just great," she said, shaking his hand off. "I'm glad to hear we've been so obvious. That just cheers me right up. Now get out of my way." She elbowed him in the side and walked past as he winced.

"Wait a minute, Kira. It's not like that at all."

She continued up the stairs without looking back at him. When she reached her office she shoved her key into the door, before realizing it was already unlocked.

She frowned. If she'd been so distracted yesterday that she'd forgotten to lock her door, maybe it was a good thing Jake had disappeared from her life.

She stepped inside and stopped. Someone had been in her office. The stack of papers she'd left on her desk was in a different place. She leafed through them. They were in a different order, as well.

Dropping her briefcase, she tugged at a drawer in the file cabinet. Still locked.

Her hands shook as she reached into her purse for the key to the file cabinet. When she opened the top drawer, it screeched with the fingernails-on-a-chalkboard sound of metal grinding on metal. It didn't take long to figure out why.

The tiny bar that locked the file cabinet was scraping against the metal rail that held the file folders. As if the lock had been opened only part way.

Or had been forced open and broken.

The scratches on the metal file cabinet were obvious when she looked for them. As were the tiny marks around the lock. Someone had jammed a sharp instrument into it and forced the drawer open.

Her heart pounded as she stared down at the row of manila folders. Someone had been in here while she was gone. Someone had stood at her file cabinet, thumbed through her files.

Reading them.

Her stomach rolled. She wrote in careful shorthand after a session with a patient, always aware that files could be subpoenaed. But her private notes, the ones no one ever saw, were in the files, as well. She hadn't bothered to separate them. She'd never expected someone to break into her file cabinet.

Pulling the vandalized drawer open all the way, she began thumbing through the folders. It didn't take long to realize she couldn't tell if any files were missing.

Think. After a moment, she pulled out her appointment book. Starting with the day before, she looked at the file of every patient she'd seen.

It didn't take long to find the file her intruder had been after.

Jake's. Her scribbled notes were out of order, as if someone had rifled through them and shoved them too hastily back into the folder.

Why?

Why would anyone care what Jake told her? Why commit a crime to find out?

What was going on? Only police officers and their support personnel would be able to do this. Someone she and Jake worked with had read his files.

Jake needed to know. She needed to warn him.

She flew down the stairs. Their personal problems didn't matter. They needed to figure out what to do.

She stopped abruptly. She couldn't run into the bull pen like a crazed person. The one who'd broken into her office would know she'd found out.

Taking a deep breath, she smoothed her hands down her skirt, made sure her hair was in place. Only when she was sure she looked calm did she walk into the bull pen.

Jake wasn't there.

Mac sat at his desk, reading a file, feet up. He dropped them to the floor when he saw her.

"Kira, I'm sorry I teased you. I was totally out of line." He glanced at A.J.'s office. "A.J. straightened me out, but feel free to take a shot at me yourself."

"Where's Jake, Mac?" She spoke in a low voice, but she felt eyes drilling into her back. Was the person who'd broken into her office here right now? Was he or she watching, wondering if she was going to raise the alarm?

"He ran out for coffee. He'll be back in a few minutes." He frowned. "Is something wrong?"

"Yes," she said. Making a snap decision, she added, "Can I talk to you privately?"

"In here." Mac stood and headed for A.J.'s office.

A.J. gave Mac an exasperated look. It changed to concern when she saw Kira. "Are you okay, Kira?" she asked. "I tore a strip off him for what he said to you."

"It's fine, A.J. That's not why I'm here." She turned and closed the door. "I need to talk to Mac."

"I'll leave you alone," A.J. said.

"No. You should hear about this, too." Kira said.

"What's going on?" Mac asked.

"Someone broke into my office last night," Kira said. "The door was open when I got here this morning. I thought I'd forgotten to lock it last night. But some papers on my desk had been disturbed. And someone pried open the lock on my file cabinet."

"Any of your files missing?" A.J. asked.

"I started to look through my recent patients. I got as far as Jake's file. Someone had read through it. So far, nothing is missing."

"Hell and damnation." Mac stared at her. "Whoever did it must have been a member of the department."

"They'd have to be. Who else would be able to get to my office? Who else would want to?"

"Why would anyone read Jake's file?" Mac asked.

"I don't know."

The three looked at one another. "There's been a lot of rumbling in the department," Mac said. "Rumors of a shake-up, talk about an investigation. Everyone is jittery and on edge. The department was embarrassed publicly when it came out that Doak Talbott was getting information from someone in the department and that was why he managed to avoid being caught for so long."

"Could that be why someone looked at Jake's file?" Kira wondered.

"Maybe. Any other files disturbed?"

"I don't know," Kira said, feeling foolish. Damn

Jake for making her react with her emotions instead of her head. "As soon as I realized his file had been disturbed, I came looking for him."

"You need to go through all of your files.

"I'll send Jake up when he gets back," Mac said.

"Wait," A.J. called.

Kira looked back at her.

"We should keep this between the four of us," A.J. suggested. "At least for the time being, until we have more information. I know Mac didn't do it because he was with me all night. And we can assume that Jake didn't do it. That leaves a lot of possibilities."

"A.J.'s right." Mac stood. "We don't tell anyone else. Jake and I will handle this."

"All right," Kira said. "I'll finish looking for evidence."

KIRA WAS HALFWAY through the files when her door burst open and Jake rushed in. "Are you all right?"

Her heart thudded, but she managed to face Jake calmly. "Of course I'm all right. Why wouldn't I be?"

"Mac said someone broke in here. Is anything missing?" He spun around, looking at the furnishings.

"I don't think so. The only thing disturbed was my file cabinet." She glanced at her appointment book for the next person on her list.

She was reaching for his file when Jake slapped his hand over it. "Stop it."

"Stop what?" She glanced up at him, hoping he saw a polite question on her face and nothing more.

"Stop acting like this."

"I can't. We need to know if any of my other files have been tampered with," she said, pushing his hand away and pulling out the folder.

"I'm not talking about the files," he said, an edge of anger in his voice. "I'm talking about your attitude."

"My attitude?" she said. "What attitude is that?"

"You're acting like I'm one of the guys." He scowled. "Like we're just professional acquaintances."

"That's exactly what we are, Jake. Professional acquaintances. Colleagues."

"We're a hell of a lot more than colleagues," he said, his voice rising. "Or did I imagine kissing you the other night? Did I imagine you kissing me back?"

"Since I haven't heard from you, you've obviously forgotten the other night. So have I. Focus on the problem. Someone broke into my office to see what I'd written about you."

"Look, I know I should have called. I'm a jerk. Okay?"

"Your jerk quotient isn't the issue." She picked up his file. "You told me things about yourself that were private. Now someone in the department knows." She wrapped her arms around the folder clutching it to her chest. "I'm worried for you, Jake. We need to find out who did this. And why."

"I like that you're worried about me." He touched her face, then dropped his hand when she jerked away. "In spite of the snotty attitude."

"Of course I'm worried about you. It gives me the creeps that someone read my private notes about you."

"Yeah? What did you write in your private notes?"

"My opinions, my observations, my thoughts."

"What kind of thoughts?"

She glanced down at the file. "Private thoughts."

"I like the sound of that."

"Stop it, Jake," she said, exasperated. "This is important. Serious. Someone read your files. It could affect you in the department."

"What about you?"

"What about me?"

"Someone could blame you. Someone could say you weren't taking due caution."

"Forget about that," she said impatiently. "I'm not concerned about my job. It's about you, about how this will affect you."

"So I'm more important than your job? I like that, too."

He *was* more important than her job, and that was frightening. She scrambled to recover. "I take patient confidentiality very seriously."

"Screw patient confidentiality. So someone read my file and knows what I said to you. I don't like it, but we can't change it now. What's done is done."

He took a deep breath and stared down at her. "I made a mistake, okay? I should have called you. I didn't. Can't you let it go?"

She dropped the file onto her desk. "Why didn't you call me, Jake?"

"Do you always have to know why? Can you forget for a few minutes that you're a psychologist? Sometimes guys do stupid things, okay? Can't we just leave it at that?"

She swiveled her chair away from him. "Fine. You're a jerk and I was stupid. Now that that's settled, we need to talk about your file." She couldn't let him see how much he'd hurt her. She refused to allow herself to be vulnerable to him again.

"Not so fast." His slow voice was like silk against her nerves. "There are other things more important right now. Starting with this." He pressed his mouth to the nape of her neck.

She leapt out of her chair and turned to face him. "Damn it, Donovan! Don't do that ever again. We're in my office, for God's sake."

He held her gaze. "Yeah, we're in your office. That doesn't mean you get to set the agenda for every discussion. I'm trying to apologize to you and you're brushing me off like I'm an annoying fly."

"Fine. Apology accepted. All right?"

"No, it's not all right. Talk to me, Kira."

A wave of anger washed over her. "Fine. Let's talk about Monday night. You asked me to come home with you right before your pager went off. God help me, I was ready to say yes. I was ready to trust you with my body." And my heart. "Then you left and never looked back."

He shoved his hand through his hair. "Do you think I wanted to let you go when my damn pager went off? I had to answer it. That's my job."

"I know you had to leave. But you haven't been near a phone since then?"

"It's complicated," he muttered. "I stayed at the

hospital on Monday night while Lewis had surgery. I had to tell his wife what happened."

"Is he all right? I thought he was recovering well. Is there something else wrong?"

"No, other than the piece of his liver he's missing, he's doing good. That's not the point."

"Then what *is* the point?"

"The point is…" He shoved his hands in his pockets. "The point is I've had a lot on my mind. I've been pushing you. I thought I should give you a little space."

"Did I ask you for that?" The scene in the darkness, the heat and need… "There were a lot of things I wanted that night, but space wasn't one of them."

Her throat closed. "Was this a game for you, Jake? Was I a challenge until I gave in?"

"It's not a game. I'm attracted to you. You're a beautiful, complex, fascinating woman."

"Then why didn't you call me? Did you want me to beg? Is *that* the game? Just so you know, I don't beg. Ever."

"No?" His expression grew heated. "I bet I could make you beg." His gaze drifted down her body, paused at her breasts. "Oh yeah. I want to hear you beg." His voice deepened. "You can definitely make *me* beg."

"Oh, for heaven's sake." She rolled her eyes, although everything inside her tightened. "Stop it."

"Not going to happen." He paced around the office, then stopped in front of her again. "Look. I'll come over to your house tonight, after Lexie's in bed. I want to talk to you with no distractions."

"Sorry, Jake, I'm busy."

"Are you?" He touched her cheek. "I never thought you were a coward."

She moved away from him, her anger stirring again. "You think I'm lying? You're not important enough for a lie. I have plans with Lexie and Brian."

"All night?"

"Tonight is the grand finale to the week of elegance." She wanted to bite her tongue. She hadn't meant to let that slip out. It implied a closeness that no longer existed.

"The grand finale? What are you wearing?"

"That's none of your business."

"Is it as elegant as that dress you wore Monday?"

"Elegant is not my thing. Sneakers and gym shorts are more my speed."

"That dress you had on the other night was elegant."

"It was revealing. There's a big difference."

"Whatever, I liked it."

"I could tell," she said dryly. "Now go away, Jake. I need to make sure no one else's file has been ransacked."

He lounged against the wall. "You think this is over?"

"Of course not," she said, holding up his file, deliberately misunderstanding him. "We need to figure out who did this."

He smiled. "That was quick, Kira. But you know I wasn't talking about the damn file."

She tossed it onto her desk. "Give it up, Jake."

"I'm a real persistent guy, Kira." He leaned forward. "I don't give up. You might want to keep that in mind."

She crossed her arms. "I'm willing to bet I'm at least as stubborn as you."

"Oh, yeah?" He moved around the desk.

"Yes." She stared at him, defying him to come closer. He ignored her.

"I like it when you go all tough-guy on me," he said. "When you give me that I-dare-you-to-touch-me look." He ran his hands up her arms and smoothed his thumbs over her neck. The rasp of his skin against hers made her legs tremble. "It's like waving a red flag in front of a bull."

He grazed his lips across hers, lingered for a moment. When her lips softened and she began to open to him, he moved his mouth down her neck, gave a tiny bite. "I can't help myself," he whispered.

He stepped back and let her go. As he headed for the door, he said over his shoulder. "You think you're stubborn? You haven't seen stubborn yet, babe."

CHAPTER THIRTEEN

KIRA POURED the grape juice into her teapot, arranged the cookies on her mother's Wedgwood plate and glanced at Lexie. "What do you think, Lex? Is our tea ready? Do we need anything else?"

Lexie scrutinized the table. "You're 'sposed to have finger sandwiches at tea. But it's okay that we don't," she added hastily. "I don't want to eat any fingers."

Kira swallowed a laugh. "They're not made of fingers, honey," she said. "They're just small sandwiches." She held out her hand. "Let's go make cucumber sandwiches."

Lexie crinkled her nose. "That sounds icky."

"We'll give it a try."

Twenty minutes later Lexie rearranged the cookies and cast a doubtful look at the cucumber sandwiches. "When is Uncle Brian going to be here? I'm hungry."

"He should be here any minute," Kira said. *Brian, don't do this to Lex. Don't forget about her tea party.*

Lexie skipped toward the living-room window and tripped on the hem of her dress. "It's too long, Mommy," Lexie said, pulling on the fabric.

"Let me fix it."

For the grand finale, Lexie had chosen a short, sheer nightgown she'd found in Kira's drawer. Kira had forgotten about it years ago.

She pulled the filmy material over the blue sash Lexie wore, black chiffon billowing over Lexie's SpongeBob SquarePants T-shirt. The smiling yellow sponge peeked out from the lace on the nightgown's bodice.

As she straightened Lexie's dress, she heard a car door slam and gave her daughter a hug. "That must be Uncle Brian now," she said.

The front door opened and Brian walked in, followed by Jake. Both of them wore tuxedos and had top hats set at jaunty angles. They carried walking sticks.

Jake rolled his hat off his head and down his arm, catching it in his hand and bowing deeply. "Good evening, ladies."

Kira's heart lurched. His shoulders seemed wider in the tailored jacket, and his blond hair gleamed against the black material. He was elegance personified.

She didn't look away quickly enough, and Jake caught her eye.

She forced herself to smile at Brian. "Wow, Bri. You put me and Lex to shame."

"Hey, it's the week of elegance," Brian said. He glanced at Jake. "We thought we should go all-out."

"Uncle Brian!" Lexie breathed. "You look beautiful!"

Kira's irritation at Jake's presence melted as Lexie

ran to Brian and hugged him. "Yeah, Bri," Kira said, recovering her poise. "You clean up real good."

Lexie leaned away from Brian and examined him from head to toe. "What are you wearing?"

"This is a tuxedo. It's what guys wear to fancy affairs like this." He swept his top hat off and bowed to her. "What do you think?"

"I like it!" Lexie said. She studied Brian, then looked at Jake. "You look beautiful, too, Mr. Jake."

"Why, thank you, Miss Lexie." He kissed her hand. "You're ravishing tonight. Your dress is amazing."

Kira watched Jake smiling down at her daughter. She could resist his teasing, his sexy appeal. But she had no defenses against the charm he lavished on Lexie.

Lexie giggled. "It's Mommy's dress."

Jake looked at Kira, his eyes gleaming. "I'm sure she'd look equally exquisite in it."

"Watch it," Kira muttered under her breath to Jake.

"I picked out Mommy's dress," Lexie said, eyeing the brown velvet halter gown with satisfaction.

"It was a fine choice," Jake assured her. His eyes followed the V of its neckline. "And it fits really well."

Kira smoothed down the brown velvet and resisted the impulse to pull the bodice up. The halter gown's neckline was more plunging than she remembered. "Why don't you show Brian our tea?" she said to Lexie.

As soon as they were out of earshot, she turned to Jake. "What are you doing here?"

He swung the cane and tipped the hat. "Being elegant. Can't you tell?"

"Okay, the tuxedos were a great idea. A little over the top, but Lexie liked it." She eyed the sexy man in front of her. "Don't do this to me, Jake. Don't blow me off one day, then act like you're part of the family the next. I thought we'd settled this in my office today."

"We didn't settle anything, other than that I'm a jerk."

"There's *one* thing we can agree on."

"I thought Lexie would get a kick out of the tuxedos. And she did ask me to the grand finale the other night."

"I'm sure she forgot all about it." She gave him a thin smile. "It's not like she was expecting you to call."

"Ouch. You're a hard woman, Kira."

"You have no idea."

"Anyway, I'll bet she didn't forget. Kids remember more than you think they do."

"It doesn't matter. Kids are resilient. She would have gotten over it and forgotten all about you."

"How about you?"

"Hardly," she said, trying to keep her voice light. "I see you almost every day at work."

"Exactly. I can't forget about you, either."

"Why are you doing this?" she asked quietly. "Do you expect me to fall into your hands like a ripe peach?"

"A guy can hope, can't he?" He leaned closer. "You know what I do with peaches?"

"What?" The word came out of her mouth before she could stop herself.

"I take a bite and roll their sweetness around on my tongue for a while. Tasting it. Sucking it. Then I lick the juice as it runs down my hand."

"Stop it," she whispered. Brian and Lexie were giggling together in the kitchen, but they could back into the living room anytime.

"Do you really want me to stop?"

"Of course I do." She took a step away from him. Away from his intoxicating scent. Away from the intensity in his eyes.

"Are you sure?" His gaze traveled down her body, then back up. "You look like you want me to…"

"Jake! My daughter and my brother are in the next room."

"Okay. I'm a patient guy. I can wait."

"Don't hold your breath," she managed to say, even though she was having trouble breathing.

He reached out, ran a finger up her arm, slid it beneath the halter of the dress and over her collarbone. "I warned you, Kira. I'm a stubborn guy."

He didn't fight fair. "I can't do this," she whispered.

"Sure you can." He leaned still closer. "It'll be fun, Kira."

"Fun and nothing else."

"Why not? Don't you do anything just because it would be fun? Without analyzing it to death first?"

"Not so much anymore," she said as Lexie walked into the room.

"Mommy, our tea is getting cold." Lexie stood with her hands on her hips, scowling.

"Okay, honey, I'll be right there," Kira called as Lexie stomped back to the kitchen.

"Maybe it's time you were more impulsive," Jake said.

"We can pick up where we left off on Monday night." He trailed his hand back down her arm.

"Too late. I've had time to come to my senses."

"I bet I can make you lose them again."

She saw heat in his expression and felt the answering response deep inside. He could make her lose more than her senses. And it scared her.

When she'd thought he was all flash and no substance, it was easy to dismiss him.

But now she wanted to lose herself in his possibilities.

"I'm burning up, Kira. For you," he whispered. He glanced at her chest. "Have you thought about how it'll be? What's going to happen when all this heat between us explodes?"

She'd thought of little else. "It's not the smart thing to do."

"Who wants smart?" He leaned impossible closer.

Lexie ran back into the room. "Come *on,* Mommy."

"Hey, Jake, what's the hold-up?" Brian called. "Come on, Kira. Lex is hungry."

"Hold on a second," Jake called without taking his eyes off her. "Your sister isn't sure she wants me to stay."

"The tuxedos were Jake's idea," Brian retorted, pushing past Kira to stand next to Jake. "You have to let him stay."

"What do you say, Kira?" Jake murmured.

He wasn't just asking to stay for their party. He was asking for much, much more.

She wanted him to stay. She wanted to be a little reckless and crazy.

"All right," she said finally. "I'll probably end up paying the stupid tax. But you can stay."

JAKE AND BRIAN crooked their little fingers as they drank grape-juice "tea" from delicate bone-china cups. They nibbled on the cucumber sandwiches. And they devoured the cookies. Lexie giggled as she poured. She even tried a cucumber sandwich after Jake swooned over how delicious they were.

Kira watched them as she nibbled on a sandwich. Jake was tender and careful with Lexie, and it brought down every barrier she'd erected against him. And he treated Brian like a man, not a boy. Brian sat taller in his chair, his eyes bright as he followed Jake's lead.

When all the cookies and sandwiches were gone, Jake shared a look with Brian and stood. He held out his hand to Lexie. "I think this occasion calls for some ice cream from Doogie's. What do you think?"

"Yes! Can we, Mommy?"

In for a penny, in for a pound. "Sure," Kira said. "We can take my car."

"We don't need a car," Brian said, his eyes shining.

"No? Are we going to walk downtown?"

"Nope." He grinned at Jake. "Tell them."

"Let's show them instead," Jake said.

Jake and Brian ushered them to the front door, then Brian threw it open with a flourish. At the curb was a white stretch limo.

If Kira's heart had begun to melt during tea, now it dissolved into a puddle. "Jake," she murmured.

He held her gaze for a moment before turning and elbowing Brian. "What did I tell you, Johnson? Elegance gets the girls every time."

"Is that big car yours, Mr. Jake?" Lexie asked, staring at the limo in awe.

"It is for tonight, kid. How about we ride downtown in style?"

Ten minutes later they were walking down the pedestrian mall toward Doogie's Ice Cream. Kira caught a glimpse of them in a store window—Brian and Jake in their tuxedos, her in her old velvet gown and Lexie in her nightgown. Lexie's shoes were pink flip-flops with colored glitter on the straps. As she walked, tiny red lights flashed in the soles.

They looked like the goofballs on parade. And very much like a family.

Because her heart stuttered in her chest and her breath caught in her throat, she looked away. At the same time, Lexie looked up at her. "This is the most fun ever, Mommy. Isn't it?"

"I'd say it is," Kira said with a smile. Grabbing Lexie's hand, she stopped and stared at their reflections in the window. "Absolutely."

CHAPTER FOURTEEN

As Brian clocked in at Digital City on Saturday afternoon, he breathed a sigh of relief that Redmond wasn't around. Maybe the manager had forgotten about him.

A weight lifting off his shoulders, he walked toward the loading dock. He'd been dreading another confrontation. Now he could enjoy his shift. He walked a little faster; Jenny had already clocked in.

He spotted her, dressed in her usual black, at the end of an aisle, restocking shelves. The store had gotten a big shipment last night. He and Jenny would spend their whole shift putting all the stuff away.

As he got closer, he could see white earbuds sticking out of her ears. And he could see her hips moving to the music only she could hear.

He frowned.

"Hey, Jen," he said as he touched her shoulder.

She jumped, ripping the earphones out of her ears. "Jeez, Brian. Way to sneak up on me." She shoved the wires into her pocket. "How's it going?"

Brian glanced down at the pocket. "What are you doing?"

"I'm putting this stuff away." She pointed to the

pallet of boxes. "They got a buttload of stuff in yesterday. They must be having a big sale next week."

"I'm not talking about that." He nodded toward her hip. "What did you just put away?"

"Nothing."

"Aw, Jen." Brian felt sick to his stomach. "It was an iPod, wasn't it?"

"So what if it was?" Jen stuck her chin out. "I like listening to music."

"You said they were status symbols and tools. You make fun of people who bring them to school."

"Maybe I changed my mind." She grabbed another box off the pallet. "You'd better get busy. Redmond will yell at you if he sees you standing around."

"Is he here?"

She looked at him as if he was some dork loser. "He's on the schedule, isn't he?"

"I didn't see him. I thought he changed shifts." He glanced over his shoulder, but they were alone. "We can fix this, Jen. I'll help you."

"What are you talking about?"

"The iPod thing. You still have the box at home, don't you? We can put it all back and put it on the shelf somewhere. They'll think it got misplaced."

Her face darkened. "Do you think I stole this?" She pulled the silver-and-white iPod out of her pocket and glared at him. "Is that what you're saying?"

"What am I supposed to think, Jen? You can't afford one of those." He stared at the mp3 player.

"Maybe someone gave it to me."

"Like who? Your mom? Maybe she gave it to you the last time you saw her."

Jenny flinched. "That was really mean, Brian."

Immediately, he felt ashamed. "I'm sorry, Jen. I didn't mean it." Jenny hadn't seen her mother since the day her mom had walked out on them two years earlier. "I say stuff without thinking first."

"Sorry doesn't cut it, Brian." Her lip quivered and she swung away from him. "Leave me alone."

"Aw, Jen. I'm a creep. I can't believe I said that. I really am sorry. And I want to help." He laid a hand on her shoulder but she jerked away.

"Let's put it in your locker. Later we'll figure out how to get it back into stock."

Jenny turned to face him. "You really think I stole this, don't you?"

"I know how easy it is to get sucked back into stuff. You saw what happened to me last week."

"Do you think I'd let Jake down by stealing again?" Jenny asked, her voice fierce. "Or the rest of the group?"

"Do you think I wanted to let Jake down?" He swallowed. "It's hard working here, seeing all this stuff I can't get. Seeing people buy stuff for their kids. It must be harder for you."

"I got it from…"

"What's going on?"

Redmond. Brian whirled to face the assistant manager. "Nothing, sir. We're just figuring out the most efficient way to get all this stuff put away."

Redmond gave him the once-over before he zeroed in on the iPod in Jen's hand. "Whose is that?"

"It's mine," Brian said. "I was showing it to Jen."

Jenny shot Brian a look he couldn't interpret. "It's mine," she said.

Redmond smiled triumphantly, a knowing expression on his face. "It can't belong to both of you."

"We're sharing it," Brian said, taking a breath. "You know?"

"Yeah, I do," Redmond said. "Hand it over."

Jenny shoved it in her pocket. "No." Brian was surprised at how calm she was. "It's mine."

"Don't make me take it away from you," Redmond threatened, reaching for Jenny.

Brian stepped in front of him. "Don't touch her."

"You think you're a big man?" Redmond sneered, clearly furious, looking Brian up and down. "A few weeks behind bars will cut you down to size."

He spun on his heel and walked away. Brian didn't move until he was gone. Neither did Jenny.

"Why did you do that, Bri?" Jenny asked. There was a funny sound to her voice.

"Do what?"

"Why did you say it was your iPod? And why did you stand in front of me like that?"

"I didn't want you to get in trouble for stealing."

"But now you're going to get in trouble."

Brian shrugged, trying to act cool. Like he wasn't worried in the least. "He can't prove I stole anything."

"You were trying to protect me." Jenny looked at him, her eyes too bright.

"Of course."

He'd failed his mom by causing the car accident. He wouldn't fail Jen.

"You did that last time with Redmond, too. No one's ever tried to protect me before," Jen said. She stared at him, her eyes suspiciously wet. Wiping the back of her hand over her face, she gave him a watery smile. "Maybe you're not such a jerk after all."

"I'm sorry Redmond caught us. I shouldn't have been arguing with you. I should have waited until we were on break. Or until we were finished working."

"It's okay," Jen said.

Brian reached out, touched her cheek. It was wet from her tears. Jen looked into his eyes and he wanted to kiss her. He wanted to hug her. What would she do if he did?

Gathering his courage, he bent down and touched her mouth with his. When she didn't jerk away, he put his arms around her. He felt awkward and stupid. But then Jen put her arms around his waist. She stood there tentatively, as if she didn't know what she was doing, either.

Before he could decide what to do next, he heard footsteps in the next aisle. With a combination of frustration and relief, he let go of Jen and moved away.

Brian's heart plunged when Jake turned the corner and stopped. Behind Jake, there was another guy. Redmond brought up the rear, smirking.

"There they are, officers. The girl is the one with the iPod."

"How do you know they stole it?" Jake asked. He kept his eyes on Brian and Jen while he spoke. Brian couldn't read his expression.

"They both claimed it belonged to them. And the girl was acting suspicious."

Jake turned to the manager. "Define suspicious."

"Hiding it. Putting it away when anyone got close."

Jake stood looking at Redmond for what felt like a long time. Brian wondered what was going through his head.

When he turned to the other guy, a look passed between them. Brian couldn't figure that one out, either.

"All right. You two come with me." Jake spoke in a flat, voice and pointed to him and Jen. "Detective McDougal will talk to Mr. Redmond."

Jake turned and began walking without waiting to see if they were coming. Sick at heart, knowing they'd broken trust with Jake, Brian followed.

JAKE OPENED the door of Digital City and waited for Brian and Jenny to follow him. He skirted the unmarked car at the curb and headed across the street, struggling to control his rage. He'd wanted to punch the smirking manager who was so quick to accuse the kids.

"Where are we going?" Brian asked.

"To the park?" Jenny hurried to catch up with him. "Why are we going to the park?"

Jake waited until they were on the other side of the

street. "Because it's too stinking hot to sit in the car. And we have some talking to do."

He picked a picnic table that was out of the way and shaded by a huge red oak. He slid onto the bench and waited for Brian and Jenny to sit on the other side. They sat close together, almost but not quite touching. He guessed they were holding hands beneath the table.

"All right. Here's what the manager told me. He said the two of you stole an iPod. He said other stuff has been missing, and he suspects you've taken it." He glanced at Brian. "He called you a troublemaker."

"I am not a troublemaker!" Brian's face flamed. "He's been harassing Jenny, calling her names and stuff. I told him to stop and I guess he didn't like that."

"Yeah?" Jake turned to Jenny. "Is that true? Has Redmond been harassing you?"

Jenny shrugged. "Redmond's a jerk."

Jake studied the girl. She wouldn't quite meet his eyes, and he wondered why.

"Okay, we'll get to the harassing part later. I want the truth now. Did you two steal that iPod?"

Brian looked ashamed, Jenny uncomfortable.

"Well?"

"Yeah, I stole it," Brian said.

The words hit Jake like a punch to the mouth. Hadn't he helped Brian at all? Hadn't the group helped him?

"I'm sorry to hear that," he said.

"Brian didn't steal anything." Jen set the iPod on the table. "It's mine."

"Did you steal it?" Jenny had come to the group after she'd been caught shoplifting.

She fingered the iPod. "No. I didn't steal it. My father gave it to me."

"What?" Brian frowned. "Your father gave it to you?"

"Yeah." She stared at them defiantly. "I didn't tell you because I knew you'd say I sold out. That I let him buy me off." She swallowed once. "I really wanted it," she said in a small voice.

"What's wrong with that?" Jake asked, bewildered. "You're not happy your father gave you an expensive gift?"

Brian stared at Jenny, stunned. "It really is yours?"

Jenny nodded, looking miserable.

"Am I missing something here, or are you upset that you have an iPod?" he asked Jenny.

"I made fun of them," she whispered. "I laughed at the kids who brought them to school. I said they were sell-outs, trading their souls for expensive toys." She hunched her shoulders. "I just said that stuff because I didn't have one."

Jake relaxed. He'd dealt with this kind of drama far too often with his brothers and sister. "So you were afraid Brian would think you were a hypocrite."

"Yes."

Brian continued to stare at her, dumbfounded.

"Brian," Jake said, and the kid turned toward him.

"Yeah?"

"Do you think Jen is a hypocrite? Should she give the iPod back to her father?"

"Of course not! It's way cool."

"Okay, then. Are you two square?"

They nodded vigorously.

"That's good. Because I don't like store managers calling the police about two of my kids. You understand?"

"We understand," Brian answered, his eyes narrowed. "Why are you here, anyway? You're a detective."

"I was at the dispatch center when the call came in. When I heard your names, I said Mac and I would take it."

"What do we do about Redmond?" Brian jiggled his leg.

"Nothing. I'll tell him I've determined that the iPod belongs to Jenny and that should be it."

"Do you want to see the receipt for it?" Jenny asked. "I know my dad still has it."

Jake's heart ached for Jenny. She hadn't had a lot of trust in her life. "Of course not, Jen. I believe you."

"Just like that?" She stared at him.

"Just like that. Okay. The iPod stuff is officially history. Now tell me about the harassment."

"Don't worry about it," Jenny said, shoving the iPod in her pocket. "It's not a big deal."

"It is, too." Brian's face tightened. "He calls her names and looks at her funny. And he tried to search her."

"But he didn't. Brian wouldn't let him." Jenny raised her head, her eyes glowing. "He stood in front of me and told Redmond to back off."

"Good job, kid." Jake nodded at Brian.

Brian shrugged. "No big deal."

"It *is* a big deal," Jake said. "I'm proud of you, Bri. Your sister will be, too."

"You're not going to tell her about this, are you?"

"Why don't you want her to know?"

"Because it's not her business!" Brian kicked at the dirt. "I'm sick of answering her questions."

"Maybe if you told her more stuff she wouldn't give you the third degree. She worries about you."

"She doesn't have to. I can take care of myself."

"She'll always worry. That's the way it works."

"Jeez, Jake, why are you defending her? I thought you were on my side."

"I'm not taking sides."

"No? I think you're on her side. I saw you looking at Kira last night. I know that look."

They stared at one another, male to male. Jake nodded.

"You're right. I was looking at your sister. She was hot in that dress. Do you have a problem with that?"

Brian's jaw tightened. "Are you having sex with her?"

"That's not *your* business. Your sister and I are both adults, and our private lives are off limits."

Brian shoved at the picnic table. "I wondered why you were so friendly all of a sudden. Why you're hanging around all the time."

"Your sister isn't the only reason," Jake said, trying to keep his voice calm. He felt as though he was flailing at the edge of deep water. One false move and he'd be over his head. "I like you, Brian. You, too, Jenny. I enjoy spending time with you. And I want to help you work out your problems and stay out of trouble."

"You never came to my house before," Brian pointed out. "Until you decided Kira was hot."

"I came to your house the first time because you got arrested. Remember that?" Jake said. "The next time I came over, it was because we were going to print up those flyers for the high-school registration."

"You ate dinner at our house. I thought you were there because of me. Because you…" He stumbled off the bench and stood with his back to Jake, clenching and unclenching his hands.

"I was, Brian." Jake touched his arm. "You're a great kid. How I feel about your sister has nothing to do with how I feel about you."

"You're a cop. I've been arrested twice. You can't think I'm a great kid."

"Now you can read my mind?" Jake asked. "You've made some mistakes. We all do. But you stood up for Jenny with Redmond. You stood up for her in that bar. So, yeah." He smiled. "You're a great kid."

"I think it's kind of cool," Jenny said. "That your sister is banging Jake."

"Jenny! Can we have a little respect here?" Jake slapped his hands on the picnic table and leaned toward her. "I don't want to hear you say that again. That's crude and disrespectful."

Brian's back was rigid. "Look at me, Bri."

Brian slowly turned around.

"I will have no disrespect of your sister. Do you understand me?"

He waited until both of them nodded.

"I don't want to hear any snickering behind her back, any gossip, any speculation about her. If I do, there will be serious consequences. Is that clear?"

"Yeah." Brian stuck out his chin. "But I still think it's weird."

"You're entitled to your opinion. You're not entitled to interfere in my personal life. Or your sister's."

"She's my sister!"

"She's also an adult. You don't think she deserves a life apart from you and Lexie?"

"I guess. I never thought about it."

"Maybe it's time you did."

He stood up from the table. "Mac should be done talking to Redmond. Let's get back to the store."

As they headed back through the park, Jake looked at Brian's hunched shoulders and grim mouth. "What, Brian?"

"She's not really my sister," Brian said quietly.

"What do you mean?"

"She's my stepsister." He kicked a clod of dirt and sent it flying. "We're not, like, really related."

Jake grabbed Brian's arm and swung him around. "What do you mean, 'she's not really my sister'?"

"I'm just saying. She can dump me whenever she wants."

Jake let him go. "Man, if you weren't so pathetic, I'd have to smack you around. Kira loves you. You're her brother. Not her step-brother. Not some punk she has to tolerate. Her brother."

He took Brian by the shoulders. "If she had to choose

between you and me, she'd choose you. Without even thinking about it."

He started walking again, feeling Brian fall into step beside him. "Is that what you're going to do?" Jake asked. "Screw things up between me and Kira? Make her choose between us?"

"I couldn't make her do that."

"You don't think so?" Jake shot him a look. "Then you don't know your sister very well."

"What makes you think you do?"

"All you have to do is talk to her for five minutes to figure that out."

Brian, his shoulders hunched, hurried across the street. As he pushed open the door to Digital City, Jake put his hand on his arm.

Brian shook off his hand. "Leave me alone, Jake."

CHAPTER FIFTEEN

KIRA PICKED UP THE remote and turned off the television as the front door opened on Saturday night. Brian came in, startled when he saw her sitting on the couch.

"Oh. Hi, Kira. What are you doing here?"

"Watching a boring television show. Where did you expect me to be?"

"I don't know." He didn't meet her eyes. "Out, maybe."

"Yeah, I live such a wild life. I can see where you might think that," she said with an easy grin.

"Maybe you should go out more."

"What?" She looked at him more carefully. "Where did that come from?"

Brian shrugged. "I'm just saying."

"Well, I'm here tonight. Just like always." She continued to watch him. "How was work today?"

"Okay."

"Did Redmond give you any problems?"

"No more than usual."

"At least he let you punch in."

"Yeah, he wasn't around when I got there."

He shuffled his feet, looked around the room and began walking up the stairs. "I'll see you later."

"Goodnight," she said, watching him disappear.

Five minutes later she heard his footsteps on the stairs again. "Are you going out?" she asked.

"No." He licked his lips. "Do you have a minute?"

"I have as many minutes as you need." She turned the television off again. "What's up?"

"I didn't exactly tell you everything that happened at work today," he began. He rubbed his hands on his slacks.

"No?" He looked so nervous she wanted to wrap her arms around him the way she'd done when he was younger. "You want a soda or some iced tea?"

"I'll get them." He rushed into the kitchen. A moment later he set her iced tea on the table and folded himself onto the couch. He took a long drink of his soda.

"Redmond called the police on me today."

"What?" She threw herself beside him. "Are you all right? What happened?"

Instead of pulling away from her, he leaned into her for a moment before squirming away. He took a drink of his soda and stared at the can.

"He accused me and, ah, a girl of stealing an iPod."

"He thought you'd taken iPods from the store?"

"No. He thought we stole one together."

Kira settled back on the couch. "Why?"

"It was my fault," he said. "I thought Jen had stolen it. So I said it was mine. Then Jen said it was hers."

"You were trying to protect your friend."

"I guess." Brian shrugged.

Kira squeezed his shoulder. "That was very brave."

"I was scared," he admitted. "Until Jake showed up. Then I was even more scared. I figured he'd be mad at us."

"Was he?"

"Nah. He was mad at Redmond." Brian smiled. "It was way cool. Jake told him he had no right to search us. He really chewed Redmond a new one. The jerk didn't come near us the rest of the day." He scuffed his foot along the carpet. "It was embarrassing to walk out of the store with Jake. Like he was arresting me. You know?"

"It sounds horrible."

"Yeah, but Jake talked to us and everything's cool." He grabbed his soda and took a long drink. "I know about you and Jake."

Whoa. Her stomach twisted into a knot. "Me and Jake? What about me and Jake?"

"I know that you're, like, dating him."

"Where did you get that idea?"

"I asked Jake. He told me."

"Jake told you we were dating? And why would you ask him something like that in the first place?" Her hands were damp and she felt her face turning red.

"I saw you looking at him last night. And I saw him looking at you." He twisted his can in tight circles on the table. "I know what that look means."

"What, ah, did Jake tell you?"

"Stuff." He shrugged. "Guy stuff."

Oh, God. She hadn't been this mortified since her father had interrogated her first boyfriend.

"What kind of guy stuff?" she asked carefully.

"Just guy stuff. I'm not going to tell you," he said impatiently. "Do I ask you what you talk about with Jake?"

"I guess that's fair." She pulled one of Lexie's blocks out from under her. "And we're not actually dating. He hasn't asked me out yet."

"But you'd go if he did, right?"

"I'm not sure."

"Is it because of Lex? I'll baby-sit."

"Really? You wouldn't be upset if we went out?"

"I'm okay with it."

She flopped back against the cushions. "I was sure you'd be upset if Jake and I were dating."

He cleared his throat. "If you have to date someone, Jake's an okay guy."

"Thanks, Bri." She jostled him with her elbow. "That means a lot to me. That you approve of me dating him."

"Yeah? You really care what I think?"

"Of course I do! You and me and Lexie are a family." She smiled. " Lexie will want you to like the boys she dates, too."

He scowled. "Now that's weird. She better not bring any scumbags around here."

She laughed and to gave him a quick kiss on the cheek. "I have a feeling you'll think all of them are scumbags. That's what big brothers always think."

She saw that he was pleased, despite what he said next. "I'm not her brother."

"No, you're more a combination father and big brother." She patted his leg and stood up. "You're much more than an uncle to Lexie. You know that, don't you?"

He shrugged. "I never thought about it."

"You're always there for her. Like with the tuxedos last night. You're a huge part of her life." Leaning down, she gave him a hug. "I'm going up to bed. Would you let the dogs out again before you come upstairs?"

"Sure, Kira."

"Good night, Bri."

She headed up the stairs and into the safety of her bedroom before Brian could ask her anything more about Jake. She wasn't ready to discuss their tentative relationship with her younger brother.

KIRA SAT on the top step of the back porch on Sunday afternoon, watching Brian try to teach Lexie how to hit a baseball. During the tea party, Jake had teased her and Brian, saying that real athletes played baseball, not basketball. Ever since, Lexie had been pestering Brian to teach her.

"There you go, Lex," Kira called when Lexie finally made contact with the ball. "That's the way to do it."

Lexie jumped up and down. "Now I'm a athlete," she yelled. "Just like Jake."

Lexie had been full of Jake and the tuxedos ever since the tea party. He'd charmed both her daughter and her brother that night, teasing them, joking with them, and generally acting like one of the family.

The rest of the time he'd watched Kira with smoldering eyes. He hadn't missed a single opportunity to touch her.

He'd taken her arm when they crossed the street. He'd rested his hand in the small of her back as they waited for their ice-cream cones. And in the limo, on the way home, he'd slid his leg over just enough.

Every time they turned a corner, went over a bump, his leg pressed hers. By the time the limo arrived at the house, she couldn't speak a coherent sentence. Jake had walked them to the door, given them a cheery goodbye and left with the limo.

Kira put Jake out of her head. She'd spent far too much time already today thinking about him. "Hey Bri," she called. "What should we have for dinner?"

"I'm not hungry," he called back. "Can we wait a while? Lex and I are going to shoot some baskets."

Brian disappeared into the garage with the ball and the bat. The dogs followed him to the fence, sorry that the game of chasing the ball was over.

When he emerged with the basketball, Kira stood up. "That sounds like fun. Mind if I join you?"

Brian frowned. "Are you sure? It's pretty hot out here. You'd get all sweaty and like, gross."

"Like I've never been sweaty and gross before?"

"Why don't you just watch?" he said with a nervous look. "You can give us tips on what we're doing wrong."

"But I'd rather…" She stopped when she saw the desperation on Brian's face. What was going on? "Okay," she said. "I'll be your audience this time."

"Great," he said. He bounced the basketball on the driveway. "C'mon, Lex! Let's go play basketball."

Kira sat on the grass at the edge of the driveway and watched, yelling encouragement to Lexie and cheering whenever Brian made a good shot. When Brian missed a layup, she jumped to her feet.

"Want someone to show you how to do that, Johnson?"

Brian grinned. "I would, if there was anyone around who knew how."

Laughing, Kira sat down again. She itched to join in, to play with Lexie and Brian, but for some reason Brian wanted to do this by himself. So she forced herself to stay on the sidelines and watch.

Her daughter and her brother were having a wonderful time. There was a lot of giggling as Lexie tried to dribble and laughing when she took a shot. When the ball finally found the basket, Kira cheered wildly as Brian and Lexie high-fived each other.

A car door slammed in the street behind her, and Jake called out, "Nice shot, Lexie."

Kira spun around to see Jake walking toward them. He wore pleated khakis, a blue dress shirt and a tie that featured a cartoon coyote watching a roadrunner scamper away. The only other tie she'd seen him wear was the bow tie with the tuxedo.

He caught her staring at him. "You like what you see, Kira?" he said in a low voice as he got closer. His slow smile made her face hot.

"I'm still taking it in. This is twice in a row you've dazzled me with your sartorial splendor."

He stopped a foot away from her. "I like the dazzled part," he said, softly enough that only she could hear. "I want to keep you off balance."

He was doing a good job. "Thanks for the warning."

"I like to play fair." He smiled a sexy half smile. "Right before I pounce."

As her breath caught in her throat, Jake turned to Brian and Lexie.

"You guys are looking good," he said, glancing at Lexie's dress, white with vertical pink, blue and green stripes and a pink belt. "Great dress, Lex."

"It's my favorite," she said happily.

"It's perfect for basketball."

"What are you doing here, Jake?" Kira asked.

"I just stopped by to see how you guys were doing. I thought maybe you'd all like to grab some dinner."

His expression of careful innocence stirred Kira's suspicions. She saw Brian give him a thumb's-up.

"Nah, Jake, but thanks," Brian said quickly. "Lex and I have plans. But maybe you and Kira could do something."

"You and Lexie have plans?" Kira stared at her brother. "What plans?"

"We're going to Cheesy Pete's. She wants to show me a trick in the play area." He gave her a guileless look. "Since I wasn't there to see her last time you went."

"You're going to take Lexie to Cheesy Pete's? By yourself?" Kira stared at him. "Okay, where is the real Brian Johnson? You're clearly an alien who has stolen my brother's body."

Brian grinned. "You go ahead and have dinner with Jake." He carefully avoided looking at Jake as he called to his niece. "Hey, Lex. Let's throw a few tennis balls to the dogs before we go."

Brian and Lexie disappeared into the backyard, and she turned to Jake. "Was this your idea?"

He smiled. "Believe it or not, it was Brian's. I told him I didn't need his help setting up a date with you, but he seemed to think otherwise. He thought you would chicken out otherwise."

"I have never chickened out on anything in my life," she said, glaring at him. "And Brian knows it."

Jake laughed. "He said you'd say that, too. So I guess you're going out with me, huh?"

"Slick, Jake. Very slick."

"Hey, this was Brian's brainchild. I just followed his script."

She glanced at the basketball hoop. "No wonder he didn't want me to play with them." She smiled. "He said I would get sweaty and gross."

"I wouldn't mind sweaty. In fact, I like sweaty. As long as we're getting sweaty together."

Heat unfolded deep inside her. "I'll go change my clothes," she said quickly.

"You don't have to do that." He glanced at her cut-off shorts and the clingy, V-necked T-shirt she wore. "You look good to me."

She fingered the ragged edges of the shorts. "I don't wear these out of the house. I'll be right back."

As she turned, he ran his finger over the smooth

crescent that peeked out of the bottom of the shorts. "You can wear them for me any time."

She slapped her hand over the exposed skin. When he laughed, she flashed him a grin over her shoulder. "That's why I don't wear them out of the house."

"Wear something casual," he called after her.

Ten minutes later she came outside wearing a pair of green capris and a T-shirt. "Is this casual enough?"

"I liked the other outfit better."

"That's why I changed," she retorted.

He grinned as he slung an arm over her shoulders. "You have a mouth on you, don't you? No wonder I'm so crazy about you."

Her skin burned where he touched her, and she slipped out from the weight of his arm. "Let me say goodbye."

He shoved his hands in his pockets. "I can wait."

She felt his gaze as she walked around to the backyard. "Hey, guys," she called to Brian and Lexie, who were throwing Frisbees to the dogs. "Jake and I are leaving."

"Okay." Brian came loping over. "Don't worry about getting home or anything. Lexie and I are good." He glanced over her shoulder to where Jake stood. "And, ah, I'll make sure she gets to church in the morning."

Heat flooded her face. "That won't be necessary, Brian. I'll be here tomorrow morning."

"I'm just saying," he answered. "Have fun."

"Thanks." She walked back to Jake.

"Why are you blushing?" he asked.

"That was the most embarrassing conversation I've ever had," she muttered.

"What?"

"Brian told me he'd take Lexie to church tomorrow morning. Did you put him up to that?"

Jake started to laugh, then pretended to clear his throat when she glared at him. "No, I did not put him up to that," he said. "Do you think I'd discuss our sex life with Brian? Especially since we don't have one? Yet."

"God! I can't believe he said that to me."

He opened the truck door. "Get used to it. It's called dating with teenagers."

"I may have to rethink this whole idea."

"Too late," Jake said cheerfully. "I've got you now, and I'm not going to let you weasel out." He gave her a wicked grin. "We'll discuss the tomorrow-morning part later."

Her heart bumped against her chest and she sucked in a breath.

As they drove through the streets of Riverton, she cleared her throat. "Where are we going, Jake?"

He slid one finger down her cheek. "We're going to have some fun."

CHAPTER SIXTEEN

A FLOOD OF DESIRE slammed into Kira. She slid her hands beneath her thighs to stop them from shaking. "We are?" she managed to say.

"Oh, yeah. I have all kinds of things planned."

She swallowed. "What kinds of things?"

"Are you sure you want me to tell you?" He glanced over at her, and the lust in his expression made her throb with anticipation. "Surprises can be so much fun."

"Okay," she said. "Surprise me."

The air in the cab of the truck seemed thin. She shifted on the seat, trying to defuse the tension. If she didn't, she was going to leap across the seat and cover his mouth with hers.

It took her a moment to realize they weren't in Riverton. They were on Sheridan Road, heading south toward Chicago.

"Where do you live?" she asked, bewildered.

"I have a house in a neighborhood not far from yours."

"Then what are we doing here?" She looked around as they rolled to a stop at a stoplight. "We're almost at Lake Shore Drive."

"I told you. We're going to have some fun."

"I thought…"

"What did you think?"

"Nothing. I'm just surprised."

He smiled as the traffic light turned green. "You thought I was going to drag you to my house and jump your bones, didn't you?"

When she didn't answer, he slid one finger down her cheek to her neck. Then he skimmed over her collarbone. "Not that I haven't imagined that scene way too often." He trailed his fingers down her shirt, brushing the side of her breast. "I spend a lot of time thinking about what I want to do with you."

"Oh." She could barely say the single syllable.

"Yeah, as appealing as that idea is, it'll have to wait. You have a serious fun deficit that needs to be fixed."

"Where are we going, Jake?"

"Wait and see."

Fifteen minutes later they pulled into Navy Pier. Ten minutes after that, they were sitting in one of the cars on the enormous Ferris wheel, crowded in with four other people. Jake draped his arm over her shoulders and pulled her close. They were touching from ankle to thigh, and she was having trouble concentrating on the magnificent view.

The car swayed gently in the wind, and Jake stroked his fingers over her upper arm. He bent to whisper in her ear, "This is where you're supposed to say, 'Oh, Jake, I'm scared. Hold me tighter.'"

"I don't think so," she managed to say. "At least not in public."

His arm tightened on her shoulder, then he moved and took her hand, twining their fingers together. "I'm a patient guy," he said. "I can wait." He bent closer, his breath stirring her hair. "Can you?"

Her stomach dropped, and she told herself it was the motion of the Ferris Wheel. But when Jake brushed his mouth over her palm as he helped her out of the car at the end of the ride, her stomach dropped again.

They walked to the end of the pier and rented two pairs of in-line skates. Jake made a production of helping her lace the boots, his hands brushing over her legs as he did so. When they left the stand, Jake put his arm around her. To steady her, he said innocently.

He stayed close as they started to skate, pulling her against him to avoid joggers and bicyclists on the asphalt lakefront path. When another skater clipped her and she stumbled, Jake spun her off the path until she was back in control. After that he held her hand firmly, letting go only long enough to dodge other skaters. At the Montrose Avenue Bench, Jake rolled to a stop.

"Having fun yet?" he asked.

She grinned at him. "I am. I haven't been on skates in years. Thank you." She reached up and kissed him on the mouth. She meant to give him a quick, harmless kiss, but found herself sinking into him as his hands tightened on her arms. When she leaned closer, her skates slipped backward and she had to grab onto him to keep from falling.

"Okay, bad planning," he said as he supported her. "Maybe the skates weren't such a great idea."

"They were a wonderful idea."

"I have a lot more fun planned," he said, taking her hand again as they skated toward the lakefront.

He stopped at a concession stand and bought two ice-cream cones. As they sat on a bench in the shade, he watched her lick a bead of ice cream sliding down the cone. His eyes darkened.

"I changed my mind," he said, his voice low. "The fun portion of the day is now officially over."

Chocolate ice cream melted over her tongue. She couldn't look away. "What part of the day comes next?"

"The I'm-so-hot-for-you-I'm-about-to-explode part." He tossed her ice-cream cone into a trash container, and pulled her to her feet. "Let's go."

As they skated back toward Navy Pier, neither of them spoke. When they reached the rental stand, Jake practically threw the skates at the vendor and waited impatiently for him to retrieve their shoes. She'd barely slipped into her sandals when he snugged his hand around her waist. Holding her tightly against him, they hurried to his truck.

He didn't look at her as he maneuvered his truck back onto Lake Shore Drive. Once they were heading north, he reached over and took her hand. He pressed their palms together and slowly entwined their fingers.

She'd held hands before. It was a small thing, a casual connection between two people. Never before had her skin tingled like this. The simple intertwining of fingers flooded her with heat. Made her feel claimed.

"So." Jake cleared his throat. "You want to have some dinner?"

She tightened her hold on his hand. "I'm not hungry."

"No?" He glanced at her, his eyes heavy-lidded. "I'm starving."

"Then we'd better feed you," she whispered. "I don't want you withering away to nothing."

"Believe me, there's no chance of that," he said. "But I'll have a taste now, just to hold me."

He untangled their fingers and lifted her hand to his mouth. He nibbled on her index finger for a moment, then slowly drew it into his mouth. When he swirled his tongue around it, she had to bite her cheek to keep from moaning.

He eased her finger out of his mouth and put her palm on his thigh. Then he laid his hand over hers. She felt his heat through the material of his slacks.

By the time they pulled into the driveway of a typical Chicago bungalow on a quiet, tree-lined street, the scent and feel of Jake had crowded every other thought from her head. Jake lifted her out of the truck, letting her slide down his body as he put her on the ground.

Instead of ushering her into his house, he held her by the shoulders. "Do you want to come into my house, Kira?" he said. "It's not too late to say no."

This moment had been inevitable since the evening they'd played pool at McGonigle's. Now her body was crying out for him. "Yes," she said in a low voice. "I want to go through that door with you. I want to find out what we're going to do together."

"Everything," he whispered. "We're going to do everything together."

"Yes," she said. "That's what I want."

A wave of cool air washed over her as she stepped into the dim interior. Before she could notice anything more, he kicked the door closed and pressed her against the wall.

His mouth was ravenous. His hands roamed over her back, her hips as he gently bit at her lower lip, then sucked it into his mouth. She wrapped her arms around his neck and held on. He'd barely touched her, and desire was an insistent throbbing deep inside her.

Suddenly he tore himself away and grabbed the hem of her T-shirt. "This has to go."

He pulled it over her head, then stood looking at her in her black lace bra. His hand shook as he touched one nipple through the lacy material and watched it tighten and swell. "Sorry, babe," he said in a hoarse rasp. "As much as I love looking at you in lace, this is going, too."

He unhooked the front clasp and brushed it aside, her breasts falling into his hands. For a moment he stood there, watching as he brushed his thumbs over her nipples. Then he bent and took one into his mouth.

She twined her leg around his, trying to ease the ache he'd caused. She shoved her hands under his shirt. His skin was hot, the muscles beneath it hard. They jumped as she smoothed her hands over his chest, brushed her fingers over his taut nipples.

She needed to feel his skin against hers. Her hands shook as she tugged at the knot of his tie. Finally, impatient, she pulled it over his head and tossed it to the floor. She undid just enough buttons to pull the shirt over his head, too, then it joined the tie on the floor.

His mouth fastened onto hers again, his kiss desperate. His chest hair was soft against her skin. She rubbed against him, and he groaned into her mouth.

His hands shook as he stripped the rest of her clothes down her legs. Then he dropped to his knees and buried his face between her thighs. When his mouth touched her, she arched against him with a keening cry and climaxed.

"No," she sobbed. "Not alone. I want you inside me."

He rose to his feet and held her as she shook. "Don't worry, sweetheart. I will be next time."

She fumbled with the waistband of his slacks. Gently he pushed her hands away, unfastened the button and shoved them down his legs. She slipped her hands into his red silk boxers and cupped him. But when she pushed his boxers down his legs and followed them down, he stopped her.

"Not this time," he said in a ragged whisper. "I want this to last. I've been thinking about this for too long."

He took her hand and led her to the stairs. Halfway up, he pressed her against the wall and kissed her again.

His bedroom was cool and dark. His mouth still fused to hers, he backed her toward the bed and eased her down onto the sheets. As he kissed her, he fumbled in the drawer of the nightstand. Finally he tore open a foil packet. Before he could put the condom on, she took it out of his hands and rolled it onto him.

Braced above her, he slowly slid inside her, then laced their hands together. As he began to move, her body tightened again. "Jake," she whispered. "Oh, Jake."

He opened his eyes and smiled at her. "I want you with me, Kira. All the way."

He held her gaze as he moved inside her. And when he finally cried out her name and poured himself into her, she wrapped around him and shattered along with him.

"Stay with me," Jake whispered several hours later as she lay, sated and boneless, on top of him. He trailed his hand down her back from her neck to her hips. "All night. There's still lots of ground to cover."

She smiled against his chest. "Don't you want to save some for another day?"

"Hell, no. We'll think of new things."

She laughed as she pushed onto her elbows. His hair was tousled and she brushed it aside. "I've been itching to get my hands in your hair."

"It's all yours, Wild Thing."

Her smile faded as she held his gaze. Then she pressed a kiss to his mouth and rolled to the side. "I want to stay, too," she said softly. "But I can't."

He propped himself on one elbow. "How late can you get home and still say you didn't stay the night?"

"Brian is a pretty sound sleeper," she said with a slow smile. "He's not going to be able to tell if I come in at one o'clock or three o'clock. So that gives us," she glanced at the clock, "three more hours."

"I'd rather wake up with you," he said. "But I'm willing to compromise. How about four o'clock?"

"You drive a tough bargain."

He ran his hand down her side, down her leg. "I haven't wanted a woman to stay for a long time, Kira."

"No?"

"The last woman I spent the night with was my wife."

"What happened, Jake?"

He shrugged. "We confused lust with love, got married too young. Then my dad died and she wasn't crazy about me helping to raise my brothers and sister. I knew it was over when she started diagnosing deep psychological problems whenever I did anything she didn't like. I think we were both relieved when the divorce was final."

"I'm sorry," she said, brushing his hair off his forehead. "No wonder it was hard for you to talk to me after you shot Doak."

"But I couldn't resist you." He kissed the nape of her neck. "Especially now that I know what a wild thing you really are."

"You sweet-talker," she said, turning her head to return the kiss.

He worked his way down her back, then paused when he reached the curve of hip. "Have I told you how much I like this?" he whispered, smoothing one finger over the tattoo of a basketball hoop circled by barbed wire.

"You've mentioned it," she said with a smile.

"It's a good thing I didn't know about this before today. Now every time I see you in one of those prim little business suits, I'll know what you're hiding." He pressed a kiss to the tattoo. "And I'll want to…"

She turned and wrapped her arms around him. "That's enough talking.

"Yeah? Do you have something else in mind?"

"Come here and find out."

CHAPTER SEVENTEEN

ON WEDNESDAY of the following week, Jake came into Kira's office late in the afternoon. "Hey, gorgeous," he said, planting a kiss on her mouth.

She softened against him, opening her mouth to his kiss. Then she pushed him away, making him laugh. She was determined to keep things professional in her office.

He'd always liked a challenge.

"One of these days, you're going to drag me onto your desk and have your way with me," he said, smiling.

"You keep telling yourself that," she replied with an answering grin. "We all have our little fantasies."

"Yeah? What are yours?"

"Nothing I'm going to discuss in my office, ace."

"Okay, we'll save that for later." His smile faded. "We do need to talk, though, and we can't do it here."

"What's wrong?" She sat up straighter.

"Can we get some dinner? Do you think Brian could pick up Lexie and stay with her for a while?"

She called her brother, then locked her file cabinet and followed Jake down the stairs and into his truck. As they were pulling out of the parking lot, she said, "Okay, what's going on?"

"It's about your office break-in." He shoved a hand through his hair. "Mac and I don't have any leads. The two of us and A.J. have been watching everyone in the department pretty closely, but no one's acted any differently. From the past few weeks, anyway. Do you have any ideas? Have you noticed anything?"

"No."

He grimaced. "All the negative publicity from the Talbott case is getting to the chief. He's pushing us to kick up the clear rate. Everyone's irritable and on edge." He rolled his shoulders. "The most even-tempered guys in the department have been acting like Crowley."

"I know," she said. "Some of them have ended up in my office."

"Mac and I have been talking. I think we've come up with a way to push our burglar to make a mistake."

"What's that?"

"You and I are going to have a couple more sessions together," he said. "Our perp must be afraid I'll tell you something. After I make sure everyone knows about it, I'm going to wait in your office at night and hope he breaks in again."

"That could work, I suppose." She frowned. "But won't the guilty person suspect what you're up to?"

"I'm hoping he or she isn't thinking clearly."

"I guess it's worth a try." She rummaged in her purse and pulled out a key. "Here's my extra office key."

"Thanks, Kira." He slipped it into his pocket. "I'll let you know when I'm ready to use it."

As they turned the corner, she realized they were on his street. "I thought we were going out to dinner."

"I didn't say where we were eating." He swung the car into his driveway. Inside, Jake fired up the grill. He seasoned two steaks, then opened a bottle of wine. "Let's sit outside," he said. "I've been meaning to ask you about basketball. How did you get so good?"

She sat in one of the chairs on his deck and looked at his backyard. His grass needed cutting, but he had mounds of pink, coral and orange impatiens planted along the edges of the yard. They made it unexpectedly cheery.

He sat down next to her. "Talk to me, Kira."

She took a sip of wine and stared into the yard as the memories tumbled over each other in her mind. "My mom died when I was six, and after that it was just me and my father. He loved basketball. Some of my earliest memories are of sitting on his lap while he watched games on television. He was my first coach when I was in third grade, and it wasn't long until I loved it, too."

"Looks like he taught you well."

She smiled. "He did. He was a point guard, too. We'd play for hours at a time on the driveway."

"Then you taught Brian."

She nodded. "Our parents started dating when Brian was eight and I was eighteen, and he pestered me to teach him. My dad played a lot with him, too, but it was a special thing Brian and I did together."

"Brian said you played at St. Paul's," he said.

"I did." She smiled again, remembering. "They were three of the best years of my life."

"Three years? Why didn't you play all four years?"

She took a deep breath and set the glass down on the white table. "I got pregnant with Lexie in the summer before my senior year," she said. "Pregnant women can't play basketball at that level. So I had to quit the team. They wanted to make me a manager, but that was worse than quitting altogether."

She stared at the yard, not seeing the grass or the flowers. "I was lonely after our parents died, and Brian was in the hospital. That's where I met Lexie's father. I thought I was madly in love, and he said all the right things. But when I told him I was pregnant, he took off so fast he left a vapor trail behind."

"Bastard," Jake said, his voice hard.

She shrugged. "He was in medical school. He told me he didn't have time to be a father." She smiled bitterly. "I heard he decided on pediatrics as his specialty. I always appreciated the irony in that."

"You want me to kick his ass for you?"

She leaned over and brushed a kiss over his cheek. "My hero. But he's not worth it. I got over that loser a long time ago." Her smile faded. "Lexie has been asking about her father, and one day I'll have to tell her. But we're doing fine on our own."

"You're doing more than fine," he said. He reached over and scooped her out of the chair and settled her on his lap. "I'd say you've done a hell of a job raising your family."

"Thank you," she said. "Now you know the story of my life in all its boring detail."

"There's nothing boring about you, babe." His eyes drilled through her. "How could the wild thing be boring?"

An answering smile touched her mouth. "I guess that part's not so boring."

"So how did you end up working for the Riverton PD?"

His hand stroked her arm with a hypnotic rhythm, making it hard to concentrate on his question. "Riverton? I ended up there by default, I guess."

"How so?"

She shifted in his arms. He tucked her head beneath his chin and the side of her breast pressed against his chest. He rested his hand on her abdomen, and her muscles jumped beneath the fabric of her shirt.

"What?"

She felt him smile into her hair. "How did you end up working with a bunch of cops?"

"I wanted to start a private practice. But that takes a while and I needed to have money coming in. So I took the job."

"I'm glad you did," he said. The hand resting on her abdomen began to move in slow, almost absentminded circles, as if he didn't even realize he was caressing her.

Her body noticed right away. "So am I," she said, a little breathless.

"Yeah," he said, his voice dreamy. "You were a big improvement over John Bates, the psychologist who retired."

"Really?" she asked, moving into his caressing hand. "I thought John did a good job for the department."

He moved his hand to her thigh. "I guess John was okay. But he wasn't my type." He brushed his lips over her hair. "Then you started working."

He slipped his hand beneath the hem of her skirt, and she glanced around wildly. But she didn't see any of his neighbors. "Every day you'd come in and climb the stairs in those skirts of yours. It sure did improve the scenery."

She sucked in a breath as his hand moved higher. "That is so sexist."

"No, it's just fact. John didn't do it for me. You're sexy as hell."

"I'm glad to know I was giving you a thrill every day," she said, her voice tart.

"Sweetheart, you have no idea." His fingers brushed the edge of her lace underwear, and she stilled beneath his hand. He trailed his fingers over her thigh and traced tiny circles on her suddenly way-too-sensitive skin.

"What are you doing?" she whispered.

"Isn't it obvious?" He brushed the back of his hand against the juncture of her legs. "I'm talking to one of my colleagues about work."

"Oh, is that what we're doing?" she said, shifting on his lap. "That's good, because I've been wanting to talk about work, too." She wriggled until his erection was exactly where she wanted it. Then she lifted his hand, slid it beneath her T-shirt and put it on her breast. "I wanted to ask about the new expense-reimbursement policy. Is auto mileage an allowable charge? And how much?"

He found her nipple through the thin nylon of her bra. "That's a hard one," he whispered as he circled her nipple.

She rocked against him again. "It sure is."

He gave a strangled laugh into her hair. "You're a piece of work. Have I ever told you that?"

"You may have mentioned it." She slid her hand beneath his T-shirt and traced his hard muscles. They trembled faintly beneath her fingers.

She squirmed to get closer to him and he shuddered. "Stop moving, Kira," he said. "Or I'm going to embarrass myself like I haven't since I was seventeen."

"Really?" She moved again. "That sounds interesting."

"Kira, stop," he groaned. "You're driving me out of my mind here."

"Poor baby." She leaned forward and licked his nipple through the T-shirt. "How are you going to stop me?"

"I can think of a couple of ways." He fumbled for the clasp of her bra, and her breasts fell into his hand. Then his other hand touched the lace between her legs.

He bent his head to catch her moan in his mouth. His hands began moving, slowly at first, and she surged closer as their mouths clung together. Then he slipped beneath her panties and found her throbbing center.

"Jake," she panted. "Stop. Your neighbors can see us."

"I don't see anyone. And you should have thought of that before you started playing games," he whispered.

"You started it."

"I'm going to finish it, too." His hand moved faster and his tongue explored her mouth.

Her climax exploded through her, leaving her trembling in his arms. He held her tightly, whispering endearments into her ear.

Finally, when she could move again, she cupped his face in her hand. "Why do you always do that?" she asked. "I want you to be with me."

"I like to watch you come." He turned his head and kissed her palm. "Do you know how hot it makes me?"

"I think I have an idea," she said, adjusting herself on his lap. "But I need to do more research."

He stood up with her in his arms. "I can get behind this kind of investigation. But it's going to need more room than we have on the porch."

He carried her to the bedroom, setting her down on his bed. "The lab is now open."

JAKE ROLLED to his back several hours later, taking Kira with him. She propped herself on one elbow, a serious look on her face.

"What is it, Kira?" he said, brushing the hair away from her face.

"I was wondering," she began.

He tightened his grip on her. "Wondering what?"

"Maybe we could expand the scope of this investigation." She gave him an impish smile. "I have some ideas for new areas to explore."

His heart started beating again. "Oh, yeah? You want to tell me about them?"

She glanced at the clock. "It's getting late, and I don't want to rush through the list." She threaded her fingers through his hair and kissed him. "Showing is more fun than telling, anyway." She grinned at him as she trailed her mouth over his chest. "You can use your imagination in the meantime."

He was in so much trouble. He'd thought he could keep it light with Kira, keep her from getting attached to him.

Keep himself from getting attached to her.

But they'd made love twice tonight, and he wanted her again. He was afraid he'd always want her again.

Uneasy, he set her on the bed and sat up. "Nice idea to leave in my mind, McGinnis," he said. "You expect me to go to work under those conditions?"

She leaned off the bed, reaching for her clothes. "Put on your big-boy pants and suck it up, Donovan." She tossed his boxers at his head. "No, wait. Forget about the sucking part. I wasn't going to tell you about my ideas, was I?"

Groaning, he reached for her and she danced away from him, laughing. He sprawled on the bed and watched her get dressed. He missed her already.

"Go away with me for a couple of days," he said impulsively. "Let's go up to Door County. There's a bed and breakfast I've stayed at near Sturgeon Bay called Van Allen House. I think you'd like it."

The smile disappeared from her face. "I'd love to go with you. But I can't."

"I'll take a couple of days off," he said. I have some vacation coming."

The bed dipped as she sat beside him. "I can't, Jake." She studied his face, her own serious. "For the same reason I can't spend the night with you. What kind of example would I be setting for Brian? Or Lexie, for that matter, even though she's too young to understand. As long as I come home at night, we can all pretend that you and I have just been on a date."

He sighed and wrapped his arm around her. "I just lost my head there for a moment."

She kissed his cheek. "Besides, that kicks this whole fun thing to a new level. That wasn't the deal we made."

Thank God she was keeping her head. His head went on vacation whenever he was with her. "You're right," he said, forcing himself to smile. "I wasn't thinking."

He'd better get a grip on himself. Or he'd be in major trouble.

Something told him he already was.

CHAPTER EIGHTEEN

HE WAS in trouble.

Jake's truck rolled to a stop in front of Kira's house. He knew cops didn't do happily ever after. After their conversation a week ago, he shouldn't have needed last night's brutal case to remind him.

Dawn painted the sky pink and orange, and he sat at the curb and stared at Kira's house. They would all still be sleeping. He imagined Kira in her bed, her hair tousled, her skin warm and fragrant. He'd managed to see her every night this week, although they'd spent half the evenings at her house with Brian and Lexie.

They'd spent the other evenings at his house. But he still hadn't seen her sleep.

Maybe that was a good thing. Maybe it would make what he had to do a little easier.

He watched until he was satisfied no one was awake. Picking up the envelope on the seat next to him, he slid out the tickets. They were supposed to go to the Cubs' game today, the four of them. His mouth twisted. What had he been thinking? That they would have a little family outing?

Shoving the tickets back into the envelope, he

got out but left the engine running. Just like a getaway car.

He'd almost reached the door when one of the dogs started barking. Scooter, he thought with a grim smile. The little dog still didn't trust him.

Kira should have paid attention to her dog.

Opening the screen door, he pushed the tickets inside. Then he jogged back to his truck and drove off.

A COUPLE OF HOURS later, right on schedule, his phone rang. He woke up in the recliner, stiff and groggy, and reached for the telephone on the table next to the chair.

"Donovan."

"Jake? What's wrong? I found the tickets in the door. Are you sick?"

"I'm fine," he said, sitting up. "Mac and I caught a tough case last night. I'm not fit to be around."

"What happened?" Kira asked, her voice softening.

He hesitated. He didn't want to talk about it. The scene had already replayed in his mind too many times.

"Tell me, Jake. Please. I can hear you're upset."

He drank the last mouthful of flat beer then put the can back on the table. "We got a call about a kid who wasn't breathing. We got there right before the paramedics. It was a girl, maybe two years old. She had bruises from her neck to her knees. The parents said she'd fallen down the stairs." Sickness overtook him in a violent rush.

"Oh, no. Oh, Jake, how awful." She hesitated. "How's the little girl?"

"Not so good. She's in a drawer in the morgue."

She sucked in a breath. "I'm so sorry," she whispered.

"So are her parents. They say they're sorry they didn't watch her close enough. They're really sorry she fell down those stairs." He closed his eyes.

"I'll see you in a few minutes, Jake," Kira said, her shock evident even over the phone. "I'm coming over."

"No! Kira, wait."

After a long pause, she said, "What?"

"Don't come over here. Please." He moved the phone to his other ear. "I'm in a lousy mood."

"That's why I'm coming over. I need to be with you."

"Why? So you can be in a lousy mood, too?" He felt nothing but horror and crushing sadness. "I don't want to ruin your day."

"You won't." Her voice was gentle. "I just want to hold you."

God, he wanted her to hold him. He wanted to burrow into her softness, to wrap his arms around her and let everything go.

Which was exactly why he couldn't let her come over. "I need to be alone, Kira."

There was another pause. "Then at least come to the Cubs' game with us." Her voice trembled, then she cleared her throat. "It'll take your mind off what happened. You went to a lot of trouble to get these tickets."

"You take Brian and Lexie. Maybe Brian can use the extra ticket for his friend Jenny."

"You're just going to sit around and brood all day?"

"No. I'm going to drink a few beers while I brood."

"I'm coming over." The phone clicked as she hung up.

"Damn it!" He slammed the phone.

She was acting like she cared about him. Like she had a right to worry about him.

Like they had a relationship.

How had he let that happen?

He'd forgotten the most important rule he'd learned years ago—cops shouldn't have families. Because in a moment, in less than a heartbeat, it could be ripped apart. Destroyed completely. Wives and mothers devastated. Children growing up without a father.

He'd seen how his father's death in the line of duty had destroyed his family. His mother had never been the same. Ten years later, she still grieved for her husband.

His siblings had run wild, deliberately courting danger and destruction.

His marriage had been destroyed, his life plans irrevocably changed. And in order to support his family, he'd ended up working as a cop, just like his father.

The one job he'd sworn he'd never do.

He wouldn't do that to Kira.

He'd barely managed to get his teeth brushed before he heard her car in his driveway. He rubbed the stubble on his face, glanced at his razor, then turned and walked away. No time to shave, damn it.

He opened the door while she was still walking up the sidewalk. She walked a little faster.

"Jake," she said. She pushed through the door and pulled him close. She kissed him, and he held her tightly. He pressed a kiss to her hair, inhaled her scent, then released her.

"What are you doing here, Kira? I told you I didn't want to see you."

"I needed to see you. To tell you that I…" She closed her eyes for a moment, then looked at him. "I care about you, Jake. You're in pain, and I want to share it with you. I want to do whatever I can to make it better."

The need to reach out and fold her back into his arms was almost overwhelming. He was drowning and he wanted to grab onto her like a life raft, to let her keep him afloat.

He cared for her too much.

"The only thing I need is for you to leave me alone. Okay?" He heard the desperation in his voice and tried to disguise it. "I'm not going to inflict my bad mood on you guys. Go to the game. Have a good time." He forced himself to smile. "I'll look for you in the stands while I'm watching on television."

Kira tilted her head and watched him with that assessing look that drove him crazy. Finally she said, "There's something else going on here, isn't there? Some other reason you're pushing me away." Her voice burrowed into his heart as though it belonged there. "Talk to me, Jake. Tell me what you're thinking."

"Maybe I'm not thinking anything!" He began to panic. She was getting too close to the truth. He was getting too close to spilling it all out to her.

She let her gaze travel over him, over his unshaven face, his bare chest, his black silk boxers. When she raised her eyes, he could read her arousal in them. "You don't want to talk? Okay. We won't talk."

She stepped close and wrapped her arms around his neck. Wrapped her body around him. *Yes,* his body sighed. *This is what I want. What I need.*

He was too raw to make love with her. It would mean too much. But he couldn't let her go. "This isn't fair to you," he said into her hair.

She swept her hand down his chest, his abdomen, until she touched him through his boxers. "Really? Do you hear me complaining?"

He took a step back, then another, until his legs bumped against the recliner. "I don't want to use you to forget what happened."

"You're not using me," she whispered, sliding her hands beneath the waistband of his shorts. "Looks to me like I'm the one using you." She shoved his shorts to the floor, then pushed him backward until he fell onto the recliner. She tore off her clothes, then slid on top of him. "I want you, Jake. Make love with me."

His slid his arms around her, held her with frantic urgency. He buried his head in her neck, tasting her. When he took her mouth, her need and his own blended in a heady, dizzying whirl. "Kira," he whispered into her mouth. "I need you so much."

"I'm yours." She pressed her palms to his, locked their hands together. And when he poured himself into her, when he felt her join him, he wrapped his arms around her and held her tightly. He held her as if he would never let her go.

A long time later he felt her shiver. "Are you cold?"

She smiled into his chest. "You do like your air conditioning, don't you?" When she sat up, her smile lingered as she looked at him. Then, with a quick kiss, she slid off him and began to dress. "Put your clothes on, Jake. Let's go to the baseball game."

There was no way. He was too raw; he needed her too much. He had to put as much distance as possible between them.

He sat up and pulled on his boxers. "I'm not going to the game, Kira. I already told you that."

"Don't be so stubborn," she said, her smile fading. "You're not going to win this one."

"Oh, yes, I am. I warned you that you hadn't seen stubborn yet. I'm not going with you, Kira. Now why don't you get out of here before I say something I'll regret later."

Her mouth tightened and he could see her anger building. "Now you're being childish."

"Fine. I'm childish."

She glared at him, her eyes narrowing. "I'm not going to get into a wrestling match with you."

"Yeah, we already did that. And it didn't change my mind." He took a deep breath. He had to do it. "Look, Kira, you're not taking the hint here. I don't want to see you right now. Okay? I don't want to be around you."

The pain he saw in her eyes was almost too much to bear. But he forced himself to stay where he was. He stared at her with his cop face, expressionless and unwavering. "Get out of here."

Her mouth tightened, but her anger didn't completely hide the pain. "Congratulations. You wanted to make me angry and you've done it. So I'll get out of your house."

She pulled one of the tickets out of her back pocket and set in on the table beside the recliner, right next to two empty beer cans. "Here's your ticket, in case you change your mind."

She turned around and stalked to the door. Before she opened it, she said, "I trusted you, Jake. Trusted that we could be open with each other, count on each other. Maybe I needed the reminder that trusting someone is a bad idea."

She slipped out the door and closed it quietly. Jake stared at the ticket for a moment before picking it up and crushing it in his fist. Then he grabbed a beer can and hurled it at the wall.

A FEW DAYS LATER, Jake sat in one of the easy chairs at Starbucks. He'd gotten here early. He needed to focus on the kids, and their problems.

"Hey, Jake." Brian dropped into a chair.

Jake glanced at his watch. "Is it time for our group already?"

"No. I came early."

Jake set his coffee down. "What's up? The manager at your store giving you a hard time? Problems with Jen?"

"Nah." A tiny smile flickered over Brian's mouth. "Things are good with Jen. And Redmond has left me alone."

"That's great. So what did you want to talk about?"

"Kira."

Fear stabbed Jake, sharper than a dagger. He grabbed Brian's wrist. "What's wrong? Is she okay?"

Brian shook off his hand. "What do you care? You haven't been over since last Saturday."

He knew exactly how long it had been since he'd seen her. He and leaned back in his chair. "I've been busy. Your sister knows that."

Brian rolled his eyes. "That is so lame." He watched Jake carefully. "You made her cry, you know."

Oh, God. He didn't want to hear this. She was supposed to be angry with him. He couldn't bear to think of her, crying because of him.

"Your sister doesn't cry. She's too tough for that."

"I heard her."

"How do you know it was because of me?"

"It was Sunday night, after the baseball game." His gaze judged and condemned Jake. "Lex was real sad because you didn't come. So Kira bought her all kinds of stuff to eat. Lexie was up most of the night, barfing in the bathroom."

"Then that's why your sister was crying," Jake said desperately. "She was upset because Lexie was sick."

"She was mad at herself because Lex was sick. Because she'd let Lex have all that junk food. I was cleaning up some of the puke when Lexie told Kira she was sad because you missed all the fun we'd had. She asked Kira if you could come with us next time. That's when Kira started bawling." Brian scowled. "I told her I'd kick your ass."

Jake smothered a laugh. "Good for you, Bri. I guess I need to have my ass kicked."

Brian's posture was very protective. "Maybe I won't bother. My sister doesn't need a loser like you."

"I didn't mean to hurt her, Brian."

Brian snorted. "Like that counts. You're always telling us that what we mean to do doesn't matter. It's what we actually do that's important."

Jake looked away, ashamed that an eighteen-year-old kid had to point it out to him. He'd hurt Kira, and that was inexcusable. He should have let them drift apart naturally, the way he always did with women.

"Are you going to fix this? Where's your big words about responsibility now, Jake?" Brian sneered contemptuously.

Jake squirmed in the chair. Brian was right, damn it. He couldn't just leave things the way they were.

"So what are you going to do about it?" Brian asked again, his voice challenging.

"I'll make things right with your sister." He'd have to leave eventually, but it didn't have to be now. Hell, she'd probably get tired of him anyway in a month or two. "Okay?"

"You better not make her cry again," Brian warned, sounding very adult.

"I'll come over with some flowers or something."

"That's not going to work," Brian said flatly. "Kira's got a bad temper. She's not going to let you in the house." The teen suddenly clenched his fists fiercely. "And I don't want Lexie to see you guys fighting."

"You're right again," Jake said quietly, then struggled to give Brian a reassuring grin. "Hey, I thought I was the adult here. I guess I was wrong."

"I guess you were."

"Okay. I'll stay away from your house. I'll accidentally run into her somewhere."

Brian eyed him carefully, as if assessing his intentions. Finally he nodded. "Okay. I'll tell you where. It's the perfect place."

SEVERAL RUNNERS passed Jake as he slowed to a walk on the indoor track. He hated running inside, especially in the summer. Even during typical Chicago summer weather, when the heat and humidity could reach triple digits, he ran outside.

Only for Kira would he run in this box.

He was ashamed of himself. An eighteen-year-old kid had had to straighten him out.

So he'd apologize to Kira, crawl if he had to. He'd do whatever it took to make her forgive him. He'd even tell her part of the truth.

Then he could see her again. Kiss her again. Make love to her again.

See her smile again.

The heat between them would fade away in a few months. He always made sure it did. Then he could walk away without hurting her.

Without making her cry.

He veered off the track at the entrance and ran down the stairs. According to Brian, Kira played basketball here every Thursday. Brian said she always came home in a good mood on Thursday nights.

He heard the ball bouncing against the floor as he pushed open the door to the gym, heard the grunts and muttered curses of the men running down the court.

There was one other woman besides Kira, playing on the other team.

Right now she was swearing because she was trying to guard Kira. His wild thing was the point guard. And watching her play, he realized that, the day she'd played her brother, in spite of Brian's demand that she go all-out against him, she'd been holding back.

Jake settled on the partially opened bleachers and leaned back to watch.

CHAPTER NINETEEN

KIRA SAW JAKE THE moment he walked into the gym. She glanced up as she dribbled the ball, and a burly cop from the other team stole it from her. Infuriated, she chased after her opponent. He made a sweet jump shot, then turned to her and grinned.

"You're losing your touch, McGinnis. That was like taking candy from a baby."

She stared at him as she took the in-bounds pass. "I must be, if I let a loser like you take my ball." Narrowing her eyes as she dribbled, she said, "You want to try it again?"

He wisely let her pass as she swept down the court and laid the ball gently in the net. Running back, she forced herself to ignore Jake and concentrate on the game. He would *not* ruin this for her. The Thursday game was sacred, the only time she forgot everything but the running, the moves, the shots. The only time she was free.

Today, it was comfort and familiarity and an opportunity to lose herself in the game. To push Jake out of her mind, where he'd set up camp and lived since Sunday.

Damn him, why did he have to show up here?

After the next basket, one of the guys from the other team noticed Jake. "Hey, you want to play?" he called. "We've been a man short all night."

"Nah. I'm not in your league," Jake called back.

"We don't care," the guy said with a grin. "We'll eat you up and spit you out no matter what."

Jake got up from the bleacher bench. "How can I pass up an invitation like that?"

The guys on the other team introduced themselves. Mary Ellen Teague, the woman on their team, gave Jake a big smile. "Hi, I'm Mary Ellen."

"Jake Donovan."

"Welcome," she said with a flirtatious look. "I haven't seen you here before. Where have you been hiding?"

"I'm just trying the place out," he said. "To see if it's got what I'm looking for."

"This place has a lot to offer," Mary Ellen said, winking.

"I can see that." Jake's gaze moved past Mary Ellen to Kira.

Mary Ellen stepped in front of Jake, blocking his view. "Let's play."

Ignore him, Kira told herself as she ran down the court. But it was impossible when he stayed right next to her. When she could hear the rasp of his breath, reminding her of his whispers when they made love. When she could see the blond hairs dusting the ropy muscles of his forearm, reminding her of the sweat that glistened on his skin when they lay together, spent.

She didn't even have to look at him to know he was next to her. His scent was imprinted on her brain.

With a burst of speed, Kira blew past him. When Mary Ellen tried to pass Jake the ball, Kira leaped into the air and grabbed it before it reached him.

As Kira ran, she passed the ball to one of her teammates, running alongside her. He passed it back as she reached the basket, and she laid it in. She didn't look at Jake as she and her teammates bumped knuckles.

Mary Ellen tried her best to pass the ball to Jake, but Kira refused to allow it. Finally, one of the woman's teammates yelled, "Hey, Mel, stop flirting with the new guy and pass the ball. I'm wide open."

Mary Ellen scowled at Kira and flung the ball at the man who'd spoken. When she gave Kira a not-so-subtle hip bump as she passed, Kira responded with an elbow shot.

The next time Kira dribbled down the floor, Jake slipped in front of her. "Jealous?" he whispered, grinning. "Be still my heart."

She gave him a quick jab with her elbow as she dribbled past. "Not in this lifetime, bud."

Jake stayed closer than her shadow. Every time Kira touched the ball, Jake was on her. He stood in front of her when she tried to shoot, his hands close enough to brush her breasts. He bumped her from behind as she dribbled, grabbing her hips as if to steady her. Her temper rose as the rest of the guys made loud kissing noises at her. Finally, she spun around and snarled, "You want to foul? Fine. I'll give you some fouls."

The next time he touched the ball, she hacked his arm and snatched the ball as he dropped it. When he tried to take a shot, she stomped on his foot. When he got too close behind her, plastering himself against her body, she punched her elbow back into his abdomen. The whoosh of air leaving his lungs gave her grim satisfaction.

He was no longer grinning, and she saw simmering anger in his expression. When she jumped up for a rebound, he jumped, too, crashing hard into her. She staggered when she landed but managed to keep her feet. The next time down the court, she stuck out a foot and sent him flying.

When he stood, his knees were bright red from the burn. One of her teammates stopped play. "What's your problem, McGinnis? You know this guy or something?"

"Or something." She motioned for the ball. "Let's play."

"Uh-uh. We're done here," he said, laying the ball on the floor. He looked from her to Jake, then glanced at the other players. "We'll see you next week, McGinnis."

They scattered off the court, grabbing their bags and water bottles. Only Mary Ellen lingered. "Hey, Jake," she called. "You want to join us for a beer?"

"No," he barked. Kira watched as he composed himself with effort. "Thanks for asking, but I'll pass."

The other woman looked at Kira and shrugged. "Catch you next time, then."

"Yeah," Jake answered without looking at her.

When the door slammed behind her, leaving them

alone in the gym, Jake said "Okay, Kira. The game's over and we're going to talk."

She grabbed a towel from her bag and wiped the sweat from her face. "You want to reminisce about that little scene at your house last weekend? No problem. All you ever offered was fun. I had fun, as promised. So you're off the hook."

As she tried to move past him, he put his hand on her arm. "I hurt you. I've been kicking myself ever since."

"Not very hard, apparently. Or is your telephone broken again?"

"Jeez, Kira," he said, running his hands through his hair. "Are you always such a hard case?"

She looked at the waves of hair standing straight up and remembered telling him that she'd been dying get her hands in it. "No. Usually I'm worse."

"Please," he said quietly. "At least hear me out. Then if you decide to kick me and walk away, I'll accept it." He smiled. "Well, probably not. I'll whine and pester and beg. A lot."

"Why, Jake? So you can turn around and do the same thing next week? Fool me three times, even the village idiot gets the message."

She slammed her towel into her bag, pushed past him and headed for the door. Jake grabbed her bag and tossed it on the floor. "You can at least listen."

"Oh, you think I owe it to you? To give you a chance to explain yourself? Just like you explained yourself the last time you pushed me away?" She grabbed the ball and flung it at his chest causing him to stagger backward. "Read my lips, buddy. I don't owe you a thing. I'm pretty sure you had as much fun as I did."

"It wasn't just about fun," he said quietly as she started walking away again.

She whirled to face him. "No?" she asked, hurt and anger congealing into a hard knot of misery in her chest. "Then what was it about? It sure wasn't about trust or caring—or affection. It wasn't about sharing or respect. If it had been about any of those things, you wouldn't have shoved me out the door on Sunday morning." She tried desperately to swallow the tears that were threatening.

Her words echoed in the empty gym, and he glanced around. "I didn't mean to talk about this here. I usually like to have my fights in private."

"Too bad. You're the one who picked the gym for your little confrontation. Which reminds me. How did you find out about this, anyway?"

"I have an inside source."

"Brian," she said with disgust. "Did you pump him for details? Because if you did, I'm going to kick your tail all the way from here to Riverton and back."

"Get in line behind Brian. He came to our group meeting early to talk to me," he retorted. "Because he was worried about you. I didn't have to tell him the details. He could tell something was wrong."

Her anger eased a little. "Good for Brian, for thinking of someone besides himself. Maybe he's starting to grow up. But this is still none of his business."

"Yeah, it is. He wants you to be happy."

"I *am* happy," she said in a deadly voice. "I played basketball this evening. That makes me happy. My job makes me happy. I'm going to go home and spend time with my daughter and my brother. That makes me happy, too."

He cupped the side of her face, his fingers rough against her skin. "Is that all that makes you happy? Basketball and your job and your family? Brian wants more for you than that. And so do I."

She knocked his hand away. "You have an odd way of showing it, Jake. If what you did is your definition of making someone happy, I can live without it. And you."

"If I could do it over, I'd cut my tongue out before I said those things to you. All I can do is ask you to forgive me."

Her throat thickened with unshed tears and she swung away from him. "What am I supposed to say to that? 'Sure, Jake, I forgive you. Of course I'll stick around to give you another chance to kick me in the teeth.' Is that what you want to hear?" She wiped the hem of her shirt over her face.

"No." He came up behind her, so close she could feel the heat of his body, smell his sweat. "What I want to hear you say is, 'Yes, Jake, I'll give you a chance to explain.' That's all I want, Kira."

She swallowed, determined not to let him see her cry. She could feel his hand, hovering close to her shoulder. "Touch me and you're a dead man," she said in a low voice.

"Please. You said once you wouldn't beg. I'm not that proud. I'll do anything for you, sweetheart."

"I'm not your sweetheart," she said, furious with the tears that snaked down her face. She swiped her face on her shoulder.

Jake's arms came around her, pulling her close, pressing her face against his chest. "Yeah, you are," he whispered.

She tried to push him away, but he held on. "I'm sorry, Kira. I've missed you so much."

She struggled for a moment, then stopped. Jake wasn't going to let her go, and if she were honest, she didn't want him to. She'd let him hold her for just a minute. Until she could face him again without crying.

She didn't let anyone see her cry.

Jake stroked her hair, his fingers lingering at the nape of her neck. As he pressed a kiss to her hair, his breath drifted over her head and she shivered.

She pushed away from him. "Okay, I'll listen. Explain what was going on that day, Jake."

His eyes darkened. "I saw that baby, saw how callous and unconcerned those parents were, and I lost it. I couldn't deal with it. I wanted to walk out of that house and never look back. I hated my job and everything that went with it."

He shoved his hands through his hair. "I let Mac down. He's my partner, and I lost it in a volatile situa-tion. I'm a police officer, for God's sake. We're supposed to be cool. We're supposed to be in control. And I was neither. Thank God Mac was able to deal with it.

"What kind of police officer does that make me?" he asked. "How can Mac trust me again? What if one of those parents had been armed? What would have happened then?"

"You would have coped, Jake. I know you well enough to know that. You wouldn't let Mac down."

"I'm glad you're sure. Because I'm not."

"Why didn't you tell me this on Sunday?" she asked. "Why did you act like such a jerk?"

"I didn't want to ruin your day," he said, avoiding her eyes.

"Like you didn't ruin my week?" Her temper flared. "You said we weren't just about fun, but you're going to have to decide what you want. Do you want a relationship? Or do you just want to have fun? Because I have to say, the relationship part isn't working so well."

"What do you want, Kira?"

She wanted it all.

But she couldn't tell him that it had gone way past fun for her a long time ago. It made her feel exposed and completely vulnerable. "That doesn't matter. You're the one who doesn't do relationships."

"I'm trying." He looked away from her. "That's why I didn't want to talk to you about what happened with that baby. I don't want to let my job spill over into our relationship."

"That is so bogus," she said. She shoved him. "And that's strike three. You know damn well that I deal with the fallout of your job every day at work. You know I can handle it."

She clenched and unclenched her fists in equal parts fury and pain. "There's something else going on with you, Jake." She gave him a thin smile. "It's my job to figure out stuff like that."

"What do you want from me?" he burst out.

"I want honesty. I want you to look at me and tell me what's wrong instead of feeding me a line of bull."

He hesitated, and her heart cracked in two.

"Fine. That's all I needed to know," she said in a low voice. She and grabbed her gym bag. "I can't do this, Jake. It's not fun anymore."

She walked out of the gym, her head down, her eyes blurred by tears. The door slammed behind her.

Jake didn't follow her.

CHAPTER TWENTY

SEVERAL DAYS LATER, Kira was writing her notes when someone knocked at her door. "Come on in," she called.

Her hand stilled when the door opened and Jake walked in. After a moment, she set the pen on her desk. "Hello, Jake. What can I do for you?"

Her voice was professional and completely impersonal, and Jake scowled. "I need some time with you."

"Of course. Have a seat." She waited for him to sit. "What do you need?"

"You can cut the crap, Kira. I'm not a patient."

"No? Then what are you doing here?"

"Damn it." He jumped up from the chair and paced over to the window. "You just don't give an inch, do you?"

"Not anymore. Nothing has changed with you, so nothing has changed with me." She gripped the edge of her desk. "But I'm still the department psychologist and you're perfectly welcome here."

He swore viciously beneath his breath. Finally he looked at her, his expression hard. "Okay, we already talked about this. I made a big scene downstairs, said the suits are forcing me to see you again. When I walked up the stairs, everyone in the bull pen was laughing."

He threw himself into the chair. "If anyone in the department doesn't know pretty soon that I'm talking to you, they're either on vacation or in a coma somewhere."

"So we're pretending you're having another therapy session."

"Yeah." He shoved a lump of painted clay that Lexie had made from one side of the desk to the other. "I thought we could use the time to talk."

"Sorry. I don't do personal in here."

"What am I supposed to do? Stare at you for an hour?"

"There are magazines on that table over there." She nodded toward the far corner of the room. "Help yourself."

She looked down at her notes again, pretending to concentrate on them. His gaze burned into her, but she didn't look up. Finally, with a muttered oath, he stomped over and picked up a magazine.

An hour later, he threw it toward the table where he'd found it. "I've still got your extra key," he snarled. "I'll use it to get back in here tonight."

"Fine," she said. "Keep it until this is resolved."

She looked back down at her notes, not seeing a thing, and he finally stormed out the door.

JAKE STRETCHED OUT on the sleeping bag in Kira's office. It was four o'clock in the morning and the bull pen should be empty. Anyone on duty would be out on patrol. No voices had drifted up the stairs in a while.

He hoped their perp had taken the bait. He couldn't

do this again tomorrow, sit through another silent hour with Kira, spend the night in her office. Even now, her scent lingered in the air. It dug its claws into him, reminding him once again how badly he'd screwed up.

He was drifting in and out of sleep when the doorknob jiggled. He stood silently and shoved the sleeping bag into the corner. Then he waited in the shadows.

The lock clicked open and a figure dressed in black stepped inside and closed the door.

Holding a small flashlight, the person went to the file cabinet and tried to pry the lock open. At that moment, Jake pulled out his gun and stepped out of the shadows.

"Arms in the air. Now," he barked.

The flashlight dropped to the floor and rolled away, drawing circles of light on the wall. Holding the gun steady, Jake edged to the door and flipped the light switch. It was a man. His captive stood with his back to Jake, his hands high in the air. His arms were shaking.

"Turn around," Jake ordered.

The guy didn't move.

"*Now.*"

Slowly the man turned around.

"What the hell?" Jake stared at his boss, whose pasty face was covered with sweat. "Captain Crowley?"

"I'm putting my hands down now, Donovan."

"Keep them up there. Are you carrying?"

"No. I left my gun at home."

"You know I need to be sure."

"Do what you have to do."

Jake patted him down. When he was certain the captain didn't have a weapon, he motioned for Crowley to drop his hands, then slid his gun back into its holster.

"You want to explain what you're doing here?"

"Since you were waiting for me, I'm guessing you've figured it out."

"You wanted to read my file. Why?"

"It doesn't matter, since I didn't learn anything." Crowley shrugged. "I couldn't read her handwriting."

"What were you looking for?"

Crowley stared at Jake. "I need to know what's going on with my detectives," he said, defiantly.

"Cut the crap, Crowley. I want some answers."

"You're not going to get them."

Jake stared down at the shorter man. "I think I am," he said. "You're not in charge here. I am. You're going to tell me what's going on."

"Or what?" Crowley sneered. "You'll work me over?"

"If I have to."

Crowley held his stare a moment, then seemed to realize he was serious. He sank into Kira's desk chair like a puppet whose strings had been cut. "God, what a mess."

Jake didn't say anything. Finally Crowley looked at him. "It was the Doak Talbott thing," he said, his voice bitter. "That's what I needed to know. If Doak had told you or Mac anything about me."

"Why would we discuss you with Talbott?"

The captain looked out the window. The sky was just

beginning to lighten. "I was Talbott's informant," he said. "I was afraid he might have told you."

"And you thought I'd tell Kira?"

Crowley nodded. "You were supposed tell her about what happened. I figured if you knew about me, you'd say so."

Jake dropped into a chair. "I don't understand, Crowley. Why were you telling Talbott about our investigation? You let him stay one step ahead of us."

"You think I don't know that? You think I don't know it's my fault you didn't catch him earlier? For God's sake, it's my fault he almost shot A.J. and the boy."

"Why did you do it?"

"Doak was blackmailing me. In exchange for keeping quiet, I had to give him information."

"You jeopardized several people's lives," Jake said, his anger stirring. "Including me and my partner and the woman Mac loves. What does he know about you?"

"It's not important. He's dead. There won't be any more leaks."

"Unless someone else has the same information. What if another criminal tries to blackmail you?"

Crowley slid lower in the chair. "Are you trying to humiliate me, Donovan?"

"You humiliated yourself. What did Talbott know?"

The older man looked away, and Jake could see his jaw working. Finally he met Jake's eyes. "I'm gay."

"What?"

Crowley stared defiantly. "I said I'm gay. All right? Are you happy now?"

"And Talbott found out?"

"Yeah, Talbott found out," Crowley answered, clearly bitter.

"Why didn't you just tell him to go to hell?"

"Because everyone in the department would have known ten minutes later." Crowley seemed to shrink in the chair. "Come on, Donovan. You know how the department is. You think I would have been effective if the guys found out?"

"So you ratted out your people to Talbott to save yourself?"

"I did what I had to do. Sometimes we have to make hard choices."

"Yeah, we do," Jake said. "I've got some tough choices to make myself."

Jake stared at the man sitting in front of him, his anger rising. "Get out of here, Crowley. I don't want to look at you."

"You going to leave me twisting in the wind, Donovan? Or are you going to take over where Talbott left off?"

"I'm going to forget you said that," Jake said, holding his gaze until Crowley looked away, his face reddening. "I'm going to give you a chance to do the right thing. What you should have done instead of betraying us."

"What's that, Donovan?"

"You should have resigned," Jake said, his voice flat. "Then Talbott wouldn't have been able to blackmail you."

"I need to stay another year to get my thirty years in. I need to max out my pension, Donovan. My wife took everything when she divorced me."

"Some things are more important than money," Jake answered. "Get out of here, Captain."

Crowley held his gaze for a moment, then walked out the door.

Jake threw himself into Kira's desk chair. What the hell was he going to do now?

ON SATURDAY MORNING, Brian walked through the busy Digital City store, weaving through the racks of CDs and DVDs as he approached the door to the storeroom. He'd found Jenny's store ID in his car this morning. Redmond would get on her case if he thought she'd lost it.

He scanned all the aisles in the warehouse, but Jenny wasn't there. Frowning, he veered over to the card reader where they were supposed to clock in. Jenny had written her name on a blank card and stuck it to the bulletin board. Redmond had signed it, acknowledging that she'd come in.

Jenny was here. He started down the aisles again.

When he got close to the cage, he heard voices. Low, secretive voices. Frowning, he walked faster. No one was supposed to be in the cage. It was the room where they kept the really expensive stuff, and it was always locked.

Except it wasn't locked today. The door was cracked open and he could hear the voices more distinctly. He grabbed the handle of the door, then stopped.

The taunting voice sounded like Redmond's.

Brian backed away until Redmond said, "Notello." Was Jenny in there with him?

He pushed the door open. When he looked in, he saw the back of Redmond's head. And Jenny's face. Her eyes were closed, and tears ran down her cheeks.

Redmond's hand was up her shirt. His other one was holding Jenny's hand to the front of his pants.

Brian stood frozen for a moment, unable to believe what he saw. Then, with a roar of fury, he leaped at Redmond.

He grabbed the manager around the neck and tore him away from Jenny. Then he slammed him against the metal shelving. Redmond's head bounced off with a horrible, hollow sound, and he slumped to the floor. Brian was reaching down to grab him when Jenny pushed him away.

"Stop!" she said, sobbing. "Leave him alone, Bri."

He whirled to face her. "Stop? After what that bastard was doing to you? I'm going to kill him."

"No!" Jenny dragged him away from the unconscious man on the floor. "No," she said again when they were outside the cage. "I don't want you to get in trouble, Bri."

"I don't care about that!" He looked at the tears still pouring down her face, at her rumpled shirt and her shaking hands, and a murderous rage seized him. But when he tried to push her aside, to get back at Redmond, Jenny planted herself in front of him.

"Stop it, Bri." She grabbed his arms. "Please. Let it go, okay?"

"Jenny." He felt the tears begin to pour down his face, too, and didn't bother to wipe them away. "He was molesting you. God! How can you tell me to let it go?"

"Redmond isn't worth it."

"No, he's not worth it. But you are."

Jenny's face crumpled and she began to sob. Brian stood helpless, watching her cry, unsure what to do. Finally he put his arms around her. She grabbed onto him and held him tightly, sobbing into his chest.

They stood there while Jenny cried, Brian smoothing his hand down her back. Finally Jenny's tears tapered off, and she pushed away from him.

Her face was red and blotchy and her nose was running. "What are you doing here?"

"I came to bring your ID card." He glanced at Redmond, moaning on the floor. "Why weren't you telling him to stop?"

Jenny's eyes darted away from Brian's. "I can't tell him to stop. If I do, he'll call the police on me."

"You mean this isn't the first time he's done this?" He lunged for the door to the cage, but Jenny blocked the way.

"No, it's not the first time."

He grabbed her arm. "Jen! Why haven't you told your dad? Or Jake? Why haven't you told Jake?"

"Because if I tell, Redmond will have me arrested."

"For what?"

She looked away. "I stole some stuff when I first started working here. Redmond caught me."

"Aw, jeez, Jen."

"He said he'd have me arrested if I didn't let him…you know."

"And you believed him?"

"Yeah, I believed him. He would have called the police in a minute."

"That rat bastard. Why didn't you just quit?"

She almost lost it again. "He said he'd call the police if I tried to quit, too. He said if I got arrested again, I'd go to jail. I don't want to go to jail, Bri."

"You're not going to jail," he vowed. "We're going to tell Jake what's going on. He'll arrest Redmond."

"No! You can't tell Jake. You can't tell anyone!"

"What Redmond's been doing is wrong, Jen. I'm not going to let him get away with it."

"Please, Bri. Promise you won't tell Jake. Or anyone else. I don't want anyone to know. Okay?"

"You want Redmond to get away with this?"

"Yes." Tears poured down her face again. "I'm going to leave here and never come back. I just want to forget about it. Please. Promise me you won't tell anyone."

"I promise," he said reluctantly. "But I think it's wrong."

"It's my life."

"Okay." Brian peered through the fencing and saw Redmond stirring on the floor. "He's waking up."

Jen grabbed his arm. "You should leave."

"I'm not leaving unless you leave, too."

She looked at Redmond, struggling to his hands and knees. "All right. Let's go together."

With a last look back at Redmond, swaying on his knees, Brian let Jenny lead him away.

CHAPTER TWENTY-ONE

"IF CROWLEY won't resign, I'm not sure what we should do," Jake said in A.J.'s office the next morning.

He glanced around at Mac, A.J. and Kira. Mac reached out for A.J.'s hand. "Yeah, this is a tough one," Mac said. "Maybe he'll do the right thing."

"We can hope, but I have my doubts," Jake answered.

"Kira?" Mac turned to her. "What do you think? It was your office."

She looked cool and collected on this Saturday morning. Professional. And a million miles away from him.

"I'm not going to be responsible for ruining his career," Kira said. "Jake should decide. It was his file."

"They're your notes, Kira," Mac said. "If you let this go, it could put your job at risk."

"No, it won't. None of you is going to report me for lax security. And Crowley certainly isn't."

She stood up. "I have to get going. I trust you all to make the right decision."

With an impartial smile to all of them, she slipped out of the office and quietly closed the door.

A.J. also got up to leave. "I'm meeting a client at her house. I agree with Kira. It's your call, Jake."

When the door had closed behind her, Mac turned to Jake. "What do you say, partner? Do we lock Crowley up? Or do we give him a few days to resign?"

Jake stared out the window, Kira's words running through his head. "I hate this," he said in a low voice.

"Yeah, it's ugly. I've heard Crowley has been living in a bottle lately. Now I know why."

"I'm not talking about Crowley," he said. He got up to pace the room. "I'm talking about this job."

"The job? You hate being a cop?" Mac's voice resonated with shock.

"I never wanted to be a cop. But after my old man died, I couldn't think what else to do. All his buddies were pulling strings to get me into the academy, and I needed to bring home a paycheck. So I signed up."

Mac slumped back in his chair, staring at him. "You're a great cop. You're smart and you have natural instincts. You're good with people. Look at that group of kids you have. From what you've said, it sounds like you've turned them around. So what's the problem?"

"You know what I was going to do when I got out of college?" Jake threw himself into a chair. "I was going to be a teacher. Ironic, isn't it? A teacher is about as far from a cop as you can get."

"What brought this on? Crowley?"

"I've been thinking about it for a long time. I'm tired of making critical decisions—life-or-death decisions."

He stood and kicked the chair out of his way. "It started when I shot Talbott. God! I couldn't bear it, knowing I'd killed a man."

"It was him or us, Jake. You know that."

"Yeah, I do. And I'd shoot him again in the same situation. Wouldn't think twice. But I hate that I have to make that choice."

"So what are you going to do about it?" Mac asked.

"I don't know." He gave Mac a sideways glance. "Kira dumped me."

"I figured. You've been acting like a bear with a boil on his butt. And she hasn't been real happy, either."

"She said I was jerking her around, pushing her away every time something bad happened on the job and not telling her why. She was right."

"So level with her. Come on, Jake. How tough is that?"

"I'm still a cop. I'm not going to ask any woman to be a cop's wife."

"Sounds like you've got a choice. Let Kira walk away, or quit the department and do something different with your life." Mac shrugged. "What's more important?"

"Kira." He didn't even have to think about it. The thought was both frightening and freeing. "But I've been a cop for over ten years. What if I can't do anything else?"

"You can do anything you set your mind to, partner," Mac said.

Jake scraped up a smile. "Anyway, I can't quit. Who'd kick your rear when you need it?"

"Don't worry. A.J. has that covered," Mac said with a grin. "What you can have with Kira is more important than any job."

As Jake left the office, one of the patrol officers ran up the stairs. "Donovan?" he called. "You up here?"

"Yeah." Jake walked faster. "What's up?"

"Isn't Brian Johnson in that group of yours?"

"Yes, he is." Jake felt ill. "Why?"

"I've got a warrant here for his arrest. I thought you'd want to know."

THE CHIME of the doorbell interrupted Kira and Lexie in the middle of a puzzle. "Who could that be?" Kira pushed away from the coffee table to answer the door.

Jake stood on the doorstep.

Her heart gave a leap and settled back in her chest, beating way too fast. "Hi, Jake," she said, her voice cautious. "Come on in."

"Hi, Kira," he said soberly. He waved into the living room. "Hey, Lex. How's it going?"

"It's good. Are you here to play baseball with me? You promised you would."

"I know I did, honey, but I can't today." He looked around. "Where are Henry and Scooter?"

"They're in the yard."

He turned to Kira. "Could you ask Lex to go throw some balls for the dogs for a while?"

"What's wrong?" She studied his face, her stomach churning.

"Just have Lex go outside, Kira. Okay?"

She searched his eyes for a moment, but he was in cop mode. She couldn't read his expression.

"Lex," she said, moistening her lips. "Could you make sure the dogs are okay? Maybe get them a fresh bowl of water. It's pretty hot today."

"Okay."

Kira waited until she heard the back door close, then she grabbed Jake's arm. "What's wrong?"

"Is Brian here?"

"He's in his room. Why?"

He moved away from her. "I have to arrest him, Kira."

It felt as if he'd punched her in the gut. "What? Arrest Brian? For what?"

"He assaulted his manager at Digital City."

"That's ridiculous. He didn't even work today." She latched on to that fact. "There must be a mistake."

"There's no mistake. Redmond is at the hospital with a concussion. He says Brian hit him."

She sank onto the stairs. "No," she whispered. "I don't believe it. He's doing so much better. He hasn't lost his temper in a long time."

For the first time, Jake's expression softened. "I know. I thought he was doing better, too."

"Talk to him. I'm sure there's an explanation."

"I will. But I have a warrant for his arrest. I have to take him in."

"Without getting his side of the story?"

"That's not the way it works," he said with a touch of impatience. "Come on, Kira. You've worked in the department long enough. You know the procedure."

"He's one of your kids, Jake! You know him. You know he wouldn't assault anyone without a reason."

"I'm sure he thinks he had a reason." She saw the pain in his face. "Don't make this harder for me, Kira. I have a job to do, and right now that job is arresting Brian. You should be thanking me for being the one to come get him. They were going to send a patrol officer."

"That's supposed to make me feel better?"

"I couldn't change the warrant." Anger laced his tone. "This is the best I could do."

"Fine. I'll go get him."

She started up the stairs, but he drew her back. "I can't let you do that. I have to get him."

"You can take the rules and stick them…" She pressed her lips together. "I won't let you walk in and arrest my brother without any warning."

She shoved past him and up the stairs. Instead of following her as she'd expected, Jake waited by the door.

She knocked and Brian called, "Come in."

She pushed his door open door cautiously. He lay on his bed, hands folded behind his head, staring at her.

"Jake is here, Brian."

He pushed off the bed. "Yeah?"

She closed the door behind her and put her arms around him. "He's here to arrest you," she whispered. "Did you assault Redmond today?"

He slumped against her. "Yeah," he said, so quietly she could barely hear him. "I did."

She leaned away. "Bri! How come?"

He shrugged and moved away. "I just did, okay? I'm impulsive, remember? I do stuff without thinking first."

"This was just a wild impulse?"

He wouldn't meet her eyes. "I was sick of him hassling me."

Without waiting for her to answer, he clattered down the stairs. She raced after them.

"I'm not going to put the cuffs on you, Brian," Jake said. "Do I have your word you'll behave?"

"Yeah," he said. "Let's go."

"Wait a minute," Kira said. "I'm coming with you."

"Stay here," Jake said. "I'll call you later."

He disappeared out the door, Brian walking beside him. She watched them climb into Jake's truck and drive away.

As soon as they were out of sight, she ran to the back door and called Lexie.

KIRA PACED the small waiting room as the sun began to set. She'd been here for five hours and she still hadn't seen either Jake or Brian. Lexie was fine with the teen-aged girl across the street, and Kira wasn't budging.

She headed over to the officer sitting at the desk. "Are you sure Detective Donovan knows I'm here?"

"Yes, Dr. McGinnis," the officer said patiently. "I talked to him myself."

"Then why hasn't he come down here?"

"I'm sure he'll come down and talk to you as soon as he can. There are certain procedures he has to follow."

"Yes, I know." Kira paced the room again.

The door burst open and a teenaged girl hurried in, dressed all in black. Her hair was also black with streaks of magenta, she had several piercings in both ears, a tiny stud in her nose and a ring through her left eyebrow.

"I need to talk to Detective Donovan," she said.

"Take a number," the desk officer replied. He eyed her clothes and her hair disdainfully. He jerked his head in Kira's direction. "That lady's been waiting for him for a long time."

"It's an emergency," she said, and her lip trembled.

"What's your name?" he asked the girl.

"Jenny Notello." She sniffed. "I really need to talk to him."

The officer picked up the telephone, and the girl turned away. Kira studied her. Was she Brian's Jenny?

"Excuse me," she said to the girl. "Are you a friend of Brian Johnson's?"

The girl whipped her head around and gave Kira a suspicious look. "Who are you?"

"I'm Brian's sister, Kira."

"How'd you know about me?"

Kira tried to smile. "Brian has mentioned his friend Jenny. And he's with Detective Donovan right now."

"Brian's here? With Jake?" Her lip trembled. "What's he telling Jake?"

"I have no idea." Kira fought the urge to touch the girl, to comfort her. "Do you know anything about why he was arrested?"

The girl went white. "Brian was arrested?"

"Jake came to the house and got him."

Jenny stormed back to the desk sergeant. "I have to talk to Jake. Right now." She glowered at him. "If you don't get him, I'll go up there by myself."

"I can't interrupt him, young lady. You'll have to wait."

"I can't wait." She turned and dashed toward the stairs. The desk sergeant pushed away from the desk and yelled at her, "Come back here! You can't go up there!"

But Jenny's steps never faltered.

She could learn a thing or two from Jenny, Kira thought. She stood and hurried up the stairs, the sergeant bellowing at her to stop, too.

At the top, Kira found Mac holding on to the girl. She was trying to pull away from him. "I need to talk to Jake," she insisted. "Right now."

"Take it easy," Mac said. "He's in an interrogation room. I can't disturb him."

"You have to. It's important." Her lip started trembling again. "It's about Brian Johnson."

"Yeah?" Mac let her go. "Okay, hold on a minute. I'll see if he can come out here." He pointed to a chair at an empty desk. "Stay there until I come back."

To Kira's surprise, the girl sat down. Then the desk sergeant appeared at the top of the stairs.

"You're not allowed up here, young lady," he said. "Come with me."

Jenny lifted her chin. "Someone's getting Jake."

"You'll wait for him downstairs," he said, reaching for her. "If he wants to talk to you, he'll come get you."

Kira stepped in front of Jenny. "Mac went to get Jake," she said. "Why don't you give it a minute?"

He stopped and glared at her. "Get out of my way."

"If Jake can't talk to Jenny, we'll come back downstairs. Until then, we're waiting right here."

Just then Jake appeared from the corridor that led to the interrogation rooms. "What's going on, Jenny? This is a really bad time."

Jenny stood up, suddenly calm. "I need to talk to you, Jake. It's important." She licked her lips. "I think it has something to do with why Brian was arrested."

"Yeah?" He studied her for a moment, then nodded. "Okay, come on back and tell me what's going on."

Ten minutes later, Jake burst out of the corridor and grabbed the phone on his desk, punching at the numbers. His knuckles were white. "Give me the ER," he said.

After a moment, he said, "This is Detective Donovan with the Riverton PD. You have a patient named Redmond?"

As he listened, his face darkened. "Damn it."

Slamming down the phone, he yelled, "Mac! Where are you?"

When his partner didn't answer, he swore under his breath. Then he looked up and saw Kira.

"Kira. Thank God you're here. Take Brian and Jenny home and keep them there until you hear from me."

"What's going on, Jake?"

"I don't have time to explain." He looked at the desk sergeant. "Johnson is free to go, Spelling. He's in

Room Two. Jenny's in Three. Bring them to Dr. McGinnis, will you?"

"Where are you going?" she asked.

"To make an arrest," he said his voice angry. "Take care of Brian and Jenny."

Then he ran down the stairs.

A few minutes later Brian appeared in the hallway. His face was white, and when he saw Kira, he flew into her arms. "Jake said you were free to go," she murmured.

"Yeah?" He pushed away. "How come?"

"I don't know, but I think your friend Jenny had something to do with it."

He visibly paled. "Jen's here?"

She nodded toward the corridor. "There she is."

"Jen. What are you doing here?"

She ran to Brian and threw herself at him. "Jake arrested you. And you didn't tell him."

"Of course I didn't tell him," Brian said, folding his arms around the girl. "I promised you I wouldn't."

Kira's throat swelled as she watched them. Her little brother was turning into a man.

"I didn't think he'd arrest you," Jenny said, breaking down and crying. "I never would have made you promise if I thought he'd arrest you."

"It's okay." Brian dropped a kiss on Jenny's head.

Kira blinked away her tears. "Let's go home," she murmured. "We need to be at home."

CHAPTER TWENTY-TWO

JAKE FLIPPED on the siren and slapped the light onto the top of his truck as he tore out of the parking lot. He should have waited for Mac, but he was too angry to wait. He wanted that rat bastard child molester Redmond in a cell.

This would be his last collar as a detective. He wasn't about to let Redmond get away.

Ten minutes later he pulled to the curb in front of an apartment building. He pawed through his box of master keys and found the right one to this apartment's security doors, then slid out of the car.

A few minutes later he was standing in front of Redmond's apartment. He could hear the bastard moving around inside. Jaw tightening, he pounded on the door.

"Open up, Redmond. Police."

The person inside the apartment went quiet.

"Open the door," he yelled.

Still nothing.

Jake put his foot on the door and kicked it open in time to see Redmond scrambling toward a window.

"Stop, Redmond," Jake called. "Right now."

The store manager looked over his shoulder in

equal parts fear and defiance. "You have no right to break in here."

"Oh, yeah, I do." Jake reached him and grabbed his collar. "You're under arrest for child molestation, statutory rape and a whole bunch of other stuff." He recited Redmond's Miranda warning, then added, "We'll figure out the other stuff after you're locked up."

"I never raped her," he said. "If she said I did, she's a liar."

Jake pulled one of Redmond's hands behind his back. "I'll take that as an admission that you molested her. You're toast, Redmond. I'm putting your ass away for a long, long time."

As Jake reached for Redmond's right hand, the man slashed it toward Jake. Jake only had time to register the knife in Redmond's hand and jump backward. The sudden burning in his abdomen told him he hadn't jumped far enough.

"Damn it," Jake said, pulling his gun from his holster as Redmond tried to get past him. As the knife flashed down at him again, he fired his gun and Redmond spun away, one hand clamped over his shoulder as he fell to the floor. He dropped the knife and Jake kicked it away.

Redmond lay on the floor holding his shoulder, swearing and writhing in pain. Blood spilled through his fingers, turning them bright red. The front of Jake's shirt was turning red, as well.

Jake picked up his radio with a suddenly shaking hand and pushed the button. "Officer needs assistance," he said, in a voice he hardly recognized. "Officer down."

KIRA LOOKED IN the rearview mirror at Brian and Jenny, sitting close together in the back of her car. Neither of them spoke, but their hands clung together. Tears had dried on Jenny's face, leaving white, shimmery trails down her cheeks.

"Do you want me to take you home, Jenny?" she asked.

"No." Jenny's mouth quivered. "My dad's still drunk from last night."

"Then you can come to our house."

When they got home, Kira thanked the babysitter and loaded a movie into the DVD player. While Lexie watched her favorite movie, Kira returned to the kitchen. Brian and Jenny sat close together, talking in low voices.

She eased into a chair across the table from them, unsure of what to say. Brian held himself more like a man, now—more confident, more sure of himself. And more protective than she had ever seen him.

"Do you want to tell me what happened?" she asked.

Jenny reached for his hand, and Brian shook his head. "I can't," he said. "Jenny doesn't want anyone to know."

"It's okay, Bri," Jenny said in a faint voice. A dark flush rose up her neck. "You can tell your sister."

"Are you sure?" he asked.

Jenny nodded.

"You don't have to tell me anything," Kira said.

Brian gave her a puzzled look. "I was just arrested. And I don't have to tell you why?"

Kira laced her fingers together beneath the table.

Please, she prayed, *give me the wisdom I need to handle this.* "You were released. And yes, I want to know what happened," she said. "But it's clear Jenny is involved. I don't want you to betray a confidence or make her uncomfortable. You decide what to tell me."

Brian studied her for a long moment, then turned to Jenny. "Maybe Kira can help you," he said. "She's a psychologist."

Jenny shrugged one shoulder. "I don't need a shrink."

"I'm just saying," he answered.

"Tell her, Bri," Jenny said. "Get it over with."

Brian glanced over his shoulder, to make sure Lexie was still occupied with the movie, then told Kira what had happened that day at Digital City. "So Jen and I both left," he said, finishing the story. "The next thing I knew, Jake was here to arrest me."

"I'm so sorry that happened to you," Kira said softly to Jenny. "I'm glad Brian punched him. He deserves a lot worse."

"You're not angry?" Brian asked.

"Of course not. You did what you needed to do to stop him. You were very brave, Bri."

Kira turned to Jenny. "It might be uncomfortable for you to talk to me, since I'm Brian's sister. But you should talk to someone. Would you like me to call your parents and recommend some therapists?"

"It doesn't matter. My mom's gone," she muttered. "And my dad is too drunk most of the time to care."

Kira took Jenny's hand. "Then I'll help you arrange an appointment with someone, if you like."

Jenny shrugged. "I don't know. Maybe."

"We can talk about it in a day or two." She squeezed Jenny's hand, then let her go and turned to her brother.

"You were with Jake for a long time today," she said. "And you didn't tell him why you punched Redmond?"

"I promised Jen I wouldn't."

"I'm so proud of you, Bri. It took a lot of courage not to tell Jake. Not to save yourself by betraying Jenny's trust." She rested a hand on his shoulder. "Your mother and father would be proud of you, too. Of the man you've become. I'm just sorry they're not here to tell you themselves."

Brian's eyes filled with tears. "They wouldn't be proud," he said, his voice thick. "I'm a coward."

"Brian! You're not a coward," Kira said, shocked. "Why would you say something like that?"

"Because it's true."

"No, it's not! How can you say that?"

"I am." He wiped his arm across his eyes, glanced at Jenny, then looked away. "The car accident was my fault. It was my fault our parents were killed. And all this time I didn't tell anyone. I was afraid you'd be mad. I was afraid you'd kick me out."

"Oh, Brian." Kira grabbed him, hugging him close. "I would never kick you out, no matter what you did. And how could the accident have been your fault? You were only twelve years old."

"I was fighting with my mom," he said in a small voice. "Your dad turned around to yell at me. That's when the car went off the road."

Jenny reached for his hand, and Brian clung to it.

"And you've been carrying this around for all these years? Thinking you were to blame?" Kira brushed the hair out of his eyes. "It wasn't your fault, Bri. I don't care what was going on before the accident. You weren't responsible for driving the car. My father was. It was his job to drive safely. It wasn't your fault," she repeated, her voice fierce.

Brian hunched his shoulders. "I knew you'd say that. That's what you're supposed to say."

"It's true, Bri!" She grabbed his shirt and shook him. "It wasn't your fault." She pulled him closer. "Have you ever asked Jake about this?"

"Of course not."

"Listen to me. Jake would say the same thing. You ask him next time you see him. Okay?"

"You really don't think it was my fault, do you?" Brian said slowly.

"Of course I don't." She pulled Brian into her arms. "It was my father's fault. He shouldn't have turned around while he was driving. I'm so sorry you've carried this burden all this time. I wish you'd told me earlier." She hugged him tightly. "No wonder you've been drinking and fighting."

Brian pushed away, reaching blindly for Jenny's hand. "Maybe I like to drink and fight," he said, but a tiny smile hovered around his mouth.

"Don't be an ass, Johnson," Jenny said, smacking the back of his head.

"Smart mouth," Kira said, hugging him once more before letting him go. "I know you've fought me about this, but I don't care what you say. We're going to see a therapist together. You need to hear someone besides me tell you it's not your fault. Okay?"

"I guess." He glanced over at Jenny.

"Your sister's right," the girl said. "If you weren't driving, it wasn't your fault."

"Are you two ganging up on me?"

"Absolutely," Kira replied. "And if you don't pay attention to us, we'll nag you until you do."

"Jeez! Not that!" Brian answered, but the bruised look around his eyes was fading. He glanced at Jenny. "My sister is a champion nagger."

"I'm not so bad myself, Johnson," Jenny retorted.

Kira smiled through her tears. "There you go, Bri. What'll it be? Nagging? Or are you going to believe us?"

"Maybe I'll talk to Jake," he muttered.

"That's a great idea," Kira said. "He'll tell you the same thing. But we're still going to a therapist."

"Yeah, yeah, yeah," he said. "Jeez, Kira. You've started the nagging already."

"I just want to make sure you know we're serious."

"What happened to Jen today is more important than old stuff, anyhow," he said.

She got Brian and Jenny some sodas and some iced tea for herself, then sat back and listened to them talk about Jake, and what he'd said to them that day. Jenny said, "Man, I thought his head would explode when I told him what Redmond had been doing. I've never seen him that angry."

"You didn't see him when he arrested me," Brian said. "He was so angry he could barely talk."

"Jake is going to be proud of both of you," Kira said.

Brian shot her a glance. "Is Jake coming over tonight?" he asked.

"I have no idea. Was he going to arrest Redmond?"

"I think so," Jenny said. "After I told him what Redmond had been doing, he jumped up and ran out of the room. He had smoke coming from his butt."

The phone rang. "Kira? This is Mac."

"Hi, Mac. How are you?"

"Not good." His voice shook. "I'm at the hospital. Jake has been stabbed."

CHAPTER TWENTY-THREE

"WHAT?" Kira sat heavily in the chair.

"It was Redmond. Jake went tearing off to arrest him and didn't wait for me." Mac cleared his throat. "The friggin' idiot."

"Is he…" Kira couldn't finish the sentence.

"He was alive when the paramedics got to him. They said he was conscious. He's in surgery now."

"Are you at St. James?"

"Yeah. A bunch of us are here."

"I'll be right there."

She dropped the phone and turned to Brian. He and Jenny were watching her, alarmed.

"Jake has been stabbed," she said, surprised at how even her voice was. "He's at St. James Hospital. I'm going over there. Will you two stay with Lexie?"

"Is he okay?" Brian grabbed her by the arm. "Is it bad?"

"His partner didn't know. He was conscious when the paramedics got to him, so that's good." She hoped. "He's in surgery right now."

Brian glanced to where Lexie sat in the other room.

He didn't ask to go with Kira. He just said, "Will you call us as soon as you hear anything?"

"Absolutely. As soon as I know anything."

She grabbed her purse and ran from the house, tears streaming down her face. She made it to the hospital in record time and was out of her car almost before it had stopped. Wiping her hand across her eyes, she skidded to a stop at the reception desk. "Surgery. Where is it?"

The older woman behind the desk gave her a sympathetic look. "Do you have someone in surgery, dear?"

"Yes. How do I get there?"

"The surgery waiting room is on the third floor." As the woman gave her directions, Kira started running for the stairs. She couldn't wait for the elevator.

She heard the voices from the waiting room before she got there. Pausing in the hall to blow her nose, she walked into the room.

She recognized the cops clustered together, holding cups of coffee. Every one of them had his or her cop face on. Jake's sister, Lissa, huddled with three men who had to be his brothers and an older woman. His mother? The older woman wiped away tears.

"Mac!" She spotted him standing with A.J. and made her way through the throng. "What have you heard? Is he all right?"

Mac squeezed her hand. "We haven't heard anything more. The doc will come out as soon as she finishes the surgery."

"How long has he been in there? There must be some news."

A.J. took her hand. "Sit down, Kira," she said gently. "Don't make yourself crazy."

Kira shook her friend off. "What happened? How badly is he hurt?"

"We don't know much," A.J. said. "Only that he was stabbed. He was able to shoot Redmond. Got him in the shoulder." Her jaw tightened. "He's in surgery, too."

"Worthless piece of garbage." Mac scowled. "We found boxes of unopened electronics in Redmond's apartment." Mac's mouth thinned. "I thought there was something off that day we talked to him, when he wanted us to arrest Brian and Jen. He was trying to set the kids up to take the fall for the stolen merchandise."

"I don't care about Redmond," she said, her voice fierce. "I'll kill him myself if Jake…"

She turned away, her throat thick and her eyes burning. Kira paced the waiting room for what seemed like hours, until finally a tall, slender doctor in green scrubs arrived and looked around with a tired smile. "Are all of you here for Detective Donovan?"

Mac held Kira as Jake's family rushed the doctor.

"He's going to be fine," the doctor explained quickly, holding up her hands to quiet them. "I sutured two stab wounds. The one on his chest was pretty shallow, but it's going to hurt for a while because it cut through muscle. The one in his abdomen was deeper, but the knife didn't hit any vital organs. He'll be here for a few days so we can make sure his belly doesn't get infected, but that's about it." She smiled reassuringly. "He's a lucky guy. Sore, but very lucky."

"Can we see him?" somebody asked. Their voices bumped against each other, a chorus of concern, of love.

A family.

And Kira felt on the outside, looking in.

"He's still in recovery," said the surgeon. "One of the nurses will let you know when we take him to his room."

Kira sank into a chair as the doctor walked away. Shaking with relief, she watched as the cops relaxed. When her legs would hold her, she moved to a quiet corner of the room and called Brian.

When a nurse later came by and told them they could see Jake, everybody surged out of the waiting room. A.J. turned to her. "Coming, Kira?"

"In a little while."

Mac frowned. "You don't want to see him?"

"Of course I do." She snapped her mouth shut, ashamed she'd raised her voice. "But he'll want to see his family. And all the cops will want to make sure he's all right."

"You're the one he'll want to see," Mac said.

She stared down at her hands. "I'll wait until everyone else is finished."

"You sure?" Mac looked at her doubtfully.

"Positive."

"Okay." After Mac and A.J. disappeared, Kira tried but she couldn't sit in the claustrophobic room a moment longer. She walked through the halls until she saw the crowd of officers outside a room.

As Kira headed toward them, a nurse came from the other direction and shooed them away. "All right, you've seen Detective Donovan. Now get out of here." Her smile softened her words. "He needs to rest."

One of the patrol officers leaned in the door. "Your nurse is throwing us out, Donovan. As soon as she's gone, we'll bring you a beer."

"Thanks, man."

Jake's voice was no more than a raspy whisper. The nurse escorted everyone out a few minutes later. Kira waited until they'd turned the corner before she pushed open the door to his room.

Jake lay in the bed, hooked up to a bag of intravenous fluids. His eyes were closed, his face pale and drawn. She could see that he was wrapped in thick white bandages—even through the thin hospital blanket. The sickly yellow of the iodine scrub stained his skin.

She waited for him to open his eyes, but his slow, even breathing told her he'd fallen asleep. When she touched his hand, his skin was hot and dry.

He didn't open his eyes, didn't move. A sheet covered him to the waist and an IV line snaked out of the back of one hand. A clip fastened onto one finger. Wires from pads on his chest ran to a machine next to his bed, which beeped regularly. He looked helpless and very sick.

She curled her hand around his as her eyes filled with tears. "Jake," she whispered, "if you had died, I'd have smacked you. I never told you that I love you."

She wasn't sure if he squeezed her hand or if it was just a reflex. She clung to him and watched him breathe.

She had no idea how long she'd been there when the door opened and a nurse stepped in, stopping abruptly when she saw Kira.

"What are you doing in here? I told all you people to leave."

"I just got here."

"Well, you have to leave." When she saw the tears on Kira's face, the nurse patted her arm. "He's going to be fine, honey. He just needs sleep right now."

"I'm not keeping him awake. I'm just standing here."

"Honey, I have to do some things and you can't be in the room." Her voice was firm. "Come back tomorrow."

Kira let go of Jake's hand and walked to the door. When she looked back, the nurse was pulling the curtain around the bed, hiding him from her view.

The next day she brought Brian, Jenny and Lexie to see him. When they got to his room, he was asleep again. The kids crowded close to the bed, shocked looks on their faces. At least the leads from his chest were gone along with the beeping machine. He still had an IV line in his hand.

Lexie's mouth started to quiver, and Kira snatched her into her arms. She should have known better than to bring her daughter. But Lexie had begged and pleaded. Kira had thought seeing Jake would reassure her.

"Is Jake dead?" Lexie asked, her small voice wobbling.

"Of course not, honey," Kira answered, angry with herself. "He's just sleeping."

"Are you sure?"

"Yes, I'm sure."

Lexie struggled to be put down. "He'll wake up for us," Lexie said confidently. "I know he will."

Kira stepped away from the bed and let the kids have time with Jake. Jenny looked like she was going to cry. Brian was upset, too, although he was trying to act brave. "Cool bandages, huh?" he said to them.

Lexie patted Jake's hand, and his eyes fluttered open. It took Jake a minute to focus. When he saw the three kids, he smiled. "Hey, guys, what are you doing here?"

"We came to see you, man," Brian said.

"I told you he'd wake up," Lexie said. "He loves us too much to sleep while we're here."

"You got that right, Lex." Jake gave her a weak grin. "Great outfit you're wearing."

Lexie puffed up in her multi-colored skirt and green and yellow blouse. "I picked it specially for you."

"Yeah? I like it."

Jake looked past the kids to find her. "Kira." He smiled and held out his hand. "I'm glad you're here."

Nothing could have kept her away. She'd hardly slept last night, wondering if he was in pain, hoping someone was taking care of him. "We've all been worried," she said, gripping his hand. "The kids needed to see that you're all right."

"Just the kids?"

"Me, too," she said in a low voice. "I was…" She took a deep breath and tried to steady herself. She'd been completely distraught, and that terrified her. What had happened to the control she was so proud of? Her determination to forget about Jake? "I was scared, too," she said. "Everyone in the department was scared." She glanced at the bulky bandage on his abdomen. "How are you feeling?"

"I'll survive." Holding her gaze, he added with a tiny smile, "If you kiss it and make it better."

She managed to give him an answering smile. "Your nurse would have my head if I got my germs on you. In fact, I'd better go and head her off."

She squeezed his hand and slipped out of the room. It was too painful to see him lying there and not be able to touch him. All she wanted was to hold him, to feel his heart beating.

Leaning against the wall outside his room, she tried to compose herself. She couldn't let Brian and Lexie see her so upset. It would only frighten them.

Apparently Jake didn't realize she'd been there the day before. So he hadn't heard her whisper that she loved him.

Thank goodness. Jake getting stabbed didn't change anything. It didn't resolve the issues keeping them apart. It wouldn't make him more willing to open up to her.

It would make things worse. He'd be even more determined to keep her away from the ugly side of his job.

She stayed outside, listening to Lexie laugh, the low murmur of Brian's voice. And the reassuring sound of Jake's voice, stronger than it had been the night before.

Almost back to normal.

Just like things between them were almost back to

normal. When Jake was back on the job, they'd be professional colleagues again, exchanging greetings when they passed on the stairs and nothing more.

Who was she trying to fool?

She rested her head against the wall as tears dripped slowly down her face. Nothing would be normal, ever again.

CHAPTER TWENTY-FOUR

A WEEK PASSED, then two. Captain Crowley resigned, but the surprise of that event was muted by what had happened to Jake. He'd been released from the hospital two days after he was stabbed, and he came back to work a week after that. Cheers from the bull pen drifted up the stairs to Kira's office one morning, and she knew it meant Jake had just walked in. She half rose from her chair, then forced herself to sit back down. There was no reason to torture herself by seeing him any more than she had to.

School started the week after that, and Brian began his senior year of high school. She was thrilled when he came home the first day and said he'd decided to rejoin the cross-country team. He told her casually that the therapist he was seeing said it was a good idea, and that he'd really missed track the previous spring.

Had Jake helped Brian make that decision? Her eyes burned. She wanted to talk to Jake, to thank him for all he'd done for Brian. Instead, she wiped her eyes with the back of her hand and turned away. She'd cried more in the last few weeks than she had in the last few years.

She should be smiling, she told herself. After

blurting out his secret about the car accident that had killed their parents, the anger that had hung over Brian like a dark cloud had begun to fade. A huge burden had been lifted from his shoulders. They still didn't agree on everything, but they were both making an effort.

Lexie started kindergarten. Kira cried again when she dropped her daughter off on the first day of school, dressed in a brand-new outfit and carrying her prized Nemo backpack. The first day of school was a turning point in a child's life, and Kira had no one to share it with.

As Kira walked out of the school building with the other kindergarten mothers, she wrapped her arms around herself in spite of the stifling heat. She felt cold and hollow, as if something vital had been ripped out of her.

She knew exactly what was missing. Jake.

Brian had asked her what was going on, but she'd shrugged and said things hadn't worked out. It sounded so innocuous, so casual, as if Jake had been a dress she'd tried on and decided didn't fit quite right.

A few days after school started, Kira was in the backyard, watching Jenny play with Lexie on her *Finding Nemo* water slide. Jenny usually came over to the house after school to wait for Brian, much to Lexie's delight. She'd anointed Jenny her honorary big sister. Today, the two of them were shrieking with laughter as they ran at the water slide and went shooting down it on their bellies, water flying in every direction. Kira didn't hear Brian until he walked into the yard.

"Hey, Kira," he called.

"Hi, Brian," she said, smiling. The dogs scrambled to greet him. Brian petted them, then shifted from foot to foot, hesitant.

"You have to go see the school resource officer tomorrow," he finally said.

"What's the school resource officer?" she asked.

"The cop who works in the school every day."

"What happened?"

He rolled his eyes. "Nothing happened, Kira. The guy just wants to talk to you."

"About what?"

"I don't know," he said, hunching his shoulders and looking at his shoes. "Maybe you need to sign some papers so I can be in Jake's group again. He didn't say."

"Jake's leading your group again?" she asked, trying to sound casual.

"Of course. Who else would do it?"

"All right," she said, mentally reviewing her schedule. "What time am I supposed to be there?"

"He just said after school. I don't know how long he's there, so you should get there right away."

"Okay, Bri. I'll be there."

"Cool." He headed over to the water slide, and gave Jenny a thumbs-up. Then, still wearing his practice clothes, Brian ran at the plastic liner and went flying down it. Kira relaxed back into her chair and smiled.

THE NEXT DAY, she got to the high school just as the dismissal bell rang. Weaving around the wave of students trying to leave the building, she stopped at the reception desk and said, "I'm here to see the resource officer."

"Certainly." The gray-haired woman gave her a visitor's badge. "It's the third door down on the right."

Kira hesitated before she knocked. In spite of Brian's reassurances, she was still nervous.

"It's open," a muffled voice called.

She walked into the office and saw a man sitting behind a desk, bent over to retrieve something from the floor. Slowly he straightened.

Jake.

As she stared at him, he said, "Hello, Kira."

"What are you doing here?" she asked. "Brian told me I needed to see the school resource officer."

"You're looking at him."

"*You're* the resource officer?"

"In the flesh."

She frowned. "Are you undercover?"

"Nope. I'm not a detective anymore. This is my assignment, at least for the next year."

"You're not a detective? Is it because of your wound?" She started toward him, then thought better of it. "Did something go wrong? Were your wounds worse than they thought? Is this like being on desk duty?"

"Nothing's wrong. I'm healing just fine. I asked to be assigned here for the next year."

She stared at him. "What's going on, Jake?"

"Have a seat and I'll explain."

She took one of the two chairs in front of his desk, but instead of staying behind the desk, Jake came around and sat in the other one.

He took her hand and turned it over, examining it, running his fingers over hers. "I'm quitting the police force," he said. "I've enrolled in college and I'll get my teaching certificate at the end of this year. I'm hoping to get a job here at Riverton High." He looked up with a half grin. "I've already started lobbying the head of the social studies department."

"Jake?" She flopped back in her chair, staring at him. "I don't understand."

"Of course you don't," he said, his smile vanishing. "Because I never told you I didn't want to be a cop. I told you how I got into the academy after my dad died, but I didn't tell you it was the last thing I wanted to do."

"You're one of the best detectives in the department."

"That doesn't mean I enjoy it." He sighed. "Remember when you were grilling me after I shot Talbott? Remember how I wouldn't tell you how I felt?"

"Only too well," she said.

He rubbed his hand across his forehead. "I didn't want to admit to you, or myself, that I hated what I was doing. That I hated being a cop. Killing Talbott brought everything to the surface."

He leaned closer. "The day we were talking about Crowley—and what to do about him—I realized I didn't want to make life-or-death decisions anymore."

He smiled grimly "When I realized that, I knew I didn't belong on the police force."

"And then Redmond stabbed you."

He frowned. "Just another clue that I was in the wrong business. It was my own damn fault that I got hurt. I was so angry when Jen told me what that bastard had been doing that I didn't think. I didn't follow protocol and I got what I deserved."

"You didn't deserve to be hurt," she said. "You were doing your job."

"No, I wasn't. I wanted to beat the crap out of that bottom feeder. Make sure he'd never hurt another kid."

"There's nothing wrong with wanting to keep kids safe from people like Redmond."

"No. But there's a lot wrong with the way I did it. I'd already decided to quit. Getting Redmond seemed like the perfect ending to my police career. Instead, we landed in the hospital."

"I'm sorry you've been so unhappy," she murmured.

His slow smile made her stomach flip. "My time on the police force hasn't been completely unhappy," he said. "There's a lot I've enjoyed. I like the guys I work with. I got a lot of satisfaction out of helping people, out of closing cases. And I met a woman on the job. A woman I'm crazy about."

"Really?" It was all she could manage to say with her heart crowding into her throat.

"Yeah. Want me to tell you about her?"

"Yes," she said, her voice barely more than a breath.

"She's sexy and smart. She has a big helping of

attitude, a mouth that doesn't quit and she's sexy as hell. She's got more love inside her than any woman I've ever met. And did I mention how sexy she is?"

"She sounds like one of those disgustingly perfect women. Certainly not anyone I know."

"Kira." He took her hand. "Can you ever forgive me? You were right on target with everything you said. I *wasn't* being straight with you. I *was* pushing you away every time something bad happened on the job. I was an all-around jerk." He brought her hand to his mouth, kissed her palm. "I don't deserve you, but I'm hoping you won't realize that."

"What are you saying, Jake?"

"I'm saying that I wasn't giving our relationship a chance. I shoved you away every time you got close. But not anymore."

He leaned closer, his expression tender. "I love you, Kira. You're everything I want, and everything I thought I could never have. I couldn't ask you to be the wife of a cop. I'd sworn that I wouldn't do that to any woman, ever." He touched her cheek. "That's why I was pushing you away so hard. I was afraid of what would come out of my mouth."

"You want a relationship? You want more than fun?" she asked.

"Oh, I want fun," he said in a low voice. "Lots and lots of fun. I want to fall asleep with you at night and wake up with you in the morning. But I also want to make a family with you, Brian and Lexie—and any other children we're lucky enough to have."

He stood and pulled her into his arms. "I love you, Kira. Marry me. Please."

"Yes, I'll marry you. I love you, Jake. I tried to tell you so many times, but I couldn't make the words come out of my mouth."

"No?" His knowing smile made her heart jump. "Was that some stranger in the hospital who wandered into my room and told me she loved me?"

"You heard that?"

"You think I'd sleep through that? Not a chance, babe."

"These last few weeks have been killing me," she said, smiling slowly. "Trying not to beg. I told you once I never begged. I was lying."

"I like the sound of that," he said, and she saw the passion in his eyes. He grabbed a briefcase from behind the desk. "Let's go somewhere and discuss that in depth."

She wrapped her arms around his neck and pressed against him, pouring herself into a kiss. "I'll have to take a raincheck on the begging. Life is getting in the way." She trailed her mouth down his neck, felt his pulse leap beneath her lips. "Lexie is at her babysitter's and Brian comes home from practice ready to eat the furniture. I have to go."

She pulled away from him enough to study his face. "This is what you're getting into," she warned. "Are you sure you want an instant family?"

"Too late to ask me that," he said, cupping her face in his hands. "I already love Lexie, and Brian is like a kid brother." He brushed a kiss over her mouth. "Don't think you can get rid of me that easily."

"You're going to have to let me go long enough to take care of Brian and Lexie." She backed away, regretfully. "When Brian told me I had to see the resource officer, I had no idea wild monkey sex was on the agenda."

"Oh, it's on the agenda." He trailed one finger down her chest, grinning at her. "But I can wait until we take the kids out for dinner and tell them our news. How about Cheesy Pete's?"

"Not Cheesy Pete's." She shuddered. "That's a little more fun than I can take."

"Sweetheart, there's no such thing as too much fun," he said draping his arm across her shoulders as he steered her toward the door. "And I'm going to spend the rest of my life proving it to you."

Two months later, Jake followed Kira and the kids into their house and pulled the door closed. "Less than twenty-four hours to go," he said to Kira, pulling her close for a kiss.

"I'm counting the minutes," she murmured as she nuzzled his neck. "I wish that had been the wedding and not just the rehearsal."

"I'll make it worth the wait," he whispered against her lips.

"Man, you two," Brian said, rolling his eyes. "Give it a rest, will you? You're kind of sickening."

"You better watch it, Bri," Jake said with a grin. "Or I'll exercise my big-brother rights and pound you."

"Bring it on, old man," Brian said, trying to look tough. "I'll take it easy on you."

"Me, too," Lexie squealed as she leaped at Jake. "I want to wrestle with Brian and Daddy."

Kira's eyes blurred as she watched the three of them on the floor, laughing and giggling. She got mushy every time Lexie called Jake Daddy. Lexie had even brought Jake to kindergarten show and tell, explaining that having Jake for her daddy was even better than her classmate Jeremy's deer skull.

Finally, when Jake lay stretched out on the floor, panting, Kira said, "Okay, Lex, go get ready for bed. Tomorrow is a big day."

"Can I try on my dress again?" Lexie asked. "To make sure it still fits?"

"Sure, Lex," Jake said. "Then come downstairs. I have something to go with it."

"What?" she demanded, jumping on him. "What do you have?"

"Wait and see," he said with a mysterious smile.

Minutes later, Lexie came flying down the stairs. The green velvet dress with the wide pink ribbon around the waist fluttered around her. "It still fits," she announced happily.

"Come on over here, Lex," Jake said, pulling a jeweler's box out of his pocket. "I've got something for you to wear with that dress tomorrow."

"A present?" Lexie danced from foot to foot as she opened the box. "A heart," she breathed. "And it has writing on it. What does it say?"

"Show it to your mom," Jake said. "She'll tell you."

Lexie handed Kira the box. A gold heart on a

delicate chain nestled inside, with two words engraved on it.

Kira stared down at it for a long time. "It's perfect," she finally whispered. She looked at Jake, then smiled at her daughter. "It says Daddy's Girl."

"Of course I'm Daddy's girl," she said, indignant. "Who else would be his girl?"

"No one, Lex," Jake said, grabbing her in a hug. "Absolutely no one."

"Go get your pajamas on now," Kira said firmly.

"I've got something for you, too, Bri," Jake said to the young man when Lexie had disappeared up the stairs. "How do you feel about a heart engraved, Jake's Little Bro?"

Brian made a gagging motion with his hand.

"That's what I thought." Jake reached behind a chair, brought out a square box and tossed it to Brian. "I thought you might like this better."

Brian tore the paper off and his eyes got huge. "An iPod?" he whispered. "You got me an iPod?"

"Yeah, under one condition. I don't want to see white earbuds sticking out of your ears tomorrow when you're walking your sister down the aisle," Jake said, as sternly as he could muster. "Or when you're standing next to me as my best man."

When Brian looked up from the box, his eyes were wet. "Thanks." He gave Jake a fierce hug, then pulled away to stare at the box again. "Wow."

"Get out of here, Johnson," Jake said. "It's your sister's turn."

Brian leaped to his feet. "I'm going. I've got to call Jen and tell her about this."

When Brian's bedroom door closed, Kira pulled Jake close for a kiss. "Have I told you how much I love you?"

"You may have mentioned it once or twice," he said, smiling down at her. He pulled another box, identical to Lexie's, out of his pocket and put it in her hands. "I didn't forget about you."

Kira opened it. On a twin of Lexie's heart were engraved the words Wild Thing.

"Turn it over," Jake said quietly.

On the other side, it continued, You Make My Heart Sing.

"Mine, too," she whispered, going into his arms. "Because my heart is singing the same song."

"We've got a family chorus going now." He kissed her again. "Just call us the Donovan Family Singers."

HARLEQUIN®

Super Romance

OVER HIS HEAD

by *Carolyn McSparren*

HSR #1343

Single Father: He's a man on his own, trying
to raise his children. Sometimes he gets things
right. Sometimes he needs a little help....

Tim Wainwright may be a professional
educator, but since his wife died he
hasn't had a clue how to handle his own
children. Ironically, even Tim's new neighbor,
Nancy Mayfield—a vet tech who prefers
animals to people—seems to understand his
kids better than he does.

On sale April 2006
Available wherever Harlequin books are sold!

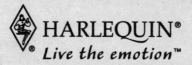

HARLEQUIN®

® *Live the emotion*™

www.eHarlequin.com   HSROHH0406

You're never too old to sneak out at night

BJ thinks her younger sister, Iris, needs
a love interest. So she does what any
mature woman would do and organizes
an Over-Fifty Singles Night. When her
matchmaking backfires it turns out
to be the best thing either of them
could have hoped for.

Over 50's Singles Night

by Ellyn Bache

HARLEQUIN®
Super Romance

UNEXPECTED COMPLICATION

by Amy Knupp

HSR #1342

A brand-new Superromance author
makes her debut in 2006!

Carey Langford is going to have a baby. Too
bad the father's a louse, and she has to do this
alone. Fortunately, she has the support of her
best friend, Devin Colyer. If only Devin could
accept the child's paternity and admit his true
feelings for Carey....

On sale April 2006
Available wherever Harlequin books are sold!

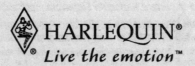

HARLEQUIN®
Live the emotion™

SWEET MERCY

by Jean Brashear

RITA® Award-nominated author!
HSR #1339

Once, Gamble Smith had everything—and
then the love of his life decided, against
medical advice, to have his child. Now he is a
man lost in grief. Jezebel Hart can heal him.
But she carries a secret she wants to share—one
she knows Gamble isn't ready to hear, one
that could destroy what the two of them have
together.

On sale April 2006

Available wherever Harlequin books are sold!

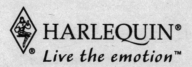

HARLEQUIN®
Live the emotion™

COMING NEXT MONTH